Flight
Renee MacKenzie

Flight

Renee Mackenzie

An Affinity Romance

Affinity
eBook Press
NZ

2015

Flight
© by Renee MacKenzie 2015

Affinity E-Book Press NZ LTD
Canterbury, New Zealand

1st Edition

ISBN: 978-1-927328-87-3

Editor: Day Peterson
Cover Design: Irish Dragon Designs

Acknowledgments

I would like to thank my family at Affinity E-Books Press for having faith in my books and reissuing *Flight*. A special thanks to Julie, Mel, and Nancy for making me feel right at home. Thanks to Mel for the formatting and Nancy for the cover. I would also like to thank my past publisher, Emily Reed, for first bringing out this book. Thanks to my Blue Feather Books editor, Day Petersen, for her exquisite editing and immense patience with me, and to the incomparable Nann Dunne for the line edit. Blue Feather Books is no longer in business, but I will forever be grateful to them for giving me a chance.

Thanks to my family and friends, especially my mom, Carol. My early readers, Deb Nichols, Dan Hallman, and Kathy Dyke gave me much appreciated encouragement and critiques. Writing about the 80s reminded me of great times in high school and beyond, making feel especially inspired by my closest high school friends, especially Valerie, Dawna, and Jo.

My writing group in Augusta, GA was the single most instrumental factor in giving me the courage and motivation to write *Flight*, so thank you Karin Gillespie, Steve Fox, Gretchen Hummel, Rhonda Jones, Kyle Steele, Nancy Clements, Donna Jackson, and Rhian Swain.

Dedication

For Pam, always

Table of Contents

Also by Renee MacKenzie

Nesting

Confined Spaces

23 Miles

Chapter One

Summer 1983

The lopsided headlight cast an upward beam as the motor scooter rounded the corner from Princess Anne Road and pulled up beside the lighted marble fountain. Kate stared toward it and clasped her library book tighter to her chest, unable to look away now that she'd finally come face-to-face with the woman she'd been watching for months.

The young woman's smooth, tanned legs easily balanced the scooter, and she sat with her torso erect. She wore her thick, dark hair pulled back in a ponytail, leaving her face unframed and her neck exposed. The illumination coming from beneath the surface of the fountain reflected onto her skin, a rich mocha with a touch of cream. Kate's eyes met hers, and the playfulness she found there made her heart race.

"You go to school here," the woman said.

Kate nodded.

"Get on, rich girl," she said, patting the seat behind her.

"Get on?"

"Unless you're scared."

"Scared of what—a little scooter?" Kate's short laugh was drenched in nervousness.

1

"Or of me." She gave Kate a challenging look, a smile that came as much from her eyes as it did from her full lips.

"You're not wearing a helmet."

"Don't have one. Come on. I promise to keep you safe." Teasing danced in her dark eyes. "Safe and sound."

Kate climbed on behind as gracefully as possible. Her library book jabbed into her thigh until the woman relieved her of it and tossed it into a small wire basket on the front of the scooter.

I can't believe I'm doing this, Kate thought. She never did anything spontaneous. Still, it wasn't as if she were being impulsive; she'd thought about it a million times. And she'd given herself permission to meet the woman if ever she had the chance.

"Pick up your feet. I don't want you to scuff up your rich-girl shoes."

Kate lifted her feet and situated them beside the driver's. "They aren't rich-girl shoes," she said over the rumbling of the engine. All she had to do was look at the other cars in student parking to be reminded that she and her Plymouth Arrow did not fit in at Lillian Wilde College. "I only came here because I got a scholarship."

"Ah. What's your name, smart-girl?" the woman asked.

"Kate."

"I'm Lana." She gunned the scooter, and Kate held on tighter.

Five minutes later, Lana switched off the engine and they coasted to a stop behind the darkened marina. The only sounds were their breathing and the gentle lapping of water against the boats.

"You aren't scared of the dark, are you?" Lana asked.

Kate shook her head. Even with the engine off, she felt phantom vibrations from the scooter.

Lana swung her left leg over the seat, shifted her weight, and pivoted around to face Kate. The moon off the water gave just enough light for her to see Lana's gaze drinking her in.

Kate swallowed hard.

"Scared now?" Lana asked.

"No," Kate lied.

When Lana rested her hand on Kate's leg, the heat surged up her thigh and into her gut, as intense as an electric current. For a second, Kate thought they'd been hit by lightning, but there wasn't a cloud in sight. Kate touched a smudge on Lana's neck. "You have something smeared here."

"Must be paint. I'm an artist."

"Oh wow. That's cool. I've seen you around a lot. Do you live near the college?"

Lana gave a dazzling smile. "Enough about me."

She ran a finger along Kate's arm, and Kate marveled at how their skin tones contrasted. The tanned finger that caressed Kate's pale forearm sent a shiver through her. She imagined how they would look embracing, Lana's dark hair entwined with Kate's blonde.

Lana leaned forward, brushed her lips lightly across Kate's, and returned to linger. Kate had never been so aware of her own mouth—its outline, its every nerve ending. Its hunger.

"Is this okay?" Lana's question warmed Kate's cheeks.

"Yes."

Her lips found Kate's again, and Kate repeated her consent. "Yes."

Lana's tongue teased Kate's mouth, and Kate's lips parted to allow it in. Lana flicked her tongue against the edges of Kate's teeth, and Kate felt it like a caress over her

3

entire body. When Lana's tongue probed Kate's mouth, Kate gripped Lana's arms and pulled her closer.

Lana pulled away slightly. "Have you ever been with a girl before?"

Kate hesitated. She didn't want her inexperience to turn Lana off. She looked into the brown eyes and whispered, "No."

Lana held her gaze. "But you've thought about it?"

Kate smiled. "A lot."

Lana trailed kisses along her jawline and down her neck. "I want to kiss and touch every inch of you," Lana murmured.

"Yes, please," Kate begged.

"But not here, not now." Lana kissed her nose. "Think about this. About me. Give me your phone number, and when I call you, you'll see me again only if you're sure this is what you want."

"I'm sure now," Kate said.

"Then you'll be even surer tomorrow." Lana pivoted around to face forward and started the scooter. "Hold on tight."

Chapter Two

"Boyd, get off me. You're heavy," April whispered. He groaned and rolled away from her.

She sat up on the edge of the futon and looked down at her boyfriend. Boyd Smith was cute, in that sunburned, sun-bleached sort of way. His hair was long in the back and more than a little sloppy-sexy. His eyes were a tired, faded green. The light hair on his thick forearms reminded April of wheat. After partying, she liked to stretch out beside him and stare at his arms, to get lost in thoughts of that pale down tickling her sides whenever he held himself over her and knocked his bony hips into hers, moaning and muttering about how hot she was and then crashing to sleep beside her.

April slipped into her Calvin Klein jeans and checked her dirty blonde, feathered hair in the mirror on the way out of the bedroom. Music and light pulsated in the living room, where music videos blared from the new cable TV.

She wished they'd spend some time watching the videos at Joey's. Part of her liked to be hidden away with Boyd, but another part wanted to be out in the living room with Joey and the others, watching the cool videos. Her own neighborhood in York County didn't get cable yet, so it was still new to her.

The sleeve of a wadded-up sweatshirt stuck out from under a couch cushion, across from where Joey had sat earlier, his feet on the coffee table. Her eyes wandered to a bong-water stain on the carpet, and she dimly remembered the night Boyd had spilled it after smoking too much and drinking even more.

Joey's apartment was quiet. Everyone else was gone, except a guy whose name she'd forgotten. Maybe it was Don, or Doug. He was propped up against the living room wall with his cigarette burned down to the filter, charring the skin between his fingers. His mouth was open and a needle dangled from his arm. A big wet spot had spread across the crotch of his pants.

April's legs went wobbly. She thought she might fall but couldn't move. A pungent smell dragged her back to the basement shower in Hillsboro. She was nine years old again and her cousin Bobby was opening the shower curtain. He hadn't shaved in days and smelled like beer. She hadn't been able to move then, either.

"Damn," Boyd said. Giving April a questioning look, he walked past her and nudged the guy's leg with his foot. "Yo, dude, you okay?" The guy didn't move, so Boyd squatted beside him and checked for a pulse. "Shit. He's toast."

He's dead? April looked around in panic, chest pounding, breath coming faster and faster.

"This is not cool," Boyd said.

He paced the room then went into the kitchen for a beer. April hugged herself and didn't answer when he asked if she wanted something to drink.

Why was this happening? She had a major case of cottonmouth and felt sex-dirty, and she just wanted to go back to the futon to stare at Boyd's wheat-hair while he half-dozed and half-touched her.

Boyd walked back into the living room and took a swig of beer before setting the can on the table. "Okay," he said, "we'll put the guy in the car and take him somewhere so no one can connect him to us or Joey."

"Shouldn't we call someone?" April asked.

"Why, so we can get busted? We're not all minors like you, baby. The rest of us would get into real trouble." Boyd shook his head. "Besides, it's too late for the guy now."

He looked down at his feet, grunted at his socks, and shuffled into the bedroom. When he came out, he hopped on one foot while trying to tie the desert boot on the other. Falling against a chair, he cussed, finished tying the lace, and strode to where April was still hugging herself and rocking slightly.

Boyd grabbed the guy under the arms and tried to drag him toward the door. He stopped after only a few feet. "He's too heavy to take all the way to the car." He took a gulp from his beer, and his mouth twisted. "Okay, I got it. Help me," he said.

April stared at the wet spot on the guy's crotch, cringing as she thought about her cousin Bobby urinating on himself as he fell to the ground.

"April," Boyd yelled. "Come on, we have to move him."

She scooted the floor lamp out of the way as Boyd grabbed the body under the arms and pulled it across the room. When she opened the door, she squinted against the unnatural glare of the outside lights.

Boyd's eyes darted from one apartment door to another as he dragged the deadweight to the bottom of the stairs. "I need you to actually help me, April."

Tears spilled down her face, and she couldn't make herself look at the guy sprawled on the concrete floor.

"I'm sorry, baby," Boyd said. "Please help me. I can't do this by myself."

She stepped over the body and positioned herself next to Boyd. She put her mind on autopilot, just as she had that last time in Hillsboro, when her dad had ordered her and Katie out of the basement.

"One step at a time," Boyd said. They heaved him up the first step then the second and third. "Doing good," he said.

Once on the next landing, Boyd rounded the corner with the body and lodged it against the railing by apartment 202, where they left him for someone else to find.

Chapter Three

Kate stretched out under her sheet and pulled the coolness of the cotton up over her head to block out the morning sun seeping through her curtains. Eyes closed, she pressed her fingers to her lips. It hadn't been a dream. She still felt Lana's lips on her own.

She took a deep breath and tried to identify Lana's scent. It was a blend of honeysuckle and a chemical. She figured the honeysuckle was perfume, and the other was some kind of paint thinner or cleaner. Lana was an artist. An artist who wouldn't tell Kate where she worked or lived.

Kate reached for the cassette player on her nightstand and flipped it on. The tape inside had been a source of courage when she'd been trying to define the quaking she felt inside every time she saw Lana sputtering around the periphery of the campus on her scooter. Pressing the rewind button, she counted. *One-one-thousand, two-one-thousand...* When she got to thirteen-one-thousand, she hit Stop, then Play.

Crimson and Clover started out slowly, but the beat was unmistakable. Kate's heart skipped a beat of its own.

Oh, God, Kate thought. The song—building and repeating, faster and harder, sweeter and scarier—was a lot like kissing Lana at the marina.

People described butterflies in their stomach, but birds or bats or the whole winged world were doing their thing in her belly.

The voice on the cassette was sweet, yet possessed an edge of craving that perfectly matched Lana's expressions and words and breath-stealing touch. When the song mentioned love, Kate felt the wings stir and stretch, trying to unfold and expand inside her.

The song ended and the silence taunted her, making her want to fill the void with Lana's scent and sounds.

When Kate got up, she made her bed as she'd done every morning since she was old enough. She let her hand linger as she smoothed out the white bedspread, then she quickly moved away, not wanting to be tempted to crawl back in and spend more of the morning thinking of the night before.

The small refrigerator Kate's dad had bought her didn't hold a lot, but it held enough to allow her to stay in her room for a few meals instead of trekking downstairs so often. She opened the door and pulled out a can of lemonade, her favorite indulgence. She loved the combination of sweet and tart. Her insides jolted to attention. *Lana. Sweet and tart.* God, would every little thing from now on make her think of Lana?

She ignored the plums on the second shelf as she took a deep breath and closed the fridge. The fruit would have her making all kinds of comparisons to Lana, driving her crazy and keeping her from getting anything done.

Deciding on cereal, she ate it right out of the box, not bothering with a bowl or milk. That would be one less dish to have to clean up.

She stretched the phone cord as far as she could toward the bathroom doorway. Staring at the phone, she decided not to shower yet. It wasn't worth the risk of missing Lana's call. She would read her assignment instead: *Arthropods of Medical Importance*. She flipped through several chapters of the book until she glimpsed a chart of the life cycle of a mosquito. She cringed and quickly turned back several chapters. She didn't want to think about when she'd eventually have to study the larvae that still conjured so many childhood memories.

She placed the book in the center of her desk. Opening her notebook, she stared at the neat writing, the notes she reprinted after every lecture while they were still fresh in her mind. She was convinced that the act of rewriting them, as well as reading them out loud as she did, helped cement them in her brain.

A knot formed in her stomach. What if Lana didn't call? What if Kate was just one in a long line of girls she took to the marina on her scooter?

She read the first paragraph of her assignment several times and didn't absorb any of it. Maybe if she read on her bed. Sometimes that worked better. She relocated to the smooth bedspread. Accelerated BIO 2011 was going to be hard work, but she'd wanted to take it over the summer because Dr. Mary Stoddard, a professor she respected immensely, was teaching it. But Kate also couldn't deny she had been looking for any reason to stay in Norfolk over the summer. She hoped to finally meet the dark-complected tomboy who showed off on her scooter.

Scared now? Lana had asked. Yes, Kate had been scared. But when she gave in to Lana's lips, and Lana yielded to hers, the fear dissolved and Kate knew there was no going back.

She leaned forward and rested her head against the textbook. Maybe she could master the contents through osmosis. Then Kate lifted her head quickly, worried about Lana coming over and being able to read Chart 3-B off her forehead. "Not sexy," she told herself.

Kate jumped when the phone rang. She sprang toward the desk before remembering the phone was on the floor by the bathroom. Reversing her direction, she twisted her ankle, stumbled, and caught her balance right before diving headlong into the wall.

When she finally answered the phone, she was breathing hard. "Hello."

"You're out of breath."

"No." Kate took a deep breath. "Well, yeah."

"Ah, you've been thinking about me," Lana teased.

"No." She laughed. "Yes."

"Do you want to see me again?"

Kate knew Lana was asking if she still wanted to be with her physically. "Yes. Do you want to come here?"

"Sure."

Kate looked around at the stacks of books. At least they're neat stacks, she thought. "Okay. When?"

"How about now?"

"Now?"

"Oh, sorry. I shouldn't have assumed you weren't busy."

Kate looked down at her nightie. "No, it's not that. I just need a little time to get ready."

"Get ready for what?"

Kate blushed at the edge to Lana's voice. "I need to shower, put my homework away, stuff like that."

Lana laughed. "Okay, smart-girl, how long do you need?"

"Give me an hour."

"See you in forty-five minutes."

"Bye." Kate replaced the receiver in its cradle on the floor, but remained squatting next to it. When it rang, she picked it up and said, "Room 213." She heard Lana laugh and hang up.

Kate finished the last of her lemonade. Sweet and tart. She stripped and jumped into the shower. Lather and rinse, lather and rinse. Sweet and tart.

She stood in front of her closet and assessed the possibilities. She liked the way her corduroy OP shorts fit her, but she didn't want Lana to think she was a brand-name showoff. When she held them up to herself, she decided their fit was worth the risk.

She started to pull out a collared shirt but stopped. Even though it wasn't Izod or anything like that, it was still way too preppy. She grabbed a light blue blouse with a touch of lace at the collar. It would have to do.

After dressing, Kate glanced around. Was there anything she could do to de-geek the room? She scanned the stacks of books: nature, science, psychology. The walls were adorned with a chart of the periodic table of elements on one, a map of the world on another, and a colorful poster organizing the animal kingdom on the third. The wall behind her bed was empty.

A knock on the door surprised her. She looked at the small clock on her desk. It had only been thirty minutes since she'd talked to Lana, but Kate didn't care about the extra fifteen minutes or the way the room looked.

She opened her door. Lana leaned against the opposite wall, wearing a T-shirt and cutoff jeans, and holding Kate's library book.

"I forgot all about that." Kate nodded toward the book she'd checked out in a last-minute effort to make her presence between the library and fountain seem accidental. Her eyes remained riveted on Lana's neck and shoulders.

"You were a little distracted."

Blushing, Kate looked away.

"Can I come in?"

"Oh, yeah, sorry." Kate stood back from the door.

As she stepped into the center of the room, Lana looked around. "So, there's not a guard downstairs at the door, huh?"

"No. It's not like that here."

"Are you a hall monitor?" Lana asked in a teasing voice.

"No way." She'd played that role long enough at home with April. She surely wasn't going to do it at school, too.

Lana squinted as she studied the cover of Kate's textbook. "Medical Entomology? Damn girl, you really are smart."

Kate's face grew warm.

"What's your major?"

"Pre-vet."

"Wow." Lana wandered over to the bedside table where the tape player perched, and she picked up the empty cassette case. "You like Joan Jett?"

Kate was glad for the quick change of subject. "Yes." She stared at Lana, still not believing she was actually there with her.

"What song is your favorite?" Lana flipped the case over.

"Crimson and Clover."

"Yeah," she said in a low voice. She looked at Kate, and her expression shifted, as if their presence there together had just sunk in.

"I'm glad you're here," Kate said. She hoped Lana didn't hear the quiver in her voice.

Lana's lips parted to speak several seconds before the words actually came out. "I'm going to die if I don't kiss you very soon."

Kate's heart pounded and her head whirled. Is this how it felt to be drunk? She didn't know; she'd always figured one delinquent in the family was enough. But if that was how alcohol affected people, she finally understood the allure. "Then why are you all the way over there?"

Lana glanced to her right, down at the bed. "Why are you way over there?"

Kate had never before been so self-conscious over seven simple steps or so happy to get to the other end of them. She stood very close to Lana, and her heart raced. "Hi," she said.

"Hi, yourself."

Kate smelled mint and honeysuckle on Lana. She was surprised when the question that formed in her mind was *What does she taste like?*

"You're blushing," Lana said.

Kate's hand instinctively went to her own face, and she looked down. Lana gently lifted her chin, and Kate almost melted at the intensity she found in Lana's eyes.

"Can I kiss you?" Lana asked.

"Please." Kate struggled to breathe as Lana's mouth claimed hers. As their tongues danced, Kate thought that nothing had ever felt so right before. She'd waited forever for this moment, and it was so worth the wait.

She drew back slightly and caught her breath. Lana nibbled on Kate's lower lip and leaned away enough to pull her T-shirt over her head. Kate wasn't surprised that Lana was braless. She stared at the tanned skin that showed no bikini lines. The dark brown of the nipples made Kate wonder about the genetics that made up this beautiful woman

15

with her smooth, rich skin. But her interest in the science of it disappeared as she wondered again how Lana would taste.

"Now your shirt." Lana slowly unbuttoned Kate's blouse.

Once Kate's shirt and bra were layered with Lana's shirt at the foot of the bed, Lana leaned forward to kiss Kate. Kate gasped at the sensation of their nipples brushing.

"You okay?" Lana asked.

"Yes." She looked down and marveled at the sight of their breasts so close together.

Lana slipped her thumb under Kate's waistband and traced a path across her abdomen. She paused in the middle, at the button of her shorts. "No doubts?"

"No doubts." Kate reached for the button of Lana's shorts while Lana unfastened Kate's.

They shed the rest of their clothes, and a shudder passed over Kate.

"Come to bed," Lana said.

Kate peeled back the bedspread and sheet and slipped in. When she went to cover herself, Lana gently pushed the sheet back. "Let me see you. You're so beautiful." Lana stared down at her for several moments before positioning herself just inches above Kate, her arms bracing her weight on either side of Kate.

"You're sure?" Lana asked.

"Yes. Please." Kate licked her lips. "Cover me with your body."

Lana lowered herself and let her body barely make contact along the length of Kate's. The electric current from the night before returned, this time striking Kate in the belly and radiating between her legs. Lana allowed more of her weight onto Kate and positioned herself, left then right, to fit herself perfectly to Kate.

Kate gasped. "Oh… oh, that feels so good."

Lana pressed down harder, rubbing their wetness together. Kate arched up into her, and Lana started a rhythmic grinding that quickly drove Kate to climax. Lana pressed and rubbed harder and harder against her until Kate could feel her tense and flutter, and she, too, came.

Chapter Four

Boyd put the Gran Torino into drive as he handed the McDonald's bag to April. The smell of food made her nauseous. He steered away from the drive-thru as she handed him a sausage biscuit and grabbed a plain one for herself.

He pulled into a parking space, preferring to eat in the car, but not going too far because April always had to pee after eating.

"That's all you're gonna have?"

"Yeah." April slowly unwrapped the slick paper. She'd been thrown off balance when Boyd said he wanted to eat. It didn't seem right, not after just touching a dead person.

April took a bite and washed it down with her soda. A third of the way through the biscuit, a greasy film formed on the roof of her mouth. She fought against gagging.

Boyd had eaten both of his biscuits by the time April finished hers. She patted the corners of her mouth, trying not to wipe off her bubblegum lip-gloss. She reached behind her seat to grab her purse.

April rummaged through her oversized bag, which made her think about Boyd going through the dead guy's wallet after they'd dragged him up the stairs. She'd seen Boyd pocket some cash and what appeared to be a condom. When he realized April was watching, he stopped abruptly and pulled out the guy's driver's license and held it up. "I'm just

18

seeing what his name is." Before he could continue, April told him she didn't want to know the guy's name, or anything else about him.

She sipped her soda and hoped the caffeine would get her going. She wondered if Boyd had any Black Beauties left.

"What are you thinking so hard about?" Boyd asked.

"Do you have any speed?"

"Maybe at home." He shrugged. "You know I forget where I put stuff." He lit a cigarette, and she coughed.

She grabbed the edge of the rearview mirror and twisted it toward her with very little resistance. She wrinkled her nose in distaste and wiped her index finger beneath each eye to remove some of the smudged mascara. She stared at her reflection, focusing on her "bug eye," the lazy left one her friend Nicki swore wasn't noticeable. A childhood mosquito bite had gotten infected and almost cost April the sight in her left eye. Her dad had told her, in his stiff, awkward way, that she was lucky the eye had gone just a little off-kilter, that it could have been much worse.

April thought about putting on some blush but didn't have the energy. Smoke swirled around her, and she coughed again.

Boyd flicked his cigarette out the window. He waved his hand in front of him, impatient with the smoke or with her reaction to it, April wasn't sure which. No matter what she said, April couldn't convince Boyd cigarette smoke really did bother her head and eyes, even if reefer smoke didn't.

"Let's go to Norfolk," she blurted. She didn't know where the idea had come from.

"Why?" Boyd reached under the AM radio to the cassette player he'd installed six months earlier.

"We could surprise Katie."

Boyd's eyebrows knitted together. He ejected a cassette, flipped it over, and stuck it back in. Nothing happened. "Why would you want to do that?"

April didn't answer. The memory of the basement shower that last summer in Hillsboro nagged her. After that, Katie had been so willing to play Monopoly. Her sister had finally pulled her head out of her nature books long enough to play with April, but something about it felt off. She wanted to talk to Katie. She wouldn't say anything about the dead guy, or Bobby, or the image that fused them in her mind. No, she just wanted to be around her older sister. Maybe it would be enough to ease her increasing anxiety.

Boyd smacked the side of the cassette player. "Piece of shit," he growled. Just as he was about to hit it again, AC/DC screeched out of the speakers. He turned it down enough for April to hear him. "You aren't serious about seeing Katie, are you?"

April studied Boyd's face. He wasn't asking to be mean or hateful; he really didn't think she meant it. She forced a laugh. "No, of course not."

Boyd smiled and gave a little wink. The look turned her insides to goo. She scooted closer on the vinyl bench seat and melted into him.

He backed out of the parking space. As he pulled onto Route 17, he took April's hand into his. "You're shaking."

"Yeah," she said. "A little."

"My mom's working this weekend. We'll swing by the house and see if she's gone yet."

Boyd's mom didn't think April was good enough for her son. All April wanted was for Boyd to get his own place, for them to have somewhere to go for a little privacy. Joey was cool about letting them use his apartment, but it just wasn't the same.

They crept up the street as Boyd checked the driveway for his mom's car. Once he was sure she wasn't home, he pulled in. "Let's get you some sleep."

"Can I take a quick shower?" April asked.

Boyd showed her where the towels were and started going through his drawers, looking for the speed. April reached past him and snatched a baseball jersey from the drawer. "Thanks," she murmured.

She shut the bathroom door and flipped up both switches. She worried that the whir of the fan wouldn't make enough noise, so she turned on the sink faucet. Going to the bathroom was a natural thing, everyone did it, but the thought of Boyd hearing her bathroom sounds horrified her.

After flushing the toilet and turning off the faucet, she stripped down and grabbed her razor from her purse. The warm trickle of the shower stirred up the usual mix of tension and relaxation, but April ignored it and occupied herself instead with the tasks at hand.

She lathered her hair with Boyd's herbal-scented shampoo, thrilled with the level of intimacy she felt using his stuff. The scent of Irish Spring permeated everything as she worked it into a lather over her body. She rinsed and re-soaped her legs. When she glanced at Boyd's razor on the edge of the tub, anxiety crept up, like it always did when the memory of a different silver razor and the sting of shaving lotion tried to resurface. She grabbed her own razor and relaxed as the ridges on her Flicker pressed into her fingertips. Then the roundness of its grip reminded her of her birth control case. She hoped she'd remember to take a pill when she finished. They still had to use condoms because she'd messed up the pills so many times by forgetting to take them.

After shaving, she lathered between her legs and worked her fingers around to be sure she was thorough. Then she pulled at the small, soapy thatch of hair, dislodging a few loose ones.

Rinsed and dried, she pulled on a clean pair of cotton panties and the jersey she'd commandeered. She set her favorite spaghetti-strap tank top on the counter for later. She hesitated for a second and slipped into her cutoffs. Walking around Boyd's house in her underwear didn't feel right. If he wanted the shorts off her, he'd just have to help her wiggle out of them.

When Boyd went in to shower, April took the time to look around his room. The mattress on the floor was unmade, but not especially sloppy. A few dirty clothes were thrown in the corner of the room, but at least they were contained. Not like in Nicki's brother's bedroom. April and Nicki snuck into Peter's room on a few occasions to look for loose change or cigarettes. Peter stashed girly magazines under his mattress and dirty dishes under his bed. His room always smelled sour. But not Boyd's. Boyd's room smelled just like him—a little soap, a little sweat. A sexy combination.

It was only the third time April had been in Boyd's bedroom. She considered going through his dresser but was too tired. She stretched across his mattress. She smelled him in the sheets, so she inhaled deeper and deeper. Her head grew lighter with each exaggerated breath, until Boyd's scent swirled and mixed with a scent from April's past. She fell into a fitful sleep.

April was nine years old, running alongside the Hillsboro train, close on her sister's heels. She'd never catch up to Katie, but Katie wouldn't let too much distance grow between them; she'd much rather taunt April by being just out of reach. The dream shifted. April was no longer chasing

Katie; she was running after Bobby. And when her cousin stopped and spun around to face her, she was amazed by the wonderful way his grown-up body was lean and strong, smelling earthy and a little untidy.

In the dream, the basement wasn't musty, it wasn't cold, and April's dad didn't interrupt them. In the dream, April was in the shower as a reward, not to wash away the sting of her dad's shave cream. In the dream, Bobby took the soap from her and lathered her back, legs, and butt. He told her he loved her and would never leave. He told her he'd play Trouble or Monopoly with her anytime she wanted and wouldn't get mad when she won.

Waking, April realized she wasn't pressing her body against her cousin's; it was Boyd whispering her name, not Bobby. It was Boyd with her shorts and panties pulled down; Boyd trying to thrust himself inside her. She moaned, said no, tried to push him off. She didn't know if she was more upset by the pain of Boyd trying to fit himself into her, or by the betrayal of her mind dreaming about Bobby.

"That hurts," she said.

"It won't for long," he answered.

April closed her eyes and inhaled her cousin Bobby's scent.

A mouth pressed against hers, tongue probing, searching. It was Boyd's lips, his smooth face against hers, not Bobby's rough, stubbly skin. Disappointment tried to sneak in, but April wouldn't let it. She loved Boyd. She'd proven it again and again.

✝

"I'm starving," April said as she slipped back into her cutoffs. She followed Boyd into his kitchen and plopped onto a bar stool to watch him fiddle with his weed and rolling papers.

Boyd held up the bag. "Baby, roll us one of your good, fat ones, okay?"

Smiling, April took the pot from him and swiveled her bar stool around. She liked it when Boyd complimented her, whether it was about how good her ass looked in her Calvins or how well she rolled a joint.

Boyd stood at the opposite counter. His Levis hung low on his hips, and he wasn't wearing a shirt. Thanks to working construction with his Uncle Mark, he was in good shape. She wanted to touch the long, tight muscles running down Boyd's back, to kiss the freckles splattered across his shoulders, but couldn't move off the bar stool.

Boyd walked over to her. "Open wide."

"What is it?"

"Just remember who takes care of you," Boyd said as he slipped the capsule into her mouth. He handed her a soda, and she washed it down. After a soft kiss, he returned to the other counter.

Peanut butter and jelly sandwiches weren't April's favorite, but something about having Boyd actually fix her something to eat made it better than any feast. Boyd assembled the sandwiches and stuck the jelly knife in the sink without rinsing it. April smiled at how incensed that would make Katie.

She rolled her eyes as she wondered what Katie was doing. She wouldn't call her big sister *Kate* like she'd requested. To her, she'd always be *Katie*, no matter how grown-up or educated she got at that snooty private college in Norfolk. Her bookworm sister was taking summer classes because she wanted to. April worried about her, ever since she saw a cable show at Nicki's house that said if a girl waited too long to get a boyfriend she'd turn frigid. April was convinced that was going to happen to Katie. And April wouldn't even know if it did, since Katie hadn't been coming home weekends like she had in the beginning. Not that they saw much of each other when she did; April was busy with a life of her own now. To Boyd and his friends, she was just April, not Katie Hunter's younger sister.

✝

They hung around Boyd's house until the last moment before his mom was due home. Boyd thrust April's purse at her and stuffed his wallet into his back pocket, all but herding her out the door.

"I need to stop by Joey's for a minute, then we can do anything you want," Boyd said.

Except go see Katie, April thought.

Her pouting was eclipsed by curiosity when Boyd turned onto Joey's road. More than the usual amount of people milled around the complex. Boyd didn't park the car, just idled, until Joey saw him from the sidewalk and came over.

"What's up?" Boyd asked.

"Messed up day, man." Joey squatted near Boyd's door, swaying slightly. "Hey, girl," he said to April.

Boyd interrupted before April said anything to Joey. "What's going on?"

"That Doug guy from last night OD'd."

Last night? April couldn't believe it had been just the night before. Her energy suddenly bottomed out, and she wished she had another Black Beauty.

"Cops been hanging around, asking questions," Joey said.

April tried to catch more of what Joey was saying, but Boyd leaned out the window, making it hard for her to hear. The word *ambulance* stood out in her mind then something about dying on the way to the hospital. But she knew that wasn't right. The guy had died in Joey's apartment.

"Catch you later, dude," Boyd said.

Joey stood and took a step away from the car. "Take it easy." He headed back toward his apartment.

"What was that all about?" April asked.

"Nothing." Boyd scratched at his cheek in the nervous way he got sometimes when he was tired or wired or up to something. "Nothing at all."

April stifled a yawn. "Aren't we gonna hang out with Joey?"

"Nah." Boyd put the car in drive. He lifted his head, and his features relaxed. "Let's go to Leary's. Just like the old days."

"Leary's Lane?"

"Yeah. Remember that first night?"

She smiled. "Yeah."

He gave a decisive nod and started driving. "It'll be—"

"Romantic," she finished for him. Just like before.

But then she thought about how only teenagers went to Leary's, not mature couples like her and Boyd. And she did consider herself mature beyond her years, not like those kids she went to school with.

Chapter Five

Kate hustled into the Farm Fresh Supermarket. Lana was coming over for a late lunch before work, and Kate wanted food that was quick and easy. She didn't want to waste any precious time. Especially not on their two-week anniversary.

The woman working behind the counter in the deli department was in her early twenties. Not as pretty as Lana, Kate thought. But then again, Kate didn't think anyone was as pretty as her girlfriend.

She decided on the pasta salad, and the woman spooned it out. That woman could have a girlfriend, too. Any of the women around could. That made Kate smile.

She thanked the deli worker and hurried to the back of the store. Tiny jars of shrimp swimming in cocktail sauce were arranged in rows in the seafood department. Since it would be easy and cheap, Kate picked up two of them.

Cellophane-wrapped trays of crab caught her eye. She could mix it with the pasta salad to class it up. Also cheap and easy. She looked closer at the label and realized it was imitation crab, made from fish. She lifted it to her nose. It didn't smell fishy. She put the tray in her basket.

She paused between the dairy and meat departments. She stepped closer to the shiny metal surface of the door to the back room and noted her reflection was a collage of subdued shades of beige. Even her hair was colorless, like

27

straw. The blue of her eyes was the only other hue that was reflected.

The image reminded her of staring into the pond behind her neighbor's house, or sometimes Chisman Creek, and saying things out loud. The ritual started when she'd watched a group of tadpoles and asked them if her cat, Priscilla, would come home one day. That was before she knew her parents had given Pris away because of April's allergies. Even after the squiggly tadpoles had long become frogs and gone away to wherever frogs went away to, she'd look into the still water at her reflection for the truth. She started making statements to the water, her way of acknowledging she accepted them as fact.

"Priscilla's not coming home," she admitted one afternoon, staring into the water before closing her eyes and repeating the words.

Then it became, "Blackie's not coming back." The final statement she made to the dark water was, "Mom is never coming home." After that, she no longer wanted to acknowledge things to the pond.

She focused on her reflection in the metal door. She knew what statement she wanted to make. She watched her mouth form the words, in a soft whisper, unheard by anyone else, but liberating, nonetheless. *I am a lesbian.* She almost laughed at how easily it came to her.

She fantasized about approaching people in the store and telling them she was a lesbian. She loved the way the word lolled around in her head. She imagined going up to the redheaded bagger and saying, "Hi, I'm a lesbian," and him replying, "That's nothing. I'm Irish." Or telling the cashier the same thing, and having her respond with, "Hey, me, too," and teaching Kate the secret handshake. But all Kate said was, "Thank you," and, "Have a nice day."

As she crossed the parking lot, she fiddled with the pewter hummingbird on her key chain. It had been a graduation present from her aunt. Before that she'd kept her keys on a plain ring. When she was ten years old, she'd begged her dad for a keychain, one with a soft, purple-dyed good luck charm that she'd found dangling from a display in the country store in Hillsboro. It wasn't until they'd walked across the hump-backed bridge to their summerhouse that she realized the implications of a rabbit's foot without the rabbit attached. She'd cried the rest of the day and accidentally on purpose dropped the good luck charm down the hole of the old outhouse.

Kate unlocked the car, carefully placed her groceries onto the passenger seat as she climbed in, and leaned forward to take a deep breath. The honeysuckle-scented air freshener swung from her rearview mirror. It wasn't exact, but it was the closest she'd get to smelling Lana when Lana wasn't with her. The stiff piece of cardboard, shaped almost like a flower, was too sweet, like it was trying too hard, and it wasn't tinged with a hint of oil paint either, but it would have to do.

Kate turned the key in the ignition, and the rattle started up immediately. She'd lied to her dad the last time he'd asked if she'd had the oil changed lately. She needed to take the car in, and she would, when she found the time.

For so long, she'd only lied to her dad to cover for April. It had started right after that last summer they spent in Hillsboro, with Kate taking the blame for a broken lamp. Then she covered up the stolen liquor, the sneaking out, and the smoking. Kate had even lied to the principal about April's absences when April discovered the joys of skipping school.

But this new lying, about her car, was so uncharacteristic of Kate. Her focus wasn't on her dad, or her car, or anything but Lana. Just Lana.

✝

Kate watched the light flicker faintly on Lana's face. She'd wanted for them to eat solely by candlelight, with the curtains drawn against the afternoon sun, but even with the new votives she'd splurged on, there just wasn't enough light. She'd had to leave the desk lamp on.

"The rose is nice," Lana said.

It was a single rose she hadn't thought about getting a vase for. It sprouted out of the lemonade can in the middle of the table like a stubborn weed growing in a sidewalk crack.

"I wish you didn't have to work tonight," Kate said.

Lana smiled. "Me, too."

"You still won't tell me where you—"

"Nope," Lana interrupted with a laugh.

Kate wasn't sure whether Lana was uneasy about where she worked, or about Kate. She wondered if Lana's friends would tease her about going out with a science geek from the small, private college. She was troubled by Lana keeping so much of her life from her, but she refused to let her apprehension interfere with enjoying their lunch.

They finished the little shrimp cocktails, and Kate spooned out helpings of pasta salad with seafood delight, as she referred to the fish pretending to be crab. She took a sip of lemonade and looked up at Lana, who was chewing in slow motion as she set her fork down on the table.

Kate watched her so closely that she almost missed her own mouth with her fork. Then she bit into a chunk of the fake crab and wished she *had* missed her mouth.

"I'll spit it out if you will," Lana said from around the food in her mouth.

They both snatched up their napkins and got rid of the offending food.

"Oh, God," Kate gasped. "It must've gone bad."

Lana placed her elbows on the table. "The shrimp cocktail was good."

"Sorry about ruining the pasta salad," Kate said.

"It's no big deal. Really."

Kate's shoulders heaved upwards and crumpled back into place. Tears flowed down her cheeks.

"What's wrong?" Lana asked.

"I've ruined it all—"

Lana wiped at Kate's tears. "Everything's fine. Well..." She paused, smiling. "Maybe not the seafood stuff, but everything else." She lifted Kate's chin and forced eye contact. "It's okay."

"I wasn't going for okay. I wanted today to be perfect."

"It is."

"No, it's not." She looked away from Lana.

"What's wrong?"

"It's just that I really like you," Kate said.

"I really like you, too." Lana took Kate's hand in hers and moved her thumb along the back of it.

A shiver ran up Kate's arm. "I mean, *really* like you."

"I *really* do, too."

She couldn't tell Lana how much more than "like" she felt. "It's scary."

"The best things often are." Lana brought Kate's hand to her mouth and pressed her lips against the knuckles, one at a time. "Better?"

"Better." Kate stared into the dark eyes, thinking she saw herself. There was no place she would rather see her reflection.

†

April ran down the driveway and looked over her shoulder twice before making it to the car. She jumped in, slammed the door, and slid over next to Boyd.

The Gran Torino's tires spewed dirt as Boyd pulled away. April winced. That was one of the few things her dad complained about. And he hadn't wanted her going out to begin with.

Boyd squeezed April's thigh and took her hand. He pressed something into it. It was a Quaalude. She looked at Boyd; he was watching the road in front of them and smiling. April examined the lude.

Boyd answered her unasked question. "It's just smudged from being in my pocket with some change."

She turned it over in her hand but knew she wouldn't be able to identify the foreign substance.

"A little dirt isn't gonna kill you," Boyd said.

You have to eat a pound of dirt before you'll die, April's mom had always claimed.

April smiled, still staring at the lude. Then she kissed it and blew up toward the ceiling. *Kiss it up to God*, her mom would say.

Boyd laughed. He knew what she was doing. One night when they first started dating, she'd gotten drunk and Boyd saw her kiss a French fry up to God after dropping it. He picked at her and picked at her until she finally told him her mom's old saying. To her surprise, he didn't laugh, just looked thoughtful for a second before saying, "Okay." If

April hadn't already fallen in love with Boyd, she would have right then and there.

April popped the lude into her mouth and washed it down with a swig of Boyd's beer.

"The cooler's in the back if you want a brew."

"No. The lude will have me loopy enough."

Kiss it up to God. Did her mom still do that—whether consciously or unconsciously—as April sometimes caught herself or Katie doing? She looked over at Boyd when he turned left onto Route 17. "Aren't we going to Joey's?"

"Nope. It's Tuesday. Double feature night."

April rolled her eyes. Hadn't they already seen every horror movie ever made? In the eleven months and three days since they first started going together, every movie they'd seen reminded her of the ones before it.

Boyd patted her leg. "Admit it, you love going to the drive-in for these slash flicks."

She grabbed his beer from between his legs, took a big swig, and put it back. As she pressed the can down, she saw him squirm. A tingle washed across her. At least she was going to the double feature after a lude and not just pot. Once the lude started its magic, she wouldn't care about the movie, or about being cramped in the backseat.

Their tires crunched over the graveled lane as they drove between rows of speakers. April noted that it wasn't weekend-packed, but still pretty busy. After they had rolled down the windows and hooked up the speaker, Boyd opened a new beer.

"You want a soda?" he asked.

The word took its time coming out, and she smiled at the fogginess growing in her head. "Yeah."

When Boyd returned from the concessions, he nodded toward the backseat.

"It's not even dark yet," April said.

"So?"

"Get in, up front with me," she said with a whine.

Boyd slid into the car. He leaned over her and let loose an animal growl before pretending to devour her. She giggled and goose bumps erupted on her arms as he nibbled her neck.

"You feeling that lude?" he asked.

"Maybe."

"You feel drunk? Horny?"

"A little drunk."

Boyd laughed. "And a lot horny."

His mouth worked down her neck and found her breast. April noted to herself that even though it wasn't quite dark yet, it was okay for what he was doing. She loved the feel of his hot breath through the cotton of her spaghetti-strap tank top. When he pulled his mouth away, the dampness cooled her flesh and her nipples hardened into even smaller nuggets. She wished he'd stay there at her breasts, suck her into his mouth until she couldn't take it anymore, but he'd already moved on, his mouth on her shoulder. She wanted to pinch her nipples while he touched her, like she did lying alone in her own bed sometimes, but didn't dare touch herself in front of him.

Boyd groaned. "You're hot, aren't you?"

April breathed faster but didn't answer. She never answered. Even when she wanted to, she couldn't bring herself to say it.

"Get in back," Boyd said.

She saw double as she crawled over the seat and glided across the vinyl surface. Her skin prickled as Boyd got out of the car and ducked into the backseat with her.

†

"What the hell?" April pushed away the big finger pressing against her nose.

"Just breathe, baby. Come on, this will wake you up."

April took a deep breath through her nose, and the sharpness of the powder inside her nostril made her sit straight up. "Shit."

"Relax." Boyd laughed. "Welcome back. You were really out of it."

"What the hell was that?"

"A little crank. Just enough to wake you up."

April moved sluggishly, even if her mind was now alert. She wiped at her nose.

"It's not great stuff but should do okay for you. I think Joey pulled a fast one. This is not the same shit I sampled earlier." He stuck his hand between his legs and rearranged himself. "You were great."

"I'm glad you enjoyed yourself," she said.

Boyd helped April back to the front seat. "Thanks for finally saying it."

"Saying what?"

"You know." He started the car.

"No. I don't."

"It's so funny how you don't remember shit when you do ludes."

"Remember what?" She was losing interest in the guessing game.

He pulled her head closer and whispered with his hot breath in her ear, "Fuck me, fuck me."

She pulled away and gave him a half playful slap on his chest and a harder one on his arm. "I did not." She felt heat sear her face.

Chapter Six

"I have plums, yogurt, milk, and lemonade. Or we can get dressed and go out somewhere."

"I love plums," Lana said.

Kate started to get out of bed but hesitated. She grabbed her panties to slip them on under the sheet.

Lana laughed. "I'll get them."

She sauntered across the room, opened the fridge, and reached in. Kate's breath caught in her chest at the sight of Lana's nipples reacting to the cool air. The sparkle in Lana's eyes told Kate she knew very well the effect she was having on her.

"Get your mind off sex and tell me about your family," Lana said as she brought the bag of plums and a can of lemonade over to the bed.

"What do you want to know?"

"Siblings?" Lana asked.

"One sister. Her name's April."

"Younger, I bet."

"Yeah, how did you know?"

"You come across as an older sister. Firstborn. Brain."

Kate smiled. "How about you? An only child?"

"Yes, smarty, as a matter of fact I am." Lana took a bite of her plum. "How about your mom and dad?"

"April and I were pretty much raised by my dad. Mom took off years ago, and we haven't heard from her since."

"That has to be tough."

"We get by."

Lana studied her for a long moment then changed the subject. "How long have you wanted to be a vet?"

Kate hesitated. "Probably since I learned to say the word."

"Veterinarian," Lana said slowly, weighing each syllable.

Kate sighed. If Lana only knew the truth about Kate's failures, she'd know her for the fraud she really was. "When do I get to see some of your art?" Kate asked.

"Soon. I'm painting something for you."

"Really? Wow. What is it?"

"You'll see. It may even be ready the next time I see you."

Kate's heart pounded with the sound of "next time." She desperately needed to know each moment with Lana wasn't going to be the last.

"I can't wait," Kate said, referring to both the artwork and the "next time." "How long have you been painting?"

"Since I was old enough to ask for paints."

"I bet you're good," Kate said.

"When I was in the eighth grade, I had the most incredible art teacher. She always knew when I needed to hear something positive, whether it was as simple as my color choice or as complex as my theme."

"Everyone needs a teacher like that at least once in their life," Kate said.

"She was the only person who believed in me as an artist. And then I went to high school and became a nobody."

Lana let out a stiff laugh. "Okay, smart-girl, time for a confession."

"A confession?"

Lana leaned back against a pillow. "I didn't graduate high school."

Kate stared at her. She'd never known anyone who was a normal, functioning person who hadn't finished high school. Only flunkies like April's pothead friends were dropouts. "Really?"

"Really." Lana's stare was defiant.

Kate didn't want her surprise to be perceived as judgment, but she didn't know what else to say.

"How bad does that bother you?" Lana asked.

"It doesn't."

"Liar."

Kate shook her head. "If you're okay with it, why shouldn't everyone else be?"

"Tell me something shocking about you," Lana said.

Kate's mouth opened, but no words came out.

"Come on, play fair. It's your turn."

"There's nothing to tell." Kate fidgeted with her plum-stained napkin.

"I already know one of your secrets."

Kate looked at her. "What secret is that?"

"That you're falling in love with me."

The bats and birds started again, flapping their wings inside Kate's stomach. She couldn't speak because her heart was lodged in her throat.

Lana gave a nervous laugh. "I was just kidding."

Kate put her napkin and plum pit on the table beside the *I Love Rock and Roll* tape case. She leaned into Lana and pulled her close. Her body started to shake as Lana's mouth found her neck.

Kate held on, tighter than she ever had on the scooter.

†

"Have you ever wanted to be with a guy?" Lana asked as she snuggled against Kate.

Kate thought about her fascination with her cousin Bobby, how she would seek him out and relish his teasing attention. He made her feel special. But, as it turned out, it was a very brief fascination.

Kate tried to push away the memory of Bobby telling her he could show her a snake in the woods—the sound of his zipper scraping downward, the jerk of her arm as he grabbed her sleeve, the sting in her lungs as she bolted away to hide in the basement.

"No," Kate whispered. "I've never wanted to be with a guy." She couldn't look at Lana.

"Damn, girl, where'd you go just then?"

Kate looked up and saw the flash of a challenge in Lana's dark eyes, but there were some things even Lana couldn't draw out of her. She'd never forget what happened in that basement—what Bobby did to April as Kate watched, hidden and frozen—but she'd also never speak of it.

She started to ask if Lana had ever been with a guy. Instead, she focused on the periodic table of elements tacked to the wall. She closed her eyes. *Hydrogen, helium, lithium.* No, she chastised herself, opening her eyes. She didn't want to think of Lana with anyone else but wouldn't let herself play games of distraction either. Not while she was with Lana.

"I can't be a vet," Kate said, surprising herself with the confession.

"Sure you can, smart-girl. You, of all people, can be anything you want to be." Lana held Kate's gaze for a long moment. "You mean you don't want to be a vet?"

"I can't be. And I don't know how to tell my dad."

"I don't get it," Lana said.

"The summer after high school, I worked in a vet's office. It had never been real before then. It was just something I knew in theory."

"And you decided you didn't want to do it?"

"Mr. McGee."

Lana cocked her head.

"Mr. McGee was this cat. I'll never forget the way he clung to his big, burly owner. The poor man just cried and cried as he held his little orange cat that'd been hit by a car."

"Oh, sweetie," Lana said.

"I started sobbing so hard, I couldn't even help the vet get the cat prepped for surgery. I cried all the time. Sometimes I'd hold off until I got out to my car, but other times, I'd just start blubbering right there in the office. It was horrible."

Lana's thumb caught a tear on its way down Kate's face. "What did the vet say?"

"He was patient at first, but it never got any better." Kate pulled at a snag in the bedspread. "Eventually I just stayed in the back, cleaning up the boarding area."

"And you're still studying vet stuff?"

"Yeah. My dad's going to be so disappointed in me." Even if she often felt her existence as her father's daughter was mostly in theory for him, just as veterinarian medicine had been for her. It wasn't lost on Kate that April was the favored daughter.

Kate was relieved to finally admit she didn't know what to do about school, but she was also determined to change the subject. "I can't wait to see what you're painting for me."

✝

"You're absolutely sure your dad won't come home?"

"Absolutely." Kate glanced around the living room and tried to imagine what Lana's first impression was. "He's out of town. As usual."

Lana picked up a framed photo from the end table. "Look how cute you were."

"Were?"

"Were. *Now* you're sexy."

Kate didn't believe that, but the comment still made her blush. She stood beside Lana and pointed. "That's Dad, Mom, April, and me, of course."

Lana put the photo back. "Show me more."

"More?"

"Pictures. You do have a family photo album, don't you?"

"Yeah."

"Show me."

Kate went to the TV stand and opened the drawer nestled beneath the television. She hesitated, sure she wanted to share with Lana but uncertain of her own reaction to the pictures she hadn't looked at in years.

They settled on the itchy plaid sofa she'd always hated. She opened the album and took a deep breath.

"How sweet," Lana said.

"That's me with Blackie." She remembered how much she loved that dog, how devastated she was when he had to go away.

41

"Blackie? Um, Kate, the dog is tan."

She nodded. "I know."

Kate turned to a picture of her dad. He was wearing a suit and his hair was slicked back. He seemed taller. Was it because he was happier then, standing there with his chest all puffed up? Or because Kate had been smaller, more awestruck?

"Your dad's handsome." She glanced at Kate. "Have you told him yet that you want to change your major?"

Kate hated letting her dad down. She vividly remembered the first time she really disappointed him. Her sister had gotten mad at her for not letting her watch a rerun of *The Monkeys*. April threw a shoe across the room, and it hit the ceramic lamp their dad had brought home from a business trip. It crashed to the ground; the lampshade ripped, and the stand shattered. Kate knew immediately that she would take the blame, that being her new routine ever since that last trip to Hillsboro. And her dad was so disappointed in her, he wouldn't talk to her until the next day.

"No, I haven't told him about my major yet. But I will."

"Your mom's beautiful," Lana said when Kate flipped the page. She scrutinized Kate for a moment. "Light hair, perfect nose. You look like her."

"You think?" She leaned closer to the picture.

"Oh yeah, no doubt."

The next photo was of her mom and dad with April. Her mom held the baby, while her dad hovered protectively behind them. Kate cocked her head. Something wasn't right. Maybe it was her, not April. No, she thought, it had to be her sister. It was obvious by the sad look in her mom's eyes. She would never forget how down her mom was after April was born.

Kate pulled up the plastic that covered the tacky page of the album. It separated with a tearing sound. She stuck her fingernail under the corner of the photo and lifted it off the adhesive. She flipped it over and grew confused when she read the back. "Me, Roger, and Katie."

But the look on her mom's face... She flipped forward a few pages and found a shot with all four of them. Her dad held April, and her mom's hand rested on Kate's shoulder. Kate tightly gripped Monk-Monk, her one-eyed stuffed monkey.

Kate looked closer. There it was. The sadness she was used to after April was born. She compared it to the photo of her with her parents.

Could it be her mom was sullen after *each* of her children was born? The words flashed into her mind: Postpartum Depression. But that would change everything, right down to her secret belief that it was April's fault their mother left. Her stomach grew queasy.

"Come back to me," Lana said as she touched Kate's chin and steered her gaze to her own.

"I'm here," Kate said. She shoved the photo back in place and shut the album. Lana followed her to the drawer, where Kate quickly stashed it away again.

Lana gave her a peck on the cheek and went to the four-foot globe in the corner. "Wow," she said.

Kate followed her and grabbed the metal arc across the top, lifting it up. The globe separated at the equator to reveal a rack with cutouts for bottles that encircled an area with glasses and an ice bucket.

She ran her hand along the empty bottle holders. "I see Dad finally stopped leaving liquor around for April to steal."

"This is so cool," Lana said as she ran her hands across Africa.

Kate nodded before lowering the top. She ran her finger along the seam that split the Atlantic Ocean in two. The edge was rough where the paper had started peeling. She thought about her mom and how she'd made up travels for her after she'd left them.

Lana slipped behind her and rested her hands on Kate's waist. With her mouth close to Kate's ear, she whispered, "Hey. Something wrong?"

Kate held her breath then slowly exhaled. She would not let memories of her mom flood over her now. She couldn't.

"Want to talk about it?" Lana asked.

Kate turned to face her. "I'd rather show you my room."

Lana smiled and Kate took her hand. She closed her bedroom door behind them. Lingering by Kate's dresser, Lana picked up a tiny plastic microscope.

"I know," Kate said. "I'm such a geek."

Lana laughed then grew serious. "Do you think we spend too much time in bed?" she asked.

"What makes you think we're going to bed now just because we came into—"

Lana interrupted her with her mouth. She steered Kate backward toward the bed, lightly punctuating each step with a kiss. Once there, Lana nudged her with one finger, causing Kate to plop down.

Kate wasted no time pulling Lana on top of her. Lana laughed and knelt over her. "Scootch up."

She did, and Lana lowered herself until she covered Kate. Lana kissed her hard and deep, then her touch turned soft and sweet.

"No," Kate whispered against Lana's lips.

"No? As in stop?"

Kate smiled. "No, as in the answer to your question. No, we don't spend too much time in bed." She pulled Lana down harder on her and pressed her pelvis up to grind slowly against her.

"Oh," Lana whimpered.

"Take your clothes off. I want to see you while I touch you." She gently tugged at Lana's T-shirt.

"We shouldn't get undressed. What if your sister comes home?"

"She won't. No one will."

Lana rose up onto her knees and lifted her arms. Kate pulled Lana's shirt over her head. She cupped Lana's breasts in her palms and felt her nipples harden under the lacy bra.

"Lose *your* shirt, sweetie," Lana said. Kate complied. "Oh? No bra?"

"No bra," Kate answered. "Shorts?"

"Off." Lana giggled. "Maybe we should get up long enough to undress."

They did. Then Kate whipped down the bedspread, and they dove back in.

†

Kate hesitated as she listened. She decided the noise was just her imagination, so she resumed her light stroking of Lana.

They both jumped at the sound of the car door. Kate got out of bed and peeked around the side of the window curtain. "It's my dad." Kate turned, and the look on Lana's face made her stomach lurch.

"Oh, God." Lana jumped up and started grabbing for her clothes.

"It's okay." Kate gathered her own clothing. "We'll just get dressed and go out there like nothing's going on. He won't in a million years suspect—"

"No," Lana said. "No way." She frantically looked around. "Shit. I'll hide."

"It's no big deal, baby. He won't give it a second thought. Really."

When the front door opened, the fear on Lana's face jump-started Kate's own.

"The closet," Lana whispered. "I'll hide in the closet."

"You won't fit."

"Katie, you're home," her dad yelled from the front hallway.

Kate looked at Lana and couldn't believe how pale she'd grown. "Go," she said, pushing Lana toward the closet. "I'm sorry," she mouthed, then she shut the door. She darted to her bedroom door and turned the lock.

"I didn't expect to see you today," her dad said, his voice growing louder.

"I'm changing my clothes. I'll be right out."

She pulled her panties back on and fumbled with her shorts. She jumped when she heard clanging and a gasp come from her closet. She whispered through the louvered door that she'd be right back. Lana didn't answer.

Kate pulled her shirt over her head and unlocked the door. As she was opening it, her dad appeared at the threshold. "What a nice surprise," he said.

She glanced at her rumpled bed, then back to her dad. Still gripping his scuffed briefcase, he stood board-stiff, as usual. He showed no sign of noticing her unmade bed.

"Will you stay for dinner?" He smoothed his free hand over his dark, wiry hair.

"Sorry, Dad. I just came to get some old texts that might help with my classes."

"Everything okay at school?"

"Oh yeah. Never better." The hair on the back of Kate's neck prickled when she heard the tinkling of hangers. "Yeah," she said, a little too loudly. "School's great. But I better go. I've got a lot of homework."

The clinking grew louder, and he cocked his head. Kate's heart pounded in beat with the hangers as she tried to figure out what to say if he found Lana hiding. She didn't know if he'd be angry, or just disappointed. She was more afraid of letting him down than of getting in trouble.

"Okay," he said.

She held her breath.

"Just drive safely. How is your car running anyway? Any other strange sounds coming from it?"

She ignored the faint noise coming from her closet and lied about her car. "No, no more sounds. I'm gonna just grab those books and go."

"April will be so sorry she missed you."

Kate knew better, but nodded. "Yeah. Me, too."

Her dad smiled and disappeared into his bedroom.

Kate shut and locked her door, then she pulled Lana out of the closet. She whispered, "If you hurry and get dressed, we can leave before he comes out of his room."

"Leave? How?"

"The door would be the easiest way," Kate said with a grin.

Lana pulled on her clothes. "No way am I going through the house. I'll go out the window."

"Don't be ridiculous. He won't see you." She couldn't understand why Lana was overreacting. It hadn't been *that* close of a call.

"I'll go out the window," Lana said.

Kate reluctantly helped her, cringing at the sound Lana's feet made when they hit the hard-packed dirt below.

"I'll be right out," Kate whispered. She locked the window and started toward the door but stopped short and turned back to her bed. She pulled the bedspread up, grabbed an old Biology textbook from her bookshelf, and ran out the front door.

Lana was slumped almost to the floor when Kate got in the car. She turned the key in the ignition and prayed her dad wouldn't hear the strange sound emanating from the engine.

As Kate pulled away, she laughed. "All I could hear were the hangers moving. What were you doing in there?"

"Shaking," Lana muttered.

"Oh." She reached for Lana's hand. Lana pulled away from her and looked around wildly.

"Not here."

"No one can see."

Lana gave her a pleading look. "Not here."

"Sorry." Kate turned to watch the road, looking forward to when Lana would relax and not worry about what people thought of them being together.

She stayed in the right-hand lane, switching lanes only to let others merge onto the interstate. Kate stole a glance at Lana and struggled to resist the urge to touch her. She didn't speak until she couldn't take the silence any longer.

"One day, we'll look back at this and laugh."

Lana stiffened. "I doubt it," she said, looking straight ahead.

†

Boyd put his arm around April's shoulder, holding her too tight. He steered her out of the Things Remembered store at the mall, and April knew by his hurry he must have lifted the bracelet he'd been looking at.

He stepped in front of a large, middle-aged woman. When she moved to the side, he shadowed her.

April shrugged her way out from under the weight of Boyd's arm. She grabbed his hand. "Come on, Boyd. Let's go."

He stared at the woman. She'd frozen, her ice cream cone halfway to her mouth.

"Come on," April repeated. She tugged at his arm.

Boyd leaned closer to the woman. "Should you really be eating that?"

The woman's hand trembled, and a drop of melted vanilla dripped down her arm.

He gave her a huge smile. "Cow," he said.

April let go of Boyd's arm and walked away. He rushed up behind her and grabbed her ass.

"That was mean," April whispered.

"That was funny. Admit it." He pulled her close. "Let's get a drink at the Black Crab."

"It's the Blue Dragon."

Boyd grabbed her ass again. "Thank God for bars in malls."

"Technically it's a restaurant."

"Technically, huh? You sound like your sister." April cringed but didn't respond.

"You got your fake ID for the technically-a-restaurant?" When April only nodded, he added, "what's wrong with you tonight?"

"Nothing," she said. But something was nagging at her. She just couldn't pinpoint what. "Sorry," she whispered, knowing she shouldn't take it out on Boyd. Leaning into him as they walked through the mall, she wondered if her time of the month was coming. She was going to start keeping better tabs on that, she promised herself.

Once inside, Boyd elbowed his way to the bar and pulled out a stool for April. "What's that thing you and Nicki talk about drinking?" He rolled his eyes. "Never mind."

He told the bartender to bring them each a Long Island Iced Tea.

April sipped while Boyd slugged his and ordered another. Goose bumps were forming on her arms and legs, and she wanted nothing more than to get out of the air conditioning.

"Got something for you, babe." Boyd pulled a bracelet from his front pocket.

"Hmm, when did you get that?"

He laughed. "Put it on. Let me see how it looks." He yanked the Things Remembered tag off before handing it to her. "It's real silver."

She looked on the inside, just long enough to read "silver-plated," and draped it over her arm. When she held out her wrist so Boyd could fasten it, he didn't notice because his face was buried in his drink. She struggled but got it latched. It did look nice on her, she had to admit.

"I would have had it engraved for you, but I didn't have time." He winked.

April ran her finger along the shiny links of the too-large bracelet. She moved her finger in a circular pattern over the flat plate where the engraving would normally be.

Movement to her left caught her attention. The bartender lined up shots of amber liquid on a tray and topped them off with some Bacardi 151. Just before pushing the tray toward the waiter, the bartender lit a match to the shots.

Boyd reached for an ashtray and knocked into the waiter. A blue flame followed the alcohol up the waiter's arm.

April took a deep breath, but the waiter just patted out the flames with his hand and went about getting new shots. He was making a point of not looking at Boyd. The guy was probably afraid to.

After Boyd downed his third drink, they left the Blue Dragon. He stumbled across the parking lot. When they got to the car, April grabbed his keys.

"Hey—"

"I need to practice. If I don't start driving more, I'll get rusty."

"Better you than my car." He went to the passenger side without any further resistance.

April got in and adjusted the seats and mirror. Boyd leaned over her and started tugging at the bracelet.

"Lemme see that thing." He grabbed her arm. "Yeah, needs to be engraved." He brought it up to his mouth and started scraping his teeth against it.

"Boyd, stop. You're gonna break it."

He studied it and frowned. Then he smiled. He pushed his arm in front of April's face. "Here, engrave me. Go on, bite my arm."

"I am not going to bite you."

He shoved his arm closer until it pressed against her lips. "Brand me."

She turned her face away. "Stop it."

He grabbed her arm again and put the bracelet in his mouth. They both froze when they heard his tooth crack. "Oops," he said.

April held tight to the steering wheel as she merged onto the interstate. "White on right," she whispered. It was a mantra for her anytime they got on I-64, ever since the first time she had to drive because Boyd was fall-down drunk. She'd been buzzed, too, but at least she could stand. That first night, trying to get them home from Buckroe Beach, she had to keep reminding herself that the white line belonged on the right, and the yellow on the left. "White on right."

"Get off on 17," Boyd slurred. "Then turn into Farm Fresh."

"Farm Fresh?"

"Yeah, they got a sale on beer."

April glanced at him. "That's the last thing you need right now."

"Bullshit. I need beer. And bologna." He chuckled. "Yeah, that's right. Beer and bo-log-na." He leaned into her and tried to kiss her cheek.

"Get off me. I'm trying to drive." She stared straight ahead. She didn't want to even look at him when he was that drunk. It was bad enough that he was well on the way to obnoxious before he picked her up outside Nicki's house. The drinks at the Blue Dragon hadn't helped.

Boyd slapped at April's leg. "Here's our exit."

"I know." She turned on her blinker.

"Ah, look. Your hands are safely at nine and three."

She took her left hand off the wheel and tried to act more relaxed than she felt as she maneuvered onto Route 17. "And it's supposed to be ten and two."

"That's cool. I think ten and two's sexy."

She rolled her eyes but couldn't help smiling.

"That's my girl. I like it better when you're happy."

She pulled into the Farm Fresh parking lot and looked for a spot to park. She didn't want to be too far from the store. She knew Boyd would insist on going in himself, and the farther he had to walk, the more likely he was to get into trouble.

She started to put on the signal before turning into the space between a pick-up truck and a car, then thought better of amusing Boyd again. She'd just stolen a glance at him and turned back to look in front of her when the car jolted and she heard the crunch of metal on metal.

"Oh," she gasped.

"Not my car, baby," Boyd whined.

April struggled to put the gearshift into Park. She reached for her door handle.

"Where are you going?" Boyd asked.

"To see the damage to that car. Do we write a note, or do we go inside and ask around?"

"We leave."

"What?" she asked.

"We leave. Come on, what are you waiting for?"

"But—"

"Shit, April. Let's go." He pounded on the dashboard. "Go." She slipped it into reverse and backed up. "Faster," Boyd urged her as she went into drive.

The tires chirped as she sped up. She was shaking so hard, she almost went over the curb leaving the parking lot. All she heard was the blood pounding in her head and Boyd's laughter.

He stroked her leg. "Now we're having fun."

"We can't just leave."

"We already did." He paused. "Shiiiittt. I didn't get my beer."

When April glanced into the rearview mirror, Boyd turned to look behind them. "Oops," he teased. "I think there's a cop back there."

"Boyd, what do I do?" she asked as she looked around frantically.

"Hide. Yeah, baby, we'll hide." He bounced in his seat. "I know. Turn left up there and pull up beside that school bus parked in the empty lot."

She did as she was told, turned off the headlights, and waited. When the large sedan passed, she saw a hunched figure leaning into the steering wheel. It wasn't a cop driving slowly to find them, but an old man poking along.

April cringed. Had she really just hit another car and driven off? She looked at Boyd. Even though he'd told her to leave, she hadn't put up much resistance. She was just as bad as he was.

"False alarm," Boyd said. "Well, while we're parked, we might as well have some fun. What do you say?" he asked as he snuggled closer.

She knew there wasn't much to say.

Chapter Seven

Kate handed a spoon across her desk to Lana, then dumped half a bag of M&Ms into the yogurt. Lana laughed. "Makes me feel decadent," Kate said, and winked.

"I'll show you decadent," Lana said.

"Eat—"

Lana smiled and the corners of her eyes crinkled.

"The yogurt," Kate added. She dipped in her spoon and watched as the different colors from the candy swirled throughout the creamy whiteness.

"Which is your favorite?"

"M&M?" Kate asked.

"Yeah."

"Green." Kate looked up.

"You would say that."

"Do you think there's any truth to what they say about the green ones?" She studied the way Lana's T-shirt clung to her breasts, barely camouflaging the darkness of her nipples.

"Probably not. I haven't had M&Ms of any color in a long time, and I don't think it's affected me any."

"No, it hasn't." Kate smiled before turning her attention to fishing out a green M&M. "I'm so glad you're off tonight."

"Me, too." Lana leaned forward and took Kate's spoon into her mouth. After Kate slid the spoon away, Lana held the M&M against the roof of her mouth as she swallowed the yogurt, then she made a big production of chewing the candy. Her eyes widened. "Oh my God. It is true what they say about the green ones."

"Show me."

"I'm going to make you earn it today, sweetie."

Kate laughed. "You want me to beg? I'm not at all above that, you know."

"No, begging is way too easy. I want you to talk."

"About what—how crazy you drive me?" She moved forward to nuzzle Lana's neck, but Lana leaned just out of reach.

"Talk about you."

"There's nothing worth talking about. You talk. You're the one with all the secrets."

"Nope, first you," Lana said. "Did you always make good grades?"

"Yes."

"Did you ever do anything wrong in school?" When Kate glanced up at the periodic table tacked above the desk, Lana pounced. "Ah, you hesitate too long. That must mean you did."

"Maybe once," Kate whispered.

Lana sat forward and put her right elbow on the desk. "Okay, fess up, bad-ass."

"Not quite 'bad-ass.'"

"Tell me what you did wrong."

"It wasn't so much what I did, but what I let someone else do."

Lana crossed her arms over her breasts. "And here all this time I thought I was your first." Her smile was wicked.

Kate nudged her knee into Lana's thigh. "You know you were." She looked down. "When I was in the ninth grade, I got caught cheating on a quiz."

Lana gasped and almost aspirated an M&M. "Oh my God. You?"

"Well, I let this girl copy off me, and she let several other kids copy her."

"And the teacher saw?"

"No." Kate gave a weak smile. "The next day he had six of us stay after class. He knew we'd cheated because everyone of us got every answer correct except number twenty-five."

"Could have been a coincidence."

"We all answered a fill-in-the-blank question with the word *isotope*." When Lana shrugged, she clarified. "We weren't even studying atoms. It was freshman Earth Science." The heat of embarrassment seared her cheeks.

"Oh." Lana chuckled. "What did the teacher do about it?"

"He told us to study that night because we'd have to take another quiz the next day."

"That was pretty cool of him."

"He kept me after everyone else left, and he said in a real frustrated tone, 'You've been reading ahead.' I just wanted to die. All I could say was that I was sorry."

"Why did you let that girl look at your paper? You could have nonchalantly held your hand in the way, or turned your body to block her view."

Kate felt the warmth from her face spread down her neck.

Lana's eyes narrowed. "Was she cute?"

"Yeah, I guess so."

Lana's face erupted into a huge smile. "You let her cheat off you because you had a crush on her."

"I did not." Kate wiped her sweaty palms on her shorts. "I didn't even like girls that way back then."

"You mean you didn't understand yet that you liked girls that way."

"Yeah," she conceded.

"So, admit it. You had a crush on her."

Kate wouldn't say anything else about that dreadful experience. She would not go on to tell Lana about how she had hoped the girl would want to study with her, but that she'd instead tried to talk Kate into purposely failing the quiz just to mess with the teacher's head. And Kate wouldn't say anything about learning then how quickly beauty turned ugly when it didn't get its way.

"Your parents—I mean, your dad—didn't find out?"

Kate shook her head. *That* disappointment in her would have been devastating.

"Okay, fair is fair. Now it's your turn," Kate said. "What was the worst thing you did in school?"

Lana put her elbow back on the desk and rested her chin in her hand. "Do you remember me telling you about getting to high school and feeling totally lost?"

"Yeah."

"Well, I'd gone from having this great art teacher in the eighth grade to having this so-so guy in high school. God, I started hating art class then. And it wasn't just the teacher. The students were such idiots. They either didn't take art seriously at all, or they took it way too seriously. There I was, alone in the middle of the two extremes, virtually invisible."

When she paused, Kate offered her the last of the yogurt. Lana shook her head, took a deep breath, and continued.

"One day I got it in my mind to shake things up a little. I skipped a pep rally and snuck into the art room. I painted frantically while everyone else was in the gym and then after school was out. I was in another world, really going to it." She smirked. "I was going for Playboy Bunny but got something closer to Rubenesque."

"What was it?"

"Art." Lana smiled. "Art that was found the next morning on an easel outside of the guidance counselor's office."

"Specifically?" Kate asked.

"A woman wearing nothing but a python draped over her shoulders."

"Oh crap. Did you get suspended?"

"No one knew I did it. No one even suspected little old invisible me. Well, that's not entirely true. I'm pretty sure Mr. Pseudo Art Teacher knew it was my work."

"He didn't turn you in?"

"No. Much worse."

"What could have been worse?"

Lana's eyebrows arched. She gave an exaggerated sigh. "I guess I can't blame you. I can't expect an isotope lover to understand."

Kate arched her eyebrows right back. "I'm merely fond of isotopes. I don't love them. Now tell me what was worse than getting suspended."

"The jerk brought the painting into our class and had everyone sit in a semicircle. Then he made a big scene of slashing through the canvas over and over, saying something about us making sure never to mistake porn for art."

"What did you do?"

"I sat there and watched, like everyone else. And I decided I couldn't have anything to do with a teacher who would bow to the pressure of the administration and destroy someone's work like that. I knew I could never go back to that class, and without art, school was worthless to me."

"Shit," Kate said.

Lana jumped up and rubbed her hands together. "Let's go for a ride."

Kate sat up straighter, surprised. She felt like she should ask Lana more about the painting, but she didn't know what. So, she asked the next thing that popped into her mind. "A ride to the marina?"

"If that's what you want."

"Yes, I want."

Lana stood, held out her hand to Kate, and pulled her to her feet.

Kate allowed herself to be led toward the door until they came up to the closet. Her heart pounded. She halted and gripped Lana's hand to stop her. She used her other hand to open the closet door.

"What are you up to?" Lana asked.

"I want to play before we go."

"I thought we were playing at the marina."

"We'll play there afterward." She kissed Lana's forehead, her nose, her chin.

"Hmm. What have you got in mind?"

"A game called 'almost getting caught while getting it on in the closet.'" She backed Lana halfway into the closet. "We're hiding, afraid of getting caught but unable to control ourselves."

When Lana resisted the backward movement, Kate ran her fingers through Lana's hair. "It's just a game." She nudged Lana back another two steps. The sound of the hangers clanking made her heart race.

Lana willingly took the final step back.

Kate wasted no time undoing Lana's shorts and sliding them down her legs. "You are so beautiful," she whispered. She moaned as her fingers found their mark. "And you want me."

"Yes," Lana answered.

Kate stroked her until she felt the beginning shudder of Lana's release, then she slipped two fingers inside, harder and faster with each penetration, coaxing the orgasm from her.

Lana gasped and pulled Kate's hand away. Kate pressed closer, holding on when Lana's legs threatened to give out.

Lana reached for the button on Kate's shorts. Kate stopped her. "No, no, no. I'm waiting for the scooter."

"Oh how you love that thing," Lana said before taking Kate's earlobe into her mouth.

"Yeah."

"Tell me what you like so much about it."

Kate's face heated up. "You know."

"Refresh my memory." When Kate hesitated, Lana continued, "We aren't going anywhere until you tell me exactly what you like so much about my scooter."

"Umm, the way it feels to press against your back. To hold on tight. To feel the vibrations and know you're feeling them, too." Kate smiled at how easily the words came.

Lana sucked harder on Kate's earlobe. "Tell me more."

"Your fingers matching the lapping of the water as you move in and out of me. Straining in the dark to see the pleasure on your face. The danger of possibly getting caught." She stopped talking when Lana tensed.

Kate pulled her closer again. "I'm sorry." She didn't understand fully why she was sorry, just knew she should be. "There's no way we'd ever be seen. You know that, or you'd never have taken me there to begin with."

Lana relaxed. "I know."

"Now are you taking me for a ride, or not?"

Lana cocked an eyebrow.

"Take me for a ride and make me beg you to stop."

Lana pulled her shorts up. "Well, when you put it that way." She gave Kate a quick kiss and grabbed her hand.

They raced out the door and down the steps.

✝

Remnants of daylight painted low-lying clouds a fuzzy, muted pink. The last of the light flashed off the wings of a group of egrets on their way home to roost for the night.

Kate perched on the back of the scooter, holding onto Lana's hips. The bones pressing from beneath the denim of Lana's shorts rested in the palms of Kate's hands. Kate leaned forward and breathed in deeply. She nestled her face against the warmth of Lana's back, smiling into the softness of her well-worn T-shirt. Anticipation tingled along the path of the scooter's vibrations as they drove toward the marina.

With one hand still holding on to Lana, Kate brought the other up to her nose to rub against an itch. The strong, sweet smell of Lana on her hands made her heart race. She pressed her hand over her nose and inhaled over and over.

Something brushed against her ankle, and Kate looked down. She jerked her left foot up when she saw a small, wiry dog running alongside them. The dog barked, causing Lana to look down as she cruised the otherwise quiet residential road. Lana sped up and Kate put her foot back down. Barking, the dog stayed right with them, briefly connecting its mouth and the back of Kate's tennis shoe. Kate lifted her foot again, rocking the scooter slightly.

"Kick," Lana said.

"I can't kick a dog," Kate hollered.

"No. I mean kick at the air."

Kate squeezed her knees together and swung her left foot out. The act of tightening her thighs against Lana sent a jolt through her. Pushing that thought from her mind, she squeezed tighter and kicked again, all the while praying she wouldn't make contact with the dog.

Lana yelled, "Hang on," just as she turned sharply to the right.

Kate squeezed her thighs even tighter. Her heart thumped as the pulse grew stronger between her legs. She pressed her weight down on the seat and leaned forward slightly. At the increased sensation, she dug her chin into Lana's shoulder.

Lana straightened the bike and gunned the whining engine. Kate looked down. No dog. She looked behind them. Still no dog. She leaned further into Lana. Lana's back jerked, and Kate realized she was laughing.

"Good job," Lana said.

Kate pressed her face against Lana's back. She was exhilarated and more than ready to park in the privacy behind the boathouse at the marina. A movement to Kate's right caught her eye. A man and a woman waved their arms.

"Lana," the woman called out.

Lana's body tensed, and she turned left onto a narrow street Kate didn't recognize. In their escape from the dog, they'd ended up somewhere Kate had never been.

"Lana." The fading voice drifted up to them.

"Who's that?" Kate asked.

"Who?" Lana gunned the engine.

Kate held on tighter as Lana wove through narrow streets. They barely missed a Datsun parked on the side of the road. Lana jerked to the left, and Kate dug her fingers into the grooves between her ribs. Lana finally slowed.

"I'm almost out of gas," she said, barely loud enough to be heard over the engine. "We'll never make it all the way to the marina and back to campus."

Kate kept pressing hard against the vibrations of the scooter's seat. Disappointment drummed through her, gathering an angry momentum, but was soon overpowered by the heat building between her legs. She became both confused and excited by the blurring of the line between her anger and her need.

"That's okay." Kate was lying. Her legs shook. She was so close to release, so close to—

"I'll drop you off then," Lana said.

Kate felt as if she'd been kicked in the gut. She loosened the grip of her thighs and closed her eyes. She forced herself to envision the periodic table of elements. *Hydrogen, lithium, sodium.* She shook her head. *Magnesium—Mg. Calcium— Ca—also the abbreviation for California.* She'd played variations of this game so often over the years as a way of keeping herself from thinking about things she didn't want to face. Like the stinging knowledge that Lana was keeping Kate on the outskirts of her life.

Lana pulled up to Kate's dorm. Kate didn't want to let go of her. "Please come up?"

"I should go." Lana leaned down and fiddled with the engine. "Something doesn't sound right with this."

"Please." Kate winced at the squeak in her voice, the sound that betrayed the depth of her need. She reluctantly lifted herself off the vibrating seat. "I need to be with you."

Lana turned her head toward Kate. She stared for several long moments. "God, you're beautiful."

Kate lost herself in Lana's dark eyes.

Lana killed the engine and leaned forward for Kate to get off the scooter. As Kate swung her leg over, a sound from the left made them jump.

"Just a car backfiring," Kate said.

Lana looked toward the road. She sighed. Still looking in the direction of the noise, she restarted the scooter's engine. "I'm sorry," she said.

Kate stepped aside and watched Lana pull away. She stood there, legs weak, until the lingering puff of exhaust disappeared.

†

April settled onto Nicki's bed.

"Did you get it?" Nicki asked, plopping beside her.

"Get what?"

"The pot. Did you get some from Boyd for tonight?"

"Oh crap. I forgot." April didn't look at her best friend as she lied. She didn't want to admit that she looked forward to a night without overanalyzing, paranoia, and munchies.

"Oh well. At least Peter came through." Nicki reached under her bed and pulled out a paper bag. "Tada!"

April smiled at the two bottles Nicki's brother had procured. "Boone's Farm. Good job. Sorry about the pot."

"That's okay." Nicki sat up straighter. "I know how you can make it up to me."

"Oh Lord," April said. "I can tell this will be interesting."

"There's this guy I've been watching. God, April, he is soooo cute."

"Okay, where do you want to go?"

"I know you and Boyd think it's lame, but it'd just be for a little while." She gave a sheepish smile, lowering her head slightly for effect. "Mickey D's," she finally admitted.

"Friday night spent cruising the McDonald's parking lot in a lemon yellow Pacer? Hmm."

"Please?"

April hadn't done the cruising thing for a long time. Boyd wouldn't be caught dead there on a Friday night, even though his car would have been a hit with the high school guys. "Sure. Why not?" Hell, she thought, it might be a nice change. "I'll go under one condition."

"What's that?"

"No making out with him or anyone else with me in the car. If you two get together, you have to do it in his car. Okay?"

"Hell, yeah, that's okay. He drives a Firebird." She leaned over April and gave her a boisterous hug. "Thank you, thank you, thank you." She opened a bottle and handed a paper cup to April.

Once upon a time, Boyd brought Boone's Farm for April on their dates. Then one night he forgot, so she made do with beer, and the wine had never materialized again.

"This guy goes to Tabb High, but I'll let him slide on that since he's such a hunk." Nicki held up her cup of wine. "Here's to liquid courage. Maybe between this and my best friend for moral support, I might even talk to him tonight."

April sipped her wine, relishing its sweetness.

Nicki sashayed over to her dresser and checked her hair. "I know this guy's not as cool as Boyd, but I think I really like him."

April thought about Nicki's liquid courage. "You haven't even talked to him yet?"

"Well, no, not directly. One time, though, I was standing in a group of people where he was talking to some guys. By the way, who's Mopar?"

"Mopar is a what, not a who. It's a car thing." April threw back her head and drained her cup of wine.

"Oh." Nicki's eyes widened. "So, I shouldn't have chimed in that I love Mopar's newest album?"

"Tell me you didn't."

Nicki's face reddened. "Of course not." She finished off her wine. "Let me put on some music."

April recognized the latest Styx from the last time she had hung out with Nicki. She liked their music, even if Boyd had scoffed when she brought them up one time. She examined the poster of Rick Springfield on Nicki's wall.

"Rick is just plain gorgeous," Nicki said.

"Yes, he is." She looked closer and tried to figure out who he reminded her of.

Nicki refilled their cups. "We have time to hang out and finish this. It's not cool to get out there too early."

April laughed.

"I know, going there isn't cool any time." She nudged April's arm with her elbow. "Except for breakfast, after screwing your boyfriend all night long."

April ignored the comment. "We can go whenever you want."

"Cheers." Nicki held up her drink.

"Cheers."

†

Clusters of cars were already forming in the fast food parking lot when Nicki and April pulled up and parked in a space just outside the throng. Chunky, refinished Mustangs, sleek Camaros, and an assortment of other Fords and Chevys—all with big rear tires and shiny mag wheels—congregated beneath light posts.

April looked around and wondered whether any of the cars could be the one she'd hit at Farm Fresh. No, she would not think about it tonight. She would have fun hanging out with her best friend and not think about that other car.

"I'm going to run in and pee," April said.

"You can't leave me. What if he shows up and I look like a loser out here by myself?"

April sighed and settled back into the seat. "Okay, five minutes."

"Thanks." Nicki leaned forward to check her face in the rearview mirror. "I keep meaning to ask you—where's Boyd tonight?"

"He's seeing a guy who owes him money."

A pea green Vega drove by, and Nicki checked it out. "Don't worry, yours is still the ugliest car out here," April said.

Nicki playfully slapped April's arm. "My car is so ugly that it's cool."

"If you say so. Besides, at least you have a car." April smiled as she thought about Nicki's Pacer being so bright it practically glowed. It was so conspicuous that when Nicki drove them to Planned Parenthood to get on the pill, the entire school knew about it the next day.

Nicki pointed out the window. "There he is," she screeched. She jabbed her finger in the direction of the glossy red Firebird as it muscled its way through the parking lot.

"Thank God. My bladder's about to burst."

"Wait." She grabbed April's arm. "Let's see if he parks."

He cruised by, slowing in front of Nicki's car.

"Oh my God. He winked at me. Did you see that?"

It looked to April more like a nervous tic, but what did she know about hot guys who drove cool cars? Then she thought about Boyd, and her pulse quickened. "I really have to pee," she reminded Nicki.

April watched as the Firebird parked one row over, not far from where Joey was looking under the hood of an old, souped-up Mustang.

"Come on," April said, opening her door.

"Wait—"

"No, now. I have an idea." She jumped out and walked to Nicki's side of the car. "Come on, now's your chance."

Nicki got out and followed April.

"Hey," April said.

Joey looked up and smiled. "Hey, what's up?" He glanced around. "Is Boyd with you?"

"Are you kidding?" She laughed. "No, he's handling some business." Joey nodded.

April gestured toward the Firebird. "See that car over there?"

"Yeah. Not bad."

"We want a good excuse to go talk to that guy. For Nicki," she added. "So, I figure we could go over there like you're interested in his car, and Nicki could jump into the conversation."

Joey chuckled. "Okay." He didn't waste any time, just sauntered right over. "Yo, dude, nice car." The guy nodded. "My friend here wanted to see what it looked like on the inside." He herded Nicki in the direction of the car.

April saw the panicked expression on Nicki's face, but her bladder needed tending more than her friend did. She told Nicki she couldn't wait any longer and started to walk off.

"Hey, April, wait," Joey said, jogging to catch up. "I haven't seen you all week." He matched his steps to April's.

Since the dead guy, April thought.

"I didn't do anything to make you mad, did I?" Joey asked.

April stopped and studied his thin face. "No, of course not. We've just been real busy."

"Okay. Well, it was good seeing you."

"You, too," she said.

"And I'll tell you what." He winked at her. "I won't tell Boyd how uncool you were to be here tonight, if you don't tell him how uncool I was."

She laughed. "Deal." As he walked away, she called out to him, "Hey, Joey."

He turned back. "Yeah?"

She glanced over at a group of kids she recognized from school. They were staring at her. "I… ah…" She wanted to ask Joey specifics about the night that guy overdosed but couldn't get the words out. "Never mind."

April went in to use the restroom. When she returned to the parking lot, the Firebird was gone and Nicki was sulking in her Pacer. "Where's your hot guy?" she asked.

"He left—with his girlfriend." Nicki yanked the second bottle of Boone's Farm from beneath her seat.

"Ouch," April said.

"This place is lame anyway." Nicki felt around under her. "We forgot the cups?"

April glanced down. "I don't mind if you don't." Nicki held the bottle near her mouth.

"Go for it," April said.

Nicki pressed the bottle to her lips and chugged. Several people in passing cars did double takes.

April tried to be a little more discreet when it was her turn. She wasn't as into being seen as her best friend was.

"That Joey guy's kind of cute." She looked at April through the corner of her eye. "You know, in that too-skinny, pothead kind of way."

April nodded.

"Boyd's better looking than Joey, though. And Boyd is built," Nicki added. "You are so lucky."

April didn't answer. She watched Joey get into his Dodge Charger. His hair was shorter than Boyd's, but no less scruffy. She smiled as she recognized it was Joey that Rick Springfield reminded her of. Joey was just more rough and raw. In a good way.

Nicki took another turn chugging. She wiped her mouth across her arm. "Want to just go hang out at my house?"

"Can't think of anything I'd rather do." April smiled as she realized it was the truth. "Can we watch cable?"

"Yeah, that's cool." Nicki started her car and pulled out. April ignored the smirks from the girls standing beside the hottest cars.

They barely made it a mile down Route 17 before Nicki started pointing excitedly. "It's him—the hot Firebird guy."

"Don't you mean it's *them*—the hot Firebird guy and his date?"

Nicki took a hard right turn.

"What are you doing?" April asked.

"Following them. Let's see where they go." Nicki swerved to the right as she reached to take the bottle from April.

"Should I drive?" April asked as Nicki chugged the wine. April held on to the door handle and, for a second, even considered putting on the seatbelt.

Nicki handed her the bottle. "Just drink," she said and giggled.

The Firebird slowed down and took a right turn. Nicki slowed, too, and started to turn right also.

"No way," April said. "No way are we following them down Leary's Lane. The whole world knows you only go down Leary's for one thing. Anyone sees us down there, they'll either think we're pervs out to watch or we're lesbos."

"Les-be friends." Nicki laughed. "Ho-mo you don't," she finished the joke herself when April didn't jump in. "Don't worry. I'm only going down far enough to pull over so I can pee."

April still gripped the door handle as the Pacer drifted onto the gravel of the shoulder. The power of suggestion prevailed, and April got out, too. She grabbed a McDonald's napkin and shoved it halfway into her pocket as she crossed the ditch a few feet left of Nicki.

April squatted between two dark green bushes. Once done, she stood and reached for her shorts. A bright beam of light blinded her. "What the hell?" Her hands instinctively went to her eyes.

"Oh shit," Nicki said.

"What's going on out here?" the male voice asked.

The light left April's face, and she looked down to grab her shorts and saw that was where the light had gone. She gasped at the way the concentrated beam made her privates all but glow. When she looked up, she knew the cop's expression of embarrassed shock matched her own.

There was a loud rustling and Nicki screamed. The cop's eyes and light moved in her direction. April turned to see Nicki facedown, her bare ass the only part of her sticking out of a tangle of briars. April's mind got stuck on how yes, mooning was an appropriate term, but then she snapped out of it and yanked her shorts up.

"I'm getting pricked. I'm getting pricked," Nicki squealed.

April ran to her and tried to help her up. Her fingers dug into Nicki's fleshy thighs, and she pulled. And pulled. Finally she said, "I could use some help over here."

The cop started in their direction, and Nicki wailed, "No!" He stopped in his tracks.

Just then, Nicki came loose, and she and April tumbled backwards.

With the light on Nicki, April carefully removed a thorny twig from Nicki's mussed hair, then she plucked a few more mutinous thorns from her friend's shirt and arms. She glanced at the cop and was glad to see that as he held the light, he busied himself watching his car. April guided Nicki onto her feet, and Nicki adjusted her cutoffs.

April's hand went to her wrist, and she realized her bracelet was gone. She knelt down and started to feel around in the leaves. She'd just about given up when her knuckle grazed the hard metal. She grabbed it and shoved it in her pocket.

The cop was standing beside the Pacer when they got back to it. "You girls been drinking?"

"No, sir," they answered together.

"Who's driving?"

Nicki raised her hand about shoulder height.

"Let me see your driver's license."

She did as she was told. The cop held it up and shined his light on it. He looked at her, his eyes briefly shifting to her smudged shorts. "Go straight home. Do not pass Go. Do not collect two hundred dollars."

April stiffened at the reference to Monopoly.

"Understood?"

"Understood," they again answered simultaneously.

†

Nicki did the speed limit the entire way to her house. Boyd's car was parked across the street. All that was visible in the darkness was the tip of his cigarette. He took a drag, and his face glowed orange.

"Boyd's here," Nicki said. She got out and walked across the street.

April thought that if Nicki had any idea how rough she looked, she'd be making a beeline for the house instead of Boyd's car. April followed her across the street. She scooted across the bench seat, leaving plenty of room for Nicki to sit up front with them.

"You girls have fun tonight?"

"Hell, yeah," Nicki said. "We almost got busted, too."

Boyd's gaze shifted to the rearview mirror.

"Nothing too bad," April said.

"Boyd," Nicki lowered her voice and said, "do you have any pot?"

"Hmm," he teased. "Bet I could find something around here."

April reached to the glove compartment for the bag and papers.

"I'm one step ahead of you, baby." Boyd pulled a joint from his shirt pocket.

Nicki sat up straighter. April almost laughed at her anticipation.

They each took a hit off the joint. When it came back around to Boyd, he hit it again and put it backward in his mouth. He faced April and blew her a shotgun. She held in the smoke while Boyd took another quick hit for himself and then crooked his finger at Nicki for her to take her turn.

April sat back as Nicki leaned across her. Boyd blew another perfect shotgun hit. Nicki drifted toward him as she inhaled, and April knew Nicki was the only girl she'd allow that close to her boyfriend.

April's attention went to Nicki's neck. She saw her pulse. But there was something else.

"Nicki, what's all over your neck?"

Nicki's hand moved to feel it as she sat back against the door. "Yuck," she said. "Must be squashed blackberries."

"Blackberries aren't in season. It's too early for them." April knew that from picking them with Katie. She remembered playing Monopoly, and as always, Katie was the dog and April was the car. She remembered wanting to stop playing and instead pick the berries that left her fingers and mouth stained purple-black, but Katie said they couldn't. April hated her sister at that moment, blaming her that the briar patch was full of white blooms instead of big, juicy berries.

Boyd smirked as he examined Nicki's neck from across the front seat. "It's shit," he said.

"It has to be berries. What shit could it be?" Nicki asked.

"Raccoon shit, or possum shit," Boyd said.

The color drained from Nicki's face. "Shit?" Her eyes grew wider and wider. She catapulted herself out of Boyd's car and across her lawn.

April gave Boyd a look-what-you've-done-now frown as she got out of the car. He sat there laughing.

"Goodnight, Boyd," she said over her shoulder.

"Aw, come on," he complained.

She waved as she ran into Nicki's house, thankful that Nicki's parents were still out.

Chapter Eight

The darkness of the drawn curtains that ensured privacy also meant Kate couldn't see Lana as well as she wanted to. Kate reached over her and flicked on the bedside lamp. Studying her, she was amazed by how Lana's firm, strong body so easily transformed to soft and vulnerable with just a slight touch. It was a complete and utterly fascinating metamorphosis.

The light danced across the moisture on Lana's neck where sweat lingered in the groove above her collarbone, reflecting the lamp's glow like a tiny tidal pool warmed by the sun. Kate ran her finger through the perspiration, causing it to course down and collect in the deeper indentation in the center, between Lana's clavicles. When Kate touched her lips to Lana's neck, she wasn't sure which part of the saltiness was Lana's sweat and which was her own tears.

Loving Lana was better than Kate's first shooting star, better than any visit to the Smithsonian, better than watching a butterfly emerge from its cocoon. Loving Lana was perfect.

"You know just how to touch me," Lana said.

Kate took several deep breaths, not wanting Lana to know she was crying. "I had a good teacher."

"You did? Remind me to thank her."

"Thank yourself."

"Thank you, self." Lana rolled on top of Kate, coming face-to-face with her. She kissed Kate's damp eyelashes. "Hey, smart-girl, are you a hopeless romantic, too?"

Kate nodded.

"That's sweet."

Kate sniffled. "Sweet as in good, or sweet oh-Lord-who-have-I-hooked-up-with?"

"Sweet *very* good." Lana kissed her until Kate forgot about her tears.

Kate had also long forgotten about the insecurities of not knowing what she wanted to do with her life now that she knew beyond a doubt that it wouldn't involve working with sick animals. For the first time, the possibilities were not only endless, but also not so scary.

Kate got out of bed and went to the fridge. She pulled out a can of lemonade, shook it, and turned back to Lana. "What?" she asked in response to Lana's smile.

"Wow, sweetie, you seem to have forgotten you're naked."

Kate looked down at herself. "Hmm, I sure am." Basking in her newfound confidence, she curtsied and pretended her face wasn't growing hot as she walked back to the bed.

She nestled into the crook made by Lana's knees being pulled halfway up to her abdomen. She took a sip of lemonade and offered the can to Lana.

"No thanks."

"I have never been happier," Kate said. Lana smiled. "And I have you to thank for that." Lana's mouth twitched, and she frowned. "What?" Kate said.

"Take credit for your own happiness."

"I couldn't be this happy if you hadn't driven up to me on your scooter," Kate explained.

"But you decided to get on. And without a helmet," Lana added, lightening her tone.

Kate grew serious. "You've shown me so much."

"Only because you were ready to see. Always take credit or blame for your own state of mind."

Kate set her lemonade on the table beside the bed. She didn't care who Lana wanted to credit for her happiness, she just wanted to be around Lana every possible second. "How much longer can you stay?" Kate asked.

"About thirty minutes."

"Hmm. Then why are we still talking?"

"Get up," Lana said as she stood. Kate cocked her head. "Come on. It's your turn."

"My turn for what?"

"To almost get caught in the closet."

Kate went willingly. There was no trepidation when Lana backed Kate into the closet, kissing her hard as she did. The edges of the hangers that pressed into Kate's back felt like Lana's fingers digging into her, but Lana's hands were busy elsewhere. The fingers of one kneaded her ass, the other stroked through the wetness between her legs.

The sounds of the hangers, the insistent touch of Lana's hands, the mingling scents of their sex, and the detergent clinging to her laundry, all swirled around her, making her wetter, with more need than she would have ever thought possible. Her legs gave out as she came. Lana followed her to the floor.

"Yes, Kate, yes. Keep coming. Oh, God, you are so wonderful." Lana held Kate until she stopped shaking.

Kate sprawled across the bed when Lana went into the bathroom to get cleaned up. She stared at the light peeking from the edges of the closed door. She wished she was in there, making love to Lana in the shower, not worrying about starting something they didn't have time to finish.

She hated not being able to spend entire nights with Lana. And still not knowing much about her. But mostly, she hated not being able to totally throw off the confusion over their last scooter ride together, when Lana pretended not to know anyone had been calling to her.

Kate listened to the water running. She stretched her legs out and her foot kicked Lana's shorts. As she visualized Lana lathering and rinsing, she grabbed the shorts from the end of the bed and contemplated the weight of both the denim and her intention.

It would be so easy to memorize Lana's address off of her driver's license. Not wanting to chicken out, she hurriedly shoved her hand into Lana's back pocket. She jerked it out when the edge of the license stabbed under her fingernail.

"Damn." She thrust her hand back into the pocket and felt the slick plastic against her skin. She pinched her fingers together and started to pull it out.

"Good, my shorts." Lana stood in the bathroom doorway, struggling into her bikini underwear.

Kate held them out, holding her breath also.

"Why's your face so red?" Lana asked. "Something wrong?"

"Just missing you already." She tried to ignore the shame inflaming her cheeks.

✝

"What do you want to do today?" April asked as they drove down Route 17.

Boyd shrugged. "Whatever you want."

"We going to Joey's tonight?" April asked.

"We should do something different," he said.

April wondered why Boyd was so preoccupied. He hadn't even touched her since she'd gotten in the car. Since she wasn't in the mood for sex, she decided to use the second best way to get Boyd's attention.

"Can we go see Katie?" she asked.

"Okay."

April coughed, almost choking on her shock. "Really?"

"Yeah, why not?" His mouth twisted in thought. "We'll go to Virginia Beach while we're over there."

"Sure." She took his hand. It was pretty far out of the way, but it wasn't like they were on that side of the Hampton Roads Bridge-Tunnel often. "What's in Virginia Beach?"

"A record store where you can actually listen to cassettes before buying them."

"Any cassette?"

"Yep." His smile was big and childlike. He cut off a pickup truck as he changed lanes to pull into a parking lot.

He went into the 7-Eleven for a six-pack. April waited in the car, squinting through the sun to watch as he stood in front of the wall-sized cooler. The back of his shirt was damp. The car's air conditioner didn't work so well, but he refused to wear shorts. He never would except to swim, and that was a rarity.

When he got back into the car, he pulled a sweaty can of beer free from its plastic ring before handing her the other five to put on the floor by her feet. "You're sure you don't want one?"

"Maybe later." She didn't want to have to pee before they even made it to the tunnel.

"Why don't you call Miss Glee Club and ask her to cover for you with your dad again tonight." He slipped on his sunglasses.

"She already is. But maybe I'll call her just to double-check."

April patted her pockets and smiled at him but then looked away, self-conscious about her reflection in the mirrored lenses of his glasses.

Boyd dug into the front pocket of his jeans, pulled the lining inside-out, and held up a quarter. "You're in luck. My last one." He examined the quarter. "And tell Glee Club not to roll around in any shit tonight."

"Ha, ha," April retorted. She took the coin from him, walked over to the payphone, and dialed Nicki. "Hey, girl, whatcha up to?"

"Blow drying my hair. Where are you?"

"7-Eleven. We're getting ready to go to Norfolk." She looked back at the Gran Torino. Her gaze lingered on the freshly repaired front bumper. She quickly turned away. "What?"

"I asked if you were going to see Katie or to party."

"Hopefully both." April stared through new scratches on her sunglasses, studying the smudged glass glaring from behind the payphone. It was highly unlikely that they'd party with Katie. April was pretty sure her sister didn't even know how to party.

"I'm going to the Blue Dragon tonight," Nicki said.

"Pu Pu Platters," they said at the same time.

"Don't drink too many Flaming Volcanoes," April advised half-heartedly.

"Then why bother?" Nicki giggled.

April reminded Nicki of their cover story that she was with Nicki's family at the beach, and they said their goodbyes. Glancing at her arms, April wondered if her dad ever questioned how she could spend so much time at the beach and never get a burn or tan.

When April got back to the car, Boyd was rolling another joint. His thick fingers fumbled with the rolling paper. He was clumsy when it came to that, but real good at other things.

She remembered the first touch of his hands. She'd gotten into his souped-up car when he offered her a ride home from a party at some friend of Nicki's. They'd ended up down at Leary's Lane, making out. When his big hands found their way under her blouse, her skin prickled as the rough skin of his palms grazed her nipples.

April knew then that they would fall in love and she'd go all the way with Boyd. But it didn't happen that night because as he was fumbling with the button on her jeans, a cop car came around the corner. They took the officer's advice and went home.

April watched Boyd finish rolling the joint. He stuck it into his mouth, giving a little twist as he pulled it out, wetting it just enough to keep it together.

"Ready to go?" he asked.

"Yeah."

Boyd maneuvered the bulky car onto the interstate on-ramp at J. Clyde Morris Boulevard, and April whispered her usual mantra to herself, "White on right."

A Pinto and Datsun B-210 yielded to the roar of Boyd's engine, and he easily merged onto the interstate. The median zipped by in a deep shade of green. From this summer hue, spotlighted in the sun, rose a lone tree. As was tradition, the tree was decorated for the Fourth of July holiday that had been earlier that week. April turned her head to take in the blur of patriotic colors. Even after it was well behind them, she still conjured up the red, white, and blue, like icing on a cake but sprouting American flags instead of candles. The mysteriously hung decorations had begun to erode, a ribbon or two whittled away by every rain or windy day. Soon she'd see more green and less red, white, and blue. Maybe one or two telltale flags would survive until the next holiday. What came next... Halloween? Or was there some obscure holiday the phantom decorator would use as an excuse to show off both creativity and stealth in not being found out? No one April knew could tell her if it was one person, or many, ornamenting the one-time Christmas tree in the median of I-64 in Hampton. But holiday after holiday, year after year, garnishments showed up overnight—turkeys, goblins, Santas, flags. Once a year, banners proclaiming "Happy Father's Day" or "Happy Mother's Day" were wrapped around the tree, brightening some mom or dad's morning commute.

April wondered whether her mom ever saw the Mother's Day decorations. Did her mom ever travel this stretch of interstate? Did she see the adorned tree and think of the family she'd left behind?

Wanting her mom to vanish from her thoughts, April turned and studied Boyd's chiseled face, his stare intent as they flew down the interstate. The movement of his tongue behind his cheek convinced her he was messing with his broken tooth. "Haven't you seen a dentist about that yet?" she asked.

"Nope."

"Are you going to?"

"Nope. It doesn't hurt. I'll go if it starts hurting."

She inspected her ID bracelet, paying close attention to the scratches Boyd had made on it by trying to engrave it with his teeth.

A white Camaro pulled up beside them. Boyd glanced to his left and looked over the top of his sunglasses at the dark-haired man who nodded back at him. April braced herself just before Boyd gave his lopsided grin. His foot came down hard on the accelerator, and the Gran Torino pulled away from the Camaro. For about a second. Side by side, the Ford and the Chevy roared down the interstate.

April glanced at Boyd. A slight twitch from behind his mirrored lenses prompted her to turn forward. Boyd slammed on the brakes, and her body lurched. She put up her hands to stop her forward momentum. The dashboard stung her palms, and she smelled rubber and heard the synchronized screeching as the Camaro's tires echoed Boyd's.

The car in front of them had stopped. The driver looked back through the rearview mirror, his eyes huge. Boyd saw it, too, and he laughed and said, "Bet he shit himself, huh?"

A ribbon of red brake lights glowed ahead, stretching out to the tunnel.

"Oh well. Baby, can you hand me another beer?" Boyd slipped the empty can onto the floor behind him. Just like his dirty laundry, he kept his car trash contained to one corner. April popped the top and handed him the beer.

"Come here," he whispered.

She slid closer. "What?"

"Kiss me."

And she did, long and deep. Just as she pulled away, the Camaro's engine revved twice and the driver flicked on his right turn signal. Boyd gave a slight nod. Traffic crept forward, and Boyd let the car pull in front of him. A minute later, the Camaro squeezed into the right-most lane and exited the interstate.

April slipped off her sandal. She pressed her toes down, and the carpet beneath them sloshed. "The AC's dripping again." As if on cue, she smelled the mustiness. "Figures." Boyd flipped off the air and rolled down his window.

The car grew dank. April rolled down her window. Heat filtered in, and the damp coolness dispersed. "I hate tunnel traffic," she said.

Boyd grabbed his cigarettes from the dash and reached into his front pocket. As he pulled out his empty hand, April got the lighter out of the glove compartment and gave it to him. He lit the cigarette and handed the lighter back to her. The coolness of the silver sleeve wrapped around the Bic spread across her palm. She ran her finger along the turquoise, five-pronged leaf glued to one side. Once her skin had sucked all the coolness from the metal, she stuffed it back into the glove compartment.

Boyd made a show of blowing the billows of smoke out the window. April leaned tight against her door. He was doing a good job of keeping the smoke away from her, but that wasn't the point. Irritation grew like the perspiration forming between the back of her legs and the vinyl seat.

"Have I told you lately how much I hate traffic?"

"Yes, baby, you have," Boyd said, his voice stiff. "This isn't too bad."

The car in front of them jerked into gear; Boyd slipped the Gran Torino into drive. He took a long drag from his cigarette and flicked it out the window. He exhaled into the car, his last stand, his last show of who was really in charge.

Fighting back a cough, April ignored him, instead choosing to watch as the breeze moving through the car stirred the smoke. Frail swirls spiraled in the bright sun and dissipated against the nicotine-tinged windshield. Her eyes burned.

A few minutes later, Boyd flipped the AC back on and they rolled up the windows. The dankness disappeared by the time they emerged from the Norfolk end of the tunnel. So did the traffic. That was always the case. For no good reason, lines of cars lingered just long enough to make everyone late for whatever they had planned.

The sun splashed light on the rippled surface of the water, the scattered sailboats and fishing boats, the bridge, the other cars. A seagull flew beside them, just above the bridge railing, in its own airborne lane. April's mood brightened. "What exit do we need?"

"We get on 44, I think. I'll know it when I see it."

He managed several tricky merges, settled into a lane, and visibly relaxed. "Fire up that joint, why don't you."

April grabbed the twisted end from the ashtray and the lighter from the glove compartment. Holding the joint low, she flicked the flame at the excess paper on the end. Fire flashed and sparks flew. She leaned down and took a hit, lighting the weed.

"Don't be so paranoid," Boyd said as she handed him the joint. He sat up straight and toked with gusto, not caring who saw. He took a quick second toke and his sculpted features glowed orange.

April didn't hide the joint the next time she brought it to her mouth. She hated being on display every time it was her turn to take a hit, but did it anyhow, wondering whether the pot was going to make her overanalyze every little thing or want to eat Taco Bell and crash. She hoped for the latter.

"Shit," Boyd said, holding in the smoke. He exhaled a blue fog across the dashboard, and his voice back to normal, said, "We need a quarter for the toll."

They stared at one another for a long moment before busting out laughing. April choked, forcing smoke from her nose in rapid, short bursts. After a minute, with eyes still watering, she regained her composure and held up her hands. "Okay, okay. Let me think."

Boyd's face turned red as he laughed harder.

"Seriously," she said.

He stopped laughing long enough to take another hit and discarded the toasty little roach in the ashtray.

April crawled into the back and shoved her hand between the seat and the seatback. She remembered Boyd had lost some change out of his pockets one time when they fooled around. That was also the night the condom broke. She looked at Boyd in the rearview mirror. He damn well better not expect to use the condom from the dead guy's wallet.

Boyd looked into the mirror and winked at her. "Find one?"

Jolted back to her task, April felt around under the seat. She finally found a quarter beneath the floor mat and picked it up, also spotting a white pill a few inches to the right. Its size gave it away even before she read the 7-1-4 inscribed on it. She wondered when they'd managed to lose a Quaalude.

She crawled back up front, handed Boyd the quarter, and held up the lude for her own inspection.

"Cool," Boyd said. "Why don't you take it? Then the party can really get started."

April didn't want to be out of it for the rest of the day and most of the night just so Boyd could have sex with her while she was relaxed enough to enjoy it better. At least Boyd kept telling her she enjoyed it more; it wasn't like she actually remembered.

"No. Katie would have a fit."

"Who cares?" He smiled as he said it, taking the edge off his words.

"I do. She is my sister, even if we are so different."

"Hmm." Boyd held up the quarter, using it to point to the left side of the approaching toll plaza. "We didn't need this after all."

April nodded. She'd forgotten there were several lanes for drivers without exact change.

Boyd pulled to the right lanes. "Might as well, since we have our quarter." He glanced at April. "If you aren't gonna take that lude, put it somewhere we'll remember."

April noticed a smudge a lot like the one on the lude she'd taken a few nights earlier at the drive-in. She wondered if the other one had come from the floor, too. Oh well, she thought, a pound of dirt... She took one last look at the soiled pill and shoved it into her pocket.

Stopping beside the basket, Boyd rolled down his window. He tossed the quarter, but it hit the rim and bounced out. "Shit," he muttered.

He opened his door, leaned out, and reached under the car. As he sat back up, the car behind them honked. April saw Boyd tense for just a moment before he slowly placed the quarter into the basket. Then he shut his door, flipped the bird at the car behind them, and squealed away, trailing exhaust and leaving tread marks.

April took a deep breath. Boyd's attention on the rearview mirror prompted her to turn around. The car from the toll plaza was on their tail. Boyd touched his brakes then accelerated. The Nova stayed on them.

When Boyd hit his brakes again, the car swerved into the lane to their right. It pulled up beside them, and the driver yelled something April couldn't make out. Boyd flipped him off again and floored it.

Boyd pulled diagonal to a van in the right lane, not leaving enough room for the Nova to get by. Then he slowed down and kept just off the rear bumper on the driver's side of the van.

April grew more nervous. What if it was an undercover cop trying to get Boyd to screw up so he could pull him over? She knew that sometimes cops targeted guys with souped-up cars.

Oh shit. She swallowed hard. What if this was the car she'd hit the other night? Had it been dark blue, or green? Was it a Nova, or a... She couldn't remember. Her heartbeat sped up. So did Boyd's car.

The Nova cut sharply, crossing behind them and into the lane to their left. Before Boyd could react, the Nova pulled just far enough away to cut back over in front of them, causing Boyd to brake hard and swerve into the right lane.

April looked over at the van as it also swerved, barely making it out of their path. The van came to a bumpy stop on the shoulder of the road.

Boyd floored it and pulled beside the Nova, on its left. "Okay, motherfucker." He cut hard to the right, forcing the Nova over to keep from getting hit.

"Boyd," April yelled.

The Nova barely missed a car trying to merge into traffic. Orange cones on the periphery of some shoulder construction weren't so lucky. The Nova hit them, sending them up into the air. They rained down onto the road behind the Nova as it skidded onto the off-ramp, having no choice but to exit the toll road.

Boyd laughed. He looked at April. "Take the lude or drink a beer. Just do something to chill out."

April's hands shook as she reached down for one of the two remaining beers.

"Drink them both. It'll do you good," Boyd added.

April popped the top and took a big gulp. It tasted bitter and was getting warm, but she didn't care. She drank some more, liking the tingling that moved across her face and into her chest.

✝

The record store was smaller than April had expected. She lingered at the front display of lighters, bumper stickers, and roach clips with long, flowing feathers. She'd had one of the fancy clips once, with soft lavender plumage, but she and Boyd somehow managed to catch it on fire one night.

As April walked around, she became convinced that everyone knew she was stoned. But that was okay, they probably were, too. She looked at Boyd, who was in the Rock section of the tapes, and noticed the guy behind the counter watching her. He probably thought she was going to steal something. Maybe she would. She'd stolen a *Teen Beat* magazine years ago. Her dad or Katie would have given her the money, had she asked, but it was more fun to see if she could lift it. She did. And no one had a clue. It was almost too easy.

The New Release section distracted her. She wanted to hear something different, something they'd never play on FM 99—WNOR—Boyd's favorite radio station. She picked up a cassette, awkward in its plastic antitheft packaging. Yeah, that was it. She'd never hear that coming from Boyd's car unless she put it in the cassette player herself. And she might just do that. If he could smoke with her in the car, she could listen to Rick Springfield.

She took the cassette to the listening counter where Boyd was already wearing headphones and nodding to the beat. The young guy working the area took the tape from her and smiled. Boyd glanced over, shot the guy a look, and put his arm around April. She put on the headphones and smiled back at the clerk.

Boyd leaned over to see what April had. He frowned. "What are you, twelve?"

Several customers turned to look at them. She put a finger to her lips and pointed to Boyd's headphones. He pulled them off; she did the same.

"I knew Miss Glee Club would rub off on you sooner or later," Boyd said.

April ignored him as she caught the employee's attention. "I'll take it," she said. "And he's paying," she added, nodding toward Boyd.

†

Kate was toweling off when she heard the knock on the door. She hoped Lana had decided to call in sick to work after all.

She buttoned her shorts and slipped into a T-shirt on her way across the room. She smiled as she opened the door. "Came back for mo—"

Kate stood with her mouth open as she stared at April, who was standing in the hall.

"This is where you say, 'Come in, glad you could drop by,'" April said.

"What's wrong?" Kate looked from April to Boyd, who was leaning against the wall. "Why are you here?"

"All that schooling and you haven't learned any manners, huh?" April brushed past Kate and walked into her dorm room.

"Sorry, I just wasn't expecting to see you here," Kate said.

"Obviously." April looked around the room. "Wow, college is finally teaching you not to be so uptight. I've never seen your bed unmade without you in it."

Kate's face grew warm.

April walked over to the nightstand. She picked up the case to the Joan Jett tape and inspected it, then she put it down and pressed the Play button. It turned right back off, so she ejected the tape, flipped it, and stuck it back in. This time when she pushed the Play button, music came out. "Katie, is that rock and roll?" she asked. "Okay, who are you and what have you done with my sister?" She laughed.

Kate knew that raspy laugh. It was the same one April had let out the first time Kate had caught her smoking pot behind the house.

She'd noticed April's eyes were a little red as soon as she'd walked into the room. She stole a glance at April's left eye. This time she wouldn't let guilt seep in. Why should she worry about her part in April's childhood eye problem when lately her sister's eyes were always bloodshot anyway?

Kate's attention left April's eye and moved to her arm. A large, silver ID bracelet all but swallowed her sister's wrist. She reached past April and turned off the music. "I talked to Dad a little while ago."

April laughed again. "Isn't that just perfect."

"So, how's the beach?"

April looked around. "Not what I was expecting, but it should be interesting." She smiled. "Ah." She looked at the table of elements hanging on the wall. "Now I see something familiar. Maybe you are the real Katie Hunter after all."

The way April broke up the syllables of Kate's name brought back the familiar tune. "Ka-tie-Hun-ter, Ka-tie-Hunter." It played in her head. She fought off the memory and the accompanying resentment she felt for April.

"Damn, I got the munchies," Boyd said.

April asked Kate if she'd eaten dinner.

"No," Kate said, thinking about lunching on plums with Lana. "Not dinner."

"Let's go someplace," April said.

Kate excused herself to brush her hair and teeth. She changed into a polo shirt and put on socks and tennis shoes. The three went downstairs, and April gestured toward Boyd's Gran Torino. Boyd jingled his keys as he walked ahead of them.

April looked around. "Where's your car, Katie?"

"In student parking, behind the athletics building."

"Not running so good?" April asked.

"No, not really." She thought about how her Arrow had started sputtering and smoking a few weeks earlier.

"Is that why you haven't been coming home weekends?"

Kate didn't answer.

"Boyd can take a look at it after we eat."

His fingers strummed his leg, playing an invisible instrument. His head moved slightly to the mystery beat, and his bloodshot eyes stared nowhere in particular. "No, that's okay," Kate said.

Kate slipped into the backseat and tugged at the seatbelt. After getting it fastened, she looked up to find April and Boyd staring at her. A smirk passed between them.

"Where we going?" Boyd asked.

"Most of the decent restaurants are either out on Military Highway or Virginia Beach Boulevard," Kate said.

"Just tell me where to turn," Boyd mumbled.

"Go left out of the parking lot and follow Princess Anne."

April scooted closer to Boyd, and Kate rolled her eyes. She'd never understand what April saw in him, but who was she to judge? Not everyone was as lucky as Kate, finding *the one* the first time around. Goosebumps erupted on her arms, and she knew they were from thoughts of Lana, not the car's bad air conditioning.

Boyd gave it a little too much gas as he pulled away from the Stop sign. He tended to do everything over the top, whether it was stopping or going. Must be a guy thing, Kate thought.

They started past the strip mall where most of the Lillian Wilde students bought their beer from the convenience store. Kate stared, at first not registering the scooter chained to the No Parking sign outside the Sea Scape Bar and Grille.

"Wait," Kate said.

Boyd put on the brakes. When April reached for the dash, Kate knew it was second nature.

"What?" April asked.

"I've heard that place back there's pretty good." She pointed in the direction from which they'd come, ignoring the fact that she'd heard nothing but substandard things about the Sea Scape's food. She pretended she hadn't heard about fights breaking out there and the police being called constantly.

"I thought you wanted Military Highway."

"We don't have to go all the way out there. This should be fine," Kate said. Her heart pounded and her palms were damp. "This will be good."

"Okay," April said as she turned to Boyd. "Let's go back."

He pulled up to the building and gave the Gran Torino extra gas before turning it off. Several guys coming out of the Quick Mart looked over. They assessed the car, nodding in apparent approval before getting into an old station wagon.

The sign inside the front door told them to seat themselves, so they walked past the bar area and over to a table in the corner. The restaurant was smoky. Kate looked at April, "Is this going to bother you?"

April glanced at Boyd and told Kate, "Of course not."

Kate saw Lana the second she walked out of the kitchen. Lana held a tray of food at chin level, and Kate worried for a second that she might drop it when she saw her sitting across the room. But Lana was always so composed, and Kate grew warm at the sight of her recovering from the surprise so quickly.

Boyd and April read their menus while Kate watched Lana serve another table of diners. On her way over to them, Lana stopped at the bar where a guy drinking beer kept calling to her. The guy tried to pull her close, but she resisted him. Kate felt horrible that Lana had to endure that kind of unwanted attention just to pay the bills, when all she really wanted was to make a living painting and drawing.

"Hi, what can I bring you to drink?" Lana looked at Boyd as she spoke.

"I'll take a draft," Boyd answered. Then he leaned toward April and asked, "Want one?"

Kate started to say something about April's age but kept quiet.

"I'll need to see some ID," Lana said.

The tug of a smile played at the corner of Kate's mouth, but she repressed the urge to show her satisfaction.

April didn't look at her sister as she pulled a driver's license from the back pocket of her cutoffs.

Lana held it up to the light, and sighed. "Okay. And for you?" she asked Kate.

Kate searched Lana's eyes for the warmth, the playfulness she so loved. There was none. Just a cold stare from a waitress wanting to move on to the next customer.

"Water's fine," Kate said and looked away.

"Okay, be right back with that."

Kate set the menu on the table in front of her. She was afraid if she tried to hold it while she read, April and Boyd would see her hands shake. But April was busy running a finger along the light hair on Boyd's arm as he stared at the muted TV in the bar area.

Lana brought their drinks and set a plate of lemon wedges beside Kate's glass of water. Kate thanked her. Sweet and tart. Kate's heart thumped in her chest, but Lana still didn't acknowledge her.

By the time Lana finished taking their food orders, Boyd and April had finished their beers. Boyd asked for a large pitcher.

A ruckus from the bar grabbed Lana's attention. She went over and said something to the same guy she'd spoken to earlier. He grabbed her wrist, and the manager yelled over to Lana to get back to work.

The hush puppies were dry, the fried shrimp overcooked, and the French fries cold, but the service was good, if a little chilly.

Lana didn't look at Kate as she refilled her water. Boyd ordered a second pitcher of beer. Kate hated that April was drinking so much, and that Lana did everything but actually look her in the eyes. The evening wasn't turning out how she'd hoped.

Kate excused herself and went into the restroom. She leaned against the sink. She closed her eyes for just a second before the door opened.

Lana slipped in. Before Kate said anything, Lana had her pinned against the door. She pressed her mouth to Kate's and kissed her. Lips still grazing, Lana whispered, "You shouldn't have come here."

"I missed you." Kate pressed her body against Lana's. "Why are you ignoring me?"

"Ignoring you? I'm giving you great service." Her voice low, she added, "Aren't I?"

"Yes," Kate gasped.

Lana tensed and took a step back. "This isn't playing a game in your dorm room closet."

"I know." She pulled Lana to her.

"And you have to respect that I need to keep parts of my life separate," Lana said.

"Okay," she whispered into Lana's neck.

The bathroom door jostled against Kate's back, and Lana reeled away from her as April stumbled in.

"Damn, it's hot out there," April said, slurring her words.

April started throwing water on her face and looked into the mirror at the reflection of Kate and Lana. "Hey, I know you," she said as she almost fell over.

Lana looked around frantically, as if searching for a place to hide. "Can you handle her? I need to go."

"I've been handling her my entire life," Kate said as Lana ducked out of the restroom.

April squatted on the floor by the toilet. As she threw up, Kate held her hair out of the way. April's pale fingers gripped the toilet seat, and her bracelet clanked heavily against the porcelain.

"You're only sixteen, April. Sixteen-year-olds are supposed to be thinking about class rings and proms, they shouldn't be strung out and puking in restaurant bathrooms."

"If you're gonna lecture, just leave."

"I can't leave you like this."

"I'm actually quite self-sufficient." She hiccupped.

"Right," Kate said, unconvinced.

†

"Why was your sister so weird at dinner?" Boyd kicked a stone across the college parking lot. "Have you ever seen anyone so uptight?"

"What can I say? I didn't think we'd ever get away from her. How many times did she ask you if you were really okay to drive?"

Boyd grunted. "I'm glad I'm doing you and not your sister."

April yanked a wisp of wheat-like hair on his arm.

"Shit. What was that for?"

She didn't answer.

They got into the Gran Torino. He rubbed at the red mark on his arm. "I wish you wouldn't do that."

April bent down and kissed the area. "All better."

Boyd pulled away from the college and into the parking lot between the Sea Scape Bar and Grille and the Quick Mart. "I'm running in for cigarettes," he said. "Need anything?"

"Gum." Even though she'd brushed her teeth before leaving Katie's, her mouth was still yucky from puking at the restaurant. She hated that she'd gotten sick in front of Katie, but hell, it wasn't the first time and probably wouldn't be the last.

Boyd tapped his cigarettes against the palm of his hand as he walked back to the car. A guy sauntered out of the Sea Scape. It was the guy who'd kept grabbing at their waitress.

He sized up Boyd's car. "What you got in that?"

Boyd's face lit up. "351 Windsor."

"Hot car."

"Thanks," Boyd said and opened the car door.

Largest stock engine Ford makes, April thought, all too familiar with the chitchat.

"You got any smoke?" the guy asked.

Boyd gave a slight nod.

"You and your girlfriend should come back to my place to party. I got some beer there."

Even before Boyd nodded, April knew he would accept the offer. She hated how Boyd tended to trust anyone who complimented his car.

"You'll drive?" the guy asked. When Boyd pulled the front seat forward, the guy climbed into the back. "I'm Richie," he said.

"I'm Boyd, and that's April."

April smiled politely.

"Just take a right, and we're almost there." Richie directed Boyd through a few turns and up a dirt driveway. "Isn't much, but it's home."

April surveyed the small building. The brick on a large part of the front was several shades darker than those around it. She decided it was a garage that had been converted into an apartment, and the unmatched brick was where the garage door had been.

Richie let them in, and the first thing April noticed was that the refrigerator was no bigger than the one in Katie's dorm room. A card table with two chairs was set up under a window stuffed with a crooked air-conditioning unit.

A dressing screen, bent like an accordion in three places, stretched across the farthest corner of the narrow room. April could make out the edge of the bed behind it. The screen was wood, each section painted in intricate detail with images of tropical birds and flowers. The bright colors were a welcome contrast to the darkness of the paneled walls.

Boyd's attention was focused on an elaborate pipe on the table under the window. Richie picked it up gently for Boyd to see. A painted snake coiled around the body of the ceramic pipe, and sunbeams shot out all around it. The yellow of the beams was bright and pure, adding a hint of benevolence to the red and black of the snake.

Boyd reached for it, and Richie's voice was quiet, yet decisive as he said, "I'm the only one who smokes from this bowl. My girlfriend painted it."

Boyd nodded as if he understood, but April knew Boyd didn't get things like that. In Boyd's world, romance was never to interfere with getting stoned, drunk, or otherwise altered.

Richie motioned toward several couch cushions arranged on the floor. April sat, but Boyd hefted a baseball bat that had been propped against the wall. He took a half swing. April was relieved when he put the bat back and sat next to her. When Richie joined them, he brought three cans of beer and a red, bulbed device.

"Nice power hitter," Boyd said.

It took April a minute to understand he wasn't referring to the bat, but to the red bulb Richie held.

Boyd leaned back and pulled the bag of weed from his front pocket. He handed it to April, and she rolled a near-perfect joint.

Richie was sticking the joint inside the bulb thing when April became distracted by a painting on the wall. Red and orange swirls radiated from the center, transforming into gold streaks that made her think of the sunbeams painted on the pipe. She was transfixed by the way the painting seemed to spit sunshine.

Boyd handed her the power hitter. A trickle of smoke came from one end of the contraption, and she wished she'd paid closer attention when Boyd and Richie took their hits. *What the hell*, she thought. She stuck the smoking end into her mouth, sucked as hard as she could and squeezed the bulb. She didn't know why they bothered; she'd hardly even gotten a hit. She handed it to Richie. She didn't really need the buzz anyhow.

Boyd's cheeks were glowing a little with color, and April wondered if he'd gotten sunburned earlier in the week while working outside with his Uncle Mark.

Richie held the power hitter a few inches from his face. As he squeezed the bulb, a stream of smoke shot out of the end and he inhaled.

April looked away, trying to hide her embarrassment. Boyd was used to her doing stupid things like that, but Richie probably thought she was a total idiot. She stared at her feet. Her toes, with their chipped nail polish, came to the edge of her sandals. She looked up.

Boyd held up the power hitter, a silent offer to help her, but April held out her hand. He hesitated before handing it back to her. She knew he was wondering if she'd embarrass him again.

She held it a few inches from her mouth and cautiously squeezed the bulb, taking a deep hit as she did. As the smoke ravaged her lungs, she knew immediately why they bothered with such a contraption. She fought to hold in the smoke. When she handed the power hitter to Richie, she didn't take her eyes off the red bulb until the front door opened.

A dark-headed woman came in and went right for the small refrigerator. She pulled out a can of soda. As she turned around, she asked, "Whose car is that out front?"

April stared at the waitress from the restaurant.

"Oh," the young woman said, staring back at April.

Richie handed the power hitter to Boyd. "Come on in and party, Lana."

Lana's eyes darted around the room. "I can't stay."

"Tired again, baby?" Richie asked her.

"I'm still working on that new piece."

"You've been painting that thing forever. I've hardly seen you."

"You know how it is when I get in creative mode."

Richie looked at Boyd. "My girlfriend's a painter. Those artsy types can be hard to handle."

Boyd squeezed April's knee. "They all can be."

Lana rolled her eyes. "Well, I'm going on home. I'll see you tomorrow, Richie."

"Yeah, good night." Richie turned away to take a hit.

April watched as Lana left the converted garage. After shutting the door, Lana glanced back at April through the window.

An engine sputtered outside. April's thoughts went to seeing Katie and the waitress together in the restroom. What were they talking about? They got real quiet when April walked in. They must have been talking about her. Maybe Katie was getting the waitress to spy on April. Maybe her dad put them up to it. Or the cops. What if this was all a setup to bust them? Wouldn't that just take the cake? And what in the hell was April doing thinking stuff like "take the cake"? Only moms said shit like that. Oh Lord, April thought, maybe the pot was turning her into her mom. No, maybe Katie had already turned into their mom. Maybe Katie was gonna disappear. So what? Would it even matter? But what was Katie whispering about with the waitress? And why did Lana leave so fast like that? And wasn't that a really strange look she gave April?

"Hey, baby, what's wrong with you?"

"Huh?" April asked, turning to Boyd.

"Someone's wasted," Richie said.

Boyd laughed. "She sure is."

He held the power hitter in front of her and squeezed. She didn't want to embarrass him, so she inhaled deeply, wishing all along he'd stop squeezing the damned thing. The longer he kept the stream of smoke aimed at her, the more it became a challenge. April hated when he got like that. She hated when she got like that.

When Boyd finally ceased fire, April held in the smoke, imagining it filtering through her lungs and into her blood. Then it wasn't the pot trickling into the small vessels of her brain, but a nagging, indecipherable thought about Katie and Lana in the restroom.

April exhaled. The thought, now stuck in her throat, trapped bile with it, making her feel sick. Scanning the room, April realized for the first time that the front door was the only door, and the only window was the one beside the door. Just like the basement in Hillsboro, there was one way in and one way out.

She wanted to get out. She had to get out.

✝

"Feel better?" Boyd asked.

"Yeah." April settled back onto the cool vinyl seat. It always helped to lean her head out the window for a minute, as long as Boyd drove slowly.

Boyd switched lanes and got onto the on-ramp for the interstate. He turned on the radio, and the deejay's obnoxious voice filled the car. Boyd turned it up. April cringed. All she wanted was to sleep.

Drifting in and out, April was aware of the change from talking to music. The beat of the song hurt her head.

Boyd tapped her leg. "Listen." He pointed to the radio. "Right there."

April made a sound in her throat, knowing Boyd would take it to mean she was listening. She knew without looking exactly what Boyd would do. He'd play his invisible guitar, taking both hands off the wheel and crossing the yellow line. Normally, April would gasp, and Boyd would laugh hysterically until he overcorrected and went off the road to the right. When gravel spat up against the underside of his precious Gran Torino, Boyd would get serious and steady them between the yellow and white lines. White on right, April thought, drifting to sleep before the scene could play out.

The lights inside the tunnel woke her. She shifted her body and scooted her butt to the right so she could put her head in Boyd's lap. Boyd ran his fingers through April's hair. He can be so sweet, she thought. Then he pressed down against her head, just enough for April to feel his hardness growing beneath her. He shifted his hips, in case she didn't already understand what he wanted.

She ignored him. All she wanted in her mouth was the gum Boyd had forgotten to get when he bought his cigarettes. She tried to remember the last time they'd actually slept together, not wired nights at Joey's or dream-torn moments at Boyd's before or after having sex, but really slept.

The next time April opened her eyes, Boyd was washed in the red light of a traffic signal. She sat up and looked around.

"I'm gonna stop at Joey's and see if I can score some crank. It'll be a long week at work without it." He gave her thigh a little squeeze. "What do you want to do now?"

"Sleep." She yawned. "Maybe we can crash at Joey's."

Boyd slowed way down before pulling to a stop in front of Joey's building. "I'll tell you what—you wait here and I'll be right back."

April had barely started to protest when Boyd got out of the car and sauntered up to Joey's.

When Boyd came back out, she could tell he'd gotten what he wanted by the way his hand was tucked protectively into the top of his front pocket. He was smiling, but his eyes were darting from side to side. He got in and put the car in gear.

"Aren't we staying?" April asked.

"Not tonight. Would you rather I drop you at home, or at Nicki's to keep up the beach story?"

"It's too late for Nicki's," she mumbled.

"So, your house?"

"Yeah," she said, too tired to complain. "Just don't stop right in front of the house."

Boyd nodded. A few minutes later, he pulled into a 7-Eleven.

"What now?"

"Cigarettes."

"You just got some."

He glanced around the car before shrugging.

Boyd was halfway to the store when the guy approached him. April followed the man's finger as he pointed to a dark blue, custom Mustang. She couldn't miss the white-smudged dent in the driver's door. "Shit," she whispered. She thought about getting out of the car, about explaining to the guy, about offering to pay for the damage. But she sat there, glued to the seat.

Boyd walked back to his car and gestured to his bumper.

"Bullshit," the guy said. He bent over the bumper and started picking at the paint.

"Don't touch my fucking car."

"Fuck you." The guy stood straighter. He was at least three inches taller than Boyd. "Admit you did it. Be a man."

Boyd's fist landed on the left side of the guy's face, causing him to fall backward onto his ass. Then Boyd casually walked back to the Gran Torino and slid into the seat. As he was backing up, the guy stood. Boyd gunned the car in reverse, barely missing a woman, and threw it into drive. As they sped away, April looked back just long enough to see the guy give up his running pursuit.

"Can you believe the nerve of that guy?" Boyd started laughing.

"Damn it, Boyd."

"Lighten up, would you."

†

The Gran Torino slanted toward the passenger side when Boyd pulled onto the shoulder of the road, three houses from April's. "You can get there from here, right?"

She was still a little shaky from the encounter at the 7-Eleven, but at least the adrenaline sobered her up some. "Yeah."

He gave her a quick kiss. "You'll be okay?"

She nodded and opened the door. The momentum from the downward angle was too much for April, and the door swung wide, digging into the bank of the ditch that ran the length of all the roads in her neighborhood. She grunted as she tugged the door free. She used her body weight to push it shut and gave Boyd a little wave. He waved back and sat there until she got to her front porch. April turned to look at the Ford as it pulled away. She smiled at the thought of how sweet Boyd was to make sure she got safely into her house. She took a step forward and tripped on the edge of the sidewalk. Landing with a crack, her knee slammed against the edge of the bottom step. She brushed herself off and snuck inside, hoping her dad wouldn't be between the front door and sleep. She didn't want to explain the late hour when she was supposed to have been at the beach with Nicki. Hell, he probably wouldn't question her anyway. He'd given up on that ages ago.

Chapter Nine

Kate ran the brush through her hair and slipped into a pair of lightweight shorts. She glanced at her bra. No need, she mused, and pulled on a T-shirt.

Lana had called earlier than usual that morning. She was on her way over. Kate smiled as she thought about seeing to it that Lana made it up to her for the night before. The other bright spot in the fiasco of being ignored at the restaurant was the kiss in the bathroom. Kate's heart thumped as she thought about it. The kiss alone was worth almost getting caught. But it seemed that didn't matter, since April was so drunk she hadn't a clue about what she'd interrupted.

There was a soft knock at the door. Kate opened it slowly, as if she didn't know who'd be standing there.

"Good morning." Lana pivoted through Kate's dorm room door, keeping her backside out of Kate's view.

Kate's eyes narrowed. "What are you up to?"

"Me?" Lana's hands remained behind her back as she took several steps toward Kate.

Kate laughed at seeing the corners of a canvas poking out from behind Lana. "Yes, you. And I still can't believe you pretended you didn't know me last night."

"Do I really know you? Does anyone ever really know anyone else?" Lana asked, taking another step.

"Don't get philosophical."

"Why not? Remember when we first met, and you said—"

"Cut the crap." Kate chuckled. "Wait, what did I say?"

Lana leaned forward and kissed Kate lightly. When she spoke, she let her mouth and words tickle Kate's lips. "Oh, I don't remember word for word, but I do recall it was something brilliant. I remember every *other* word you've ever said to me, though." She kissed Kate's neck.

"Oh stop," Kate teased.

Lana gave her the whole-face smile Kate adored. "I brought you a surprise."

"You did? Wow, I didn't even notice you were hiding something behind your back."

Lana pulled out the canvas and turned it toward Kate. She held it up in front of her face for several seconds before peering over the top of it.

"Oh my God, your painting. It's beautiful." Kate gaped at the deep yellow bill and intensely bright eyes that added splashes of color to the muted tones of the bird and the water.

Her gaze shifted from the painting to Lana. The butterflies and other winged creatures took flight once again in her stomach. She loved how Lana made her flutter inside. "*You* are beautiful," Kate added.

"Great blue herons are your favorite."

"They are." Kate was amazed by the way the bird waded in its reflection in the water.

"You told me that our first night together, at the marina."

"I remember," she whispered.

"Where do you want it?"

"I'll hang it by the bed." Kate took the canvas from her and alternated staring at it and at Lana. "Beautiful."

After Kate leaned the painting against the bed, Lana came up beside her and turned her so they were face-to-face. She placed a hand on each side of Kate's face and pressed her lips to Kate's in a slow, savoring kiss. "You're terrific," Lana said as she pulled away.

Kate's heart pounded. Lana wasn't usually the verbally sentimental one, and the words made Kate smile.

"And," Lana said, "I really care for you a lot."

Lana kissed Kate again and started to move her hands from Kate's face.

Kate grabbed both of Lana's hands. "But?"

"But what?"

"You say that like there's a 'but' coming, like you're about to dump me or something."

Lana turned her hands around in Kate's and laced their fingers together. She kissed one of Kate's knuckles. "Me dump you?"

Kate squeezed her fingers together and tightly gripped Lana's.

"You're the one who'll dump me one day," Lana said, her voice low.

"Never," Kate whispered. And you'd have to be blind not to know that.

"What are your plans for today?" Lana asked.

"Loving you."

"Oh, sweetie, I've got things to do with my mother today, things I can't get out of. I just wanted to bring you the painting."

Kate looked at the white, blue-gray, and black strokes on the canvas and marveled at the lifelike image. "You are so talented."

Lana beamed.

"I guess I'm stuck studying today," Kate said.

"Sorry."

"It's okay. I'm going to call my sister, too."

"Oh?" Lana asked.

"Yeah. I want to make sure she got home okay last night."

"So, you haven't talked to her yet today?"

"No. I don't dare call too early."

"What's up with your sister anyway?"

"What do you mean?"

"She sure does like the beer, huh?" Lana looked thoughtful for a moment. "You know, there's something about her boyfriend I just don't trust."

"You got all that from serving us dinner?"

Lana gave her a quick kiss. She looked down when she started talking again. "I need you to promise me something."

That I'll love you forever? No problem. "Anything."

"Promise you won't come back around my work. They wouldn't understand there. I could lose my job or something."

"Okay."

†

The phone rang and rang. Kate figured her dad must have had to go to work for the umpteenth day in a row. She stared at the table of elements tacked to her wall and hoped April would answer the phone. Kate worried about Boyd's ability to drive the night before. He and April drank quite a bit. A barrage of rattling and rustling brought Kate's mind back to the phone pressed to her ear.

"Hello."

"Hey, you did make it home." She tried to keep her voice light. If April thought for even a second that Kate was going to lecture or pass judgment, she'd probably hang up.

"Of course I did," April said in a hoarse voice. There was more rustling in the phone. "What time is it? Wait, don't tell me. Did you need something in particular, or did you just call to give me a hard time?"

"I just wanted to make sure you made it home okay. And—"

"Listen, Katie. Thanks for calling, but it really is early."

Kate looked at the clock on her desk. "It's ten-thirty."

"Ten-thirty is early in my time zone. We'll talk later, okay?"

A click and dial tone kept Kate from saying anything else. She'd planned on telling April it had been nice to see her. But wasn't that the way it usually worked with them? Neither one seemed able to give the other the chance to move past basic civility.

✝

April's eyes burned when she opened them, so, she closed them again. She stretched out on her bed and remembered the restaurant had been smoky. So was that guy's place. Richie. Yeah, he and Boyd were both smoking cigarettes. No wonder her eyes felt like a fire pit.

She glanced at the phone beside her and squeezed her eyes shut again. Allergies and a bug eye. Why her? Why not Katie?

Katie. Perfect, responsible Katie had called earlier to make sure April got home okay.

Bile rose in her throat as she thought about Katie and the waitress in the restroom. What was her name? Lana. Yes, Richie's girlfriend, Lana.

How did Katie know the waitress? Maybe from school. Or maybe Katie hung out in the bar at the Sea Scape and didn't want to admit it. April chuckled at the absurdity of Katie hanging out in any bar.

Her knee throbbed. She thought about falling the night before and hoped it wouldn't leave a scar. April hated the thought of scars. But not Katie. When they were younger, Katie never cared if she'd get skinned up from crawling around looking at bugs or toads. Once she even made April hang out in the basement waiting for a black snake someone told her lived down there. That was in Hillsboro. The summer when… Maybe the snake was why Katie was in the basement when April went down to shower and Bobby came in and…

The phone rang again, and April was more thankful than ever that her dad let her have a phone in her room so she didn't have to get out of bed. She especially liked the idea that Katie had never had one in her room at home.

She picked up the phone and whispered, making her voice sound pitiful, just in case it was Katie calling back. "Hello."

"You sound like shit," Nicki bellowed into the phone.

"I'll only talk to you if you promise to keep your voice down."

"I promise. Rough night?" Nicki asked.

"Yeah, a little too much beer."

"I can top that."

"Oh? How many Volcanoes did you drink?"

"Only one. Because Mandy puked on our waiter and Jeannie almost got sick, too, and the manager asked us to leave. David got mad and didn't want to pay for his last drink if we couldn't stay, so they threatened to call the cops."

"Damn, I miss all the fun," April said.

"Don't feel bad. You have a great boyfriend that treats you good. You're so lucky. You have the guy and the body. I'd give anything to be as skinny as you are."

April felt breathless just listening to Nicki's long-windedness.

"Did you see Katie last night?"

"Yeah," April said. "For a little while."

"What's she up to? Has she found some computer or science geek to hook up with, some nerdy-boy she can exchange theories or algorithms with?"

April let the receiver rest on the side of her face. Could Nicki give her some insight if she tried to explain what she thought she saw in the restaurant restroom? Her decision not to bring it up had more to do with being too worn out than it did with loyalty to her sister.

"Guess who saw Susan the Narc last night."

"You?" April asked.

"Yep."

April grunted. Their freshman year, Susan Jones—Susan the Narc—told the principal that a student in Nicki's English class had drugs on them. The entire class went into lockdown, and by the time the dust settled, three guys were expelled for having pot.

"Huh?" April asked.

"I said she was at the Blue Dragon drinking like a fish."

"Susan the Narc was out drinking?"

"Yep."

"Wow, did you bitch the hypocrite out?"

"No, I'm not that spiteful. I waited until we left, and I called the police to report a rowdy teenager drinking unlawfully."

"You didn't."

"I did."

April believed it. She'd been instantly drawn to how Nicki said exactly what was on her mind and didn't take shit from anyone. Nicki had been particularly pissed about Susan ratting since Eddie Markle—the love of Nicki's fantasy life—was one of the guys in trouble. She was never just "Susan" after that, but "Susan the Narc," even to her face.

"What?" April asked.

"I said, I guess I'll let you go since you keep zoning out on me."

"Sorry. I'll call you when I'm feeling human again."

"Okay, well, take it easy," Nicki said and hung up.

April curled up in bed and tried not to think about how much her head wanted to explode. She finally forced herself out of bed when she heard the front door close and her dad's footsteps in the hall. She dragged herself into the kitchen.

Her dad sat on a bar stool, rubbing the area between his eyebrows. He looked smaller to her. It was like he'd started shrinking the summer he coldcocked her cousin Bobby in the head with the shovel after catching Bobby touching April in the shower. Over the seven years since, he'd gotten more and more distant. Each time he let April get away with something, he seemed to move another inch away from her.

He looked up when she said good morning. "Have you eaten lunch?" he asked.

Hell, she thought, I haven't made it to breakfast. "No, not yet."

"Want me to fix you something? I'm having a sandwich. I could fix you one, too."

115

"Okay. Where're you coming back from this time?"

"Denver." He pulled a loaf of bread out of the pantry.

April watched him take out turkey and cheese. When he pulled out the lettuce and tomato, she seriously doubted he'd remember she didn't like them on hers.

She felt oddly betrayed when he made her sandwich exactly the way she liked it. He even cut it diagonally.

"While I'm thinking about it," her dad said, "I talked to Kate, and she's coming home for the weekend. We thought it'd be nice for the three of us to spend the time together. You know," he added with a smile, "like a family."

"Like a family?" How dare Katie decide now that she wanted to start coming home weekends again? She just knew it was her sister's way of keeping April at home, and she resented the hell out of that. When her dad looked expectantly at her, April just shrugged.

Each bite of her sandwich threatened to come back up as she sat beside her dad and thought about Katie sticking her nose where it didn't belong. She was convinced Katie didn't want to spend time with her, she just wanted to keep her from going out with Boyd. April wasn't sure whether she was about to choke on her sandwich, or on the sudden, overwhelming desire to hurt Katie.

When April finished eating, she plodded back to her room. Not long after, she heard her dad's car pull out of the driveway. The last thing she wanted was to be stuck home for the weekend with her workaholic father and perfect sister.

April sat with her back against her pillow and picked at the scrape on her knee. The desire to lash out at Katie returned and wouldn't go away. It festered in her belly, lessened only by the sting of messing with the abrasion.

"What were you doing in that restroom last night?" she asked her absent sister. "What in the hell are you up to?"

Chapter Ten

Kate stood in her room at her father's house, facing the closet. She traced the circumference of the wooden knob with her fingertip, and her skin prickled. She smiled about finally getting Lana to lighten up about their close call. Her breath caught as she imagined the hangers nudging the back of her neck when she and Lana played their closet game.

She jumped at the movement in her peripheral vision.

"What'cha staring at the closet for, dork?" April asked.

Kate didn't turn around. She didn't want April to see the blush that the thought of Lana had brought to her cheeks. "Get out of my room." When April didn't comply, Kate risked sounding like a whiny ten-year-old. "Out."

"Your bed's rumpled."

The heat on Kate's cheeks flared hotter with the memory of yanking up the bedspread in a sloppy attempt to straighten up before rushing out to meet Lana at the car when her dad had come home unexpectedly.

Kate finally turned to look at her sister. She bristled when April scrutinized the top of her dresser. "What do you want?" Kate asked.

"I'm just spending family time with my sister. Isn't that the point?"

Kate sighed.

"Yeah, I didn't think so." April plucked the mini microscope off the dresser.

Kate's mind flashed to when Lana had studied the plastic replica. Lana's smile had beamed across the room when she'd cradled it in her hand. Later she'd told Kate she'd loved seeing that nugget of her life. It wasn't lost on Kate that she had barely seen a sliver of Lana's life.

April tossed the microscope from one hand to the other. "Now, really, Katie, aren't you a bit old for toys?"

"Put it down, and get out of my room."

"Okay, whatever. But first there's something I've been meaning to—"

"Girls."

They both jumped at the sound of their dad's voice.

"Dinner's ready," he called.

Within minutes, Kate and April sat across from one another.

"Meatloaf," their dad said. "You girls' favorite."

Kate's gaze rested on the meatloaf. Fat congealed around the bottom of the lumpy blob. But what really bothered her was her dad thinking it was both their favorite. It was April's. Always April's.

"Katie," April muttered.

Kate looked up.

April rolled her eyes and flicked her wrist in a way that was unmistakably meant to rattle the thick silver bracelet that slid halfway up her arm. "Would you please pass the mashed potatoes?"

Kate suppressed the urge to rip the bracelet off April's bony wrist before she slid the bowl of potatoes toward her sister.

"So," their dad said, "tell me about this special summer course."

Kate watched as April smashed her potatoes into her meatloaf and gravy. She swallowed hard. "It's not really dinner conversation." She didn't care if she ruined April's appetite, but it was going to be hard enough choking down her sister's favorite meal without adding talk of tick-borne diseases and sick animals.

Their dad forced a laugh. "No, I suppose not."

Kate took a bite of her potatoes as she watched April continue to mash and mix.

"This is great," their dad said. "All of us here." He smiled, and Kate thought about how forced and unnatural it appeared.

Kate wanted to read April's expression, to climb into her head and figure out what her take on this was. When April caught her staring, her eyes narrowed. Kate smiled in an attempt to convey that her look was curiosity, not judgment. In the second before April looked away, Kate knew her own expression seemed as pathetic to April as their dad's did to Kate.

Kate forced down a bite of meatloaf. Her dinner roiled around in her gut as she watched April push hers around on her plate. Resentment gnawed at her stomach. How dare April not even eat when it was her favorite meal? Kate took another bite of the food. At least she would show appreciation for their dad's effort.

Her father chewed each bite slowly and methodically, much like he did everything. After every few bites, he sipped his drink and a "hmm" drifted from him, hanging in the air briefly before fluttering down like a dying moth. Or did his guttural response sink like a stone off the dock into Chisman Creek? Or perhaps plop and float like April's flip-flop the time they were kids and April dangled her feet off the edge of the dock and let one shoe slip from her foot into the brackish water.

Kate's grip on her fork tightened as she remembered how the flip-flop bobbed up and down in the mud-brown creek. April had thrown a hissy fit until Kate sprawled across the rough wood planks, flat on her belly, and stretched her arms out as far as she could. Her hand sloshed through the cool water several times before she caught the soggy flip-flop between her fingers. When she stood up with it in her grasp, there was bird mess or crab gunk globbed on the front of her shirt.

Kate shoveled some potatoes into her mouth and reached for her glass of milk to wash it down. That's when she saw April's grin.

"What?" Kate asked.

"Oh, nothing, just now seeing why you've gotten a little pudgy."

Even though she knew April was just trying to rile her, Kate still looked down at her stomach. Then she focused on the meatloaf. She cringed at its resemblance to the gunk on her shirt that day at Chisman Creek. When she looked back up, she locked her gaze onto April's.

"What? You'd rather drink your dinner?" Kate asked. "Dad, did April tell you we had dinner together the other night?"

"Really?" He wiped the corner of his mouth with his napkin. "What did you girls have to eat?"

"It wasn't the food that was interesting," Kate answered.

April shot her a dirty look. "Katie's right, it wasn't the food. But the service was great. As a matter of fact," she said and paused to lick the potatoes from her fork, "Katie knew the waitress."

120

"I'm glad you're making friends," he said.

Kate fought to control her breathing. "April should probably make some new friends," she countered.

"Oh, but I have." She jangled her bracelet. "Boyd and I had a double-date later that night with your friend Lana and her boyfriend. Richie seems like a nice guy. They're so cute together, so happy."

Kate stared at her fork. An image of Lana's body arching up to meet hers collided with one of Lana talking to some guy at the Sea Scape's bar.

Kate's beige reflection shone back at her from the fork she still gripped. She blinked several times before putting it down. Her mind shouted, "Liar! Drunk!" but her mouth whispered, "Dinner was great, Dad."

"Cheesecake for dessert," he said "You girls' favorite."

Kate's hand trembled as she placed her napkin onto her plate. "I can't stay." She picked up her dishes and started toward the kitchen. "I have extra work to do in the lab for class." She didn't hate lying, but she did hate the way her chest tightened and her lungs fought against taking in air.

"You aren't spending the weekend?" he asked.

"No, sorry." She hesitated. "I'll clean up in here first, but then I have to go," she finally managed to say.

"Don't worry about it. I'll do that. But at least have dessert."

"I really can't," Kate answered, too loudly. She stacked her dishes in the sink and rushed into her room. Before she could shut the door, April moved in past her.

"So, what's going on?" April asked through a smirk.

Kate didn't answer.

This time when April snatched the microscope off the dresser, Kate slapped it out of her hand. It thudded onto the carpet.

"Katie, you'll break it," April taunted.

Kate walked over to it. Tears streaked her face. She placed her sneaker-clad foot over the top of it, looked at April for a moment, and pressed her weight down. The percussion from the cracking plastic ricocheted up her leg, the pinpricks of sensation a dim echo of what stabbed at her chest.

"Happy now?" Kate grabbed her bag off the corner chair and stomped past April.

Chapter Eleven

As Dr. Stoddard stood at the front of the class writing an assignment on the board, Kate fiddled with her textbook. Even though the Monday afternoon lecture was her favorite part of the course, she couldn't concentrate.

She brought her hands to her face, intertwined her fingers, and rested her nose against them. She tried to inhale the last remnant of Lana's scent. It had to be there, she thought. Beneath the soap and textbook smells, there had to be the faint reminder, the irrefutable proof of Lana's love and want and warmth.

She lowered her hands. Of course all signs were gone; she hadn't seen Lana all weekend. Lana thought she was out of town, and Kate wouldn't go to the Sea Scape to tell her otherwise.

In a daze, Kate leafed through the pages, not really believing, but knowing April couldn't just pull names out of thin air like that. *Lana's boyfriend, Richie*, April had said. This couldn't be happening to her.

She let the pages flop on their own, immediately recognizing the species when the book opened to a picture of mosquito larvae.

Kate stared at the photo. She swallowed hard and thought back to the time she had accidentally raised mosquitoes as a child. Even after she had figured out that the squirmy, wiggly things weren't sea horses, even after she ascertained April's bites were coming from her new pets, Kate had kept them. She wouldn't give them up. She couldn't bring herself to take them back to the stale, green water in the old birdbath behind their neighbor's garage.

Instead she hid the jar on the floor between her bed and the wall. Every day she watched the little creatures floating vertically near the surface of the water. She'd already given up her cat because of April. She'd already given up a slew of long-haired stray dogs because of April's allergies, and then the short-haired one because it snapped at her sister. It wasn't the dog's fault that he could tell April was bad, even way back then.

So, when the mosquito bite on April's eyelid got infected and she almost went blind in that eye, Kate secretly held her ground. She didn't dump the jar of yellowish water until the last wiggler was gone.

Kate had even lost her song to April. Ka-tie-Hun-ter, Ka-tie-Hun-ter, we-love-you, we-love-you. She remembered crying and crying the first time she heard someone singing the Katie Hunter song wrong. She didn't know who that Farrah Jocka girl was, but Katie sure didn't want her taking her song. Her mother had rocked her in her arms and explained that other people sang the song differently, but all that mattered was that *they* knew the real way.

But then the new baby came. And one day, cradling her life-like stuffed spider monkey, Kate paused in the doorway to the baby's room. Her mom held April in her arms, and her dad leaned over them. Both parents were singing Katie's song to the baby. They'd even changed the words. Ap-ril-Hun-ter, Ap-ril-Hun-ter, we-love-you, we-love-you.

Katie ran and ran and ran, and it wasn't until she was in her room, hiding behind the cedar chest stenciled with butterflies, that she realized she'd dragged her Monk-Monk through the house by its tail. Guilt and remorse had been quickly replaced by anger. She was so mad at April for stealing her song that she wanted to drag April through the house by the tail, or at least by a leg.

It was almost a relief, years later, when she found out it wasn't her song after all. Fre-re-Jac-ques, Fre-re-Jac-ques. But that didn't lessen the sting of April stealing it.

And now April had taken away Kate's joy. She couldn't stand the idea of Kate being happy, so she had to wreck it all by telling Kate about partying with Lana and her boyfriend.

It's not fair, Kate thought. She loved Lana so much; she needed Lana so much. She couldn't let anything mess it up. The tune started in her head, and she hated that she didn't know Lana's last name. But she had the solution to that problem. "La-na-Hun-ter, La-na-Hun-ter, I-love-you, I-love-you."

When she looked up, she saw Dr. Stoddard and most of the class staring at her. Kate had been humming—or singing—the song out loud. At first her face grew warm, but then she didn't care. She was in pain, and it didn't matter what anyone thought.

As she got up to leave class early, it also didn't matter to her that she'd promised Lana she'd never go back to the Sea Scape.

✝

Several bulbs on the outside sign were burned out, turning the Sea Scape into the Se Sc ap. Kate contemplated the scooter chained to the pole—the torn seat, the rusting blue body. Her breath caught as she thought about the last time she and Lana had ridden out to the marina.

Cloaked in the damp night, they'd straddled the parked but running scooter, facing each other. Its vibration picked up the beat of *Crimson and Clover* playing in Kate's head, sending the pulse racing between her legs.

"Don't ever fix this thing," Kate had whispered.

Lana raked her teeth down Kate's neck and reached behind her to rev the engine.

"Oh," Kate gasped. And, unlike in the song, she already knew she loved Lana.

Kate shook free of the memory and shivered in the heat. She stared at the front door of the Sea Scape and knew she couldn't just leave. She couldn't go back to the ignorant bliss of those nights at the marina or the days with Lana in her bed. She had to see for herself, even if she had promised not to return to the Sea Scape.

As the door shut behind her, Kate's eyes adjusted to the dim light, and she saw them at the bar. The guy stood behind Lana, his thick arms wrapped around her and Lana leaning back against him. It was just like all those times she'd stood that way with her, tucked away in Kate's dorm room.

The shock of seeing Lana with Richie was worse than catching her parents singing her song to April. And it was worse than watching from behind the camelback trunk when Bobby came into the basement that day in Hillsboro.

Kate wanted to turn and run back out into the harsh daylight. She wanted to bolt away before Lana knew that Kate knew, and everything was ruined. If she left immediately, Kate could pretend Richie didn't exist. But her feet wouldn't budge. Just like in Hillsboro. Surrounded by liquor bottles instead of dusty jars of unrecognizable preserves, the same frozen dread weighed her down.

Richie said something into Lana's neck, and Lana's laugh gathered in the corners of her eyes, crinkling the smooth skin in a way Kate had never imagined could be meant for anyone but her. For Kate, it seemed that was the worst part of the betrayal.

Lana looked up and saw Kate. Her body must have tensed, or otherwise signaled Richie, because he looked up, too. They both stared; Lana's eyes wide with surprise, Richie's unknowing and unaffected.

Something inside Kate broke, and she knew everything would be different from now on, just as she'd known it as she'd stood in the Hillsboro basement years earlier.

She stared at them until Richie smiled and said, "What's up?"

His words began to thaw her feet. She shuffled them. Then she heard her dad's voice, far away, a lifetime away. "Katie, take your sister upstairs," her dad said after hitting Bobby. Kate felt as if she'd been struck with the shovel in her dad's hand.

What's up? She wanted to scream. What's up, other than you've ruined my life?

But she didn't scream that, or anything else. She turned and ran.

†

April slipped into Nicki's car and was almost overcome by a cloud of perfume. "Whew." She waved her hand through the air.

"It'll thin out," Nicki said. She tilted the rearview mirror toward her and puckered her lips, checking her lip-gloss.

"That's a nice color," April said.

"Pink Sass. Speaking of which..." She looked down at her chest, checking out her ample cleavage. "Too bad the ass came with the tits, huh?"

April laughed, even though she wasn't really in the mood for Nicki's butt and breast comparisons.

"T.G.I.M," Nicki squealed. "Monday night two-fers at the Blue Dragon. Yep, thank God it's Monday."

Nicki put the car into gear and took off with a jerk. "So, how did you get out of family time this weekend?" she asked in a breathless rush of words.

"Katie went back to school after dinner. Once she was gone, it didn't take much effort to get Dad to let me out of prison."

"I bet you were ecstatic."

April couldn't get Katie's reaction out of her head. When she'd mentioned Lana and Richie, Katie had stared at her fork like she'd forgotten what it was for. Then she looked hurt. Then she got pissed. Yep, the full spectrum.

"So, did you go out with Boyd then?"

April nodded. "A romantic Saturday night of double feature slasher flicks."

Nicki giggled.

Yee-haw, April thought.

Nicki steadied the steering wheel with her knee as she reached behind her seat and pulled out a leather case. She swung it onto April's lap. "Pick out whatever you want to listen to."

April opened the case and ran her finger along the edges of the cassettes—everything from Olivia Newton John to Cheap Trick, but no AC/DC or Zeppelin or Skynyrd. Then she saw it—Joan Jett. She pulled it out and handed it to Nicki.

"Yeah, that'll work." Nicki stuck the tape in the player. A chorus about bits and pieces of something blared out at them. Nicki turned down the volume.

"Do you know Katie actually listens to Joan Jett?" April asked.

"Our Katie?"

"Yep, our Katie."

April wondered how her sister was doing. She'd tried to call Katie a few times but hadn't gotten an answer. The guilt went straight to her scabbed-up knee, making it throb. But maybe what she'd told Katie about Lana and Richie wasn't such a big deal after all. Maybe April hadn't quite understood what she thought she'd seen in Katie's and Lana's reflections when she'd walked in on them in the restroom.

Maybe, maybe, maybe. But April's gut knew better.

"I guess you're only out with me physically then, huh?"

"What?"

"You're zoning again," Nicki said.

"Sorry." And she was. She knew she hadn't been a good friend since the school year ended, but she needed to spend as much time as possible with Boyd. And Boyd didn't like going out with Nicki and the others because he didn't think they were cool enough. They didn't listen to the right music or hang out with the right people.

Joan Jett was singing about a little drummer boy. It seemed odd to April, but she was thrilled to hear actual singing she understood, and in a good voice. "I like this," she said, pointing at the cassette player.

"Me, too. So, what did you have to promise Boyd for him to let you come out with me again so soon?"

Let her? Something about Nicki's choice of words rubbed April the wrong way, but she ignored it. "He's beat. He works hard, and this heat really zaps it out of him sometimes."

"I'm just glad you decided to come. Maybe you can give Boyd some extra sex this weekend so we can do something again next week."

"Maybe," April said, playing along.

"He's really good in bed, huh?"

April looked at Nicki. "He's twenty. Of course he's good."

Nicki nodded her understanding, flipped the cassette over, and started singing along about how much she loved rock and roll. At the end of the song, she told April that Mandy and David were meeting them at the Blue Dragon.

"Cool," April said as she looked out the window. She thought about getting her driver's license and a car of her own soon. Boyd liked the idea of her having her license, especially since she drove sometimes when he was too drunk, but he wasn't too hot on the idea of her getting a car. When she'd brought it up, he'd scowled and said he took her everywhere she wanted to go, why did she need her own car?

It took a moment to register, but April saw Boyd's Gran Torino turn off Jefferson Avenue and into Joey's apartment complex. She glanced at Nicki to see if she'd seen it, too, but Nicki was pawing through the cassette case teetering on her lap.

When April looked back, Boyd's car was out of view. There was probably a good reason why he was going over there without her, she told herself. He probably just wanted to get some crank or pot. She didn't want to think about the fact that they hadn't hung out at Joey's lately, not since they found the dead guy.

"What else is Katie up to?" Nicki asked.

"Just studying. You know Katie." But she didn't. And, apparently, neither did April. How could she have not known that her own sister was "that way"? Had there been signs that April just hadn't paid attention to?

"April?"

"Huh?"

"Do you still have your fake license, in case we get carded?"

"Yeah. I lost the first one, but Boyd got me another."

"He is so cool. You are so lucky."

Maybe she'd feel lucky after a Flaming Volcano or two.

†

Goose bumps ran up April's arms, and she was glad she'd remembered that the Blue Dragon was always chilly and had worn her Calvin's instead of the cutoff Levis she'd contemplated.

The bartender lined up four large glasses and mixed the Flaming Volcanoes as if on an assembly line. April stared as red bled down into the orange drink. The bartender placed the drinks on a tray, sloshed Bacardi 151 on top and struck a match.

The waiter brought the drinks to their table. As he set them down, the flames started to fizzle out. April looked forward to the fruity taste, a nice change from beer.

All chatter stopped momentarily as the four teens sipped their drinks.

"Who's your favorite group, April?" David asked.

April didn't know how to answer. She knew Boyd's favorite groups, but not her own. She'd picked Joan Jett to listen to in the car with Nicki, but that was mostly because

131

she was curious about Katie liking her. She didn't have her own favorite, and that bothered her.

"Hey, April," Nicki said, "I forgot to tell you I saw Ozone at the Pat Benatar concert last week. I wish you could have come. You would have had fun."

April nodded. "I'm sure I would have."

"Who's Ozone?" Mandy asked.

April chuckled at their nickname for her one-time friend. She and Lisa Snyder had been close until their freshman year, when April started hanging out with Nicki.

"Ozone's in the sky, right?" David moved his straw to the side and took a gulp of Volcano.

"Tell them about Ozone," Nicki said, turning to April.

"You tell it." April was uneasy talking about Lisa; they'd been good friends once. She let her attention wander back to the bar, where the bartender was torching shots of booze. Her face warmed as she thought of Boyd knocking the waiter's arm when they'd been there together. She glanced down at the stolen bracelet she still wore. Then she remembered hearing that Lisa had said some unflattering things about April dating Boyd.

"Ozone is Lisa Snyder," April said.

Mandy nudged David. "Lisa Snyder."

Nicki gave them a questioning look and went on with the story. "One time in the hall between classes, Lisa came up to us at our lockers. She'd just come from gym class and asked to borrow my deodorant. When I pulled it from my bag, April saw that it was a spray and asked if it was harmful to the ozone layer."

"What did you care?" Mandy asked.

"I was just joking around," April said.

"So Lisa gets real serious," Nicki continued, "looks down her shirt at her underarm and says, 'I use that brand. I have very sensitive skin, and it hasn't harmed mine.'"

"Her what?" David asked.

"Her ozone layer, under her arm," Nicki said loudly.

"Huh?" he asked.

"Don't bother explaining it," Mandy said. "He's a guy."

David chugged his drink. "And don't you forget it."

Mandy elbowed David. "Tell them about signing Lisa Snyder's yearbook."

He fidgeted with his drink.

"Tell them, or I will," Mandy said.

"But you'll embellish."

"That's my point. Tell them."

"Sophomore year," he said, "Lisa and I— Well, I thought we had some chemistry between us. So when we exchanged yearbooks, I thought I'd be cool, and I wrote in hers something about us hooking up."

"You wrote that you were dying to get in her pants," Mandy said.

"Not in those exact—"

"I read it," she reminded him.

"Okay, in those exact words. So, we traded back and she'd written about how sweet and kind I was. She'd signed off with 'Peace in God, Lisa.'"

Mandy laughed, and some of her drink went up her nose, almost choking her.

"Serves you right," David said.

"The best part," Mandy said and snorted, "was when Lisa's mom called David's, and he had to apologize."

"No, the best part was when I gave up on good girls and started dating you."

"Ah, how romantic," Nicki said. "Am I the only one not getting laid?" She took a big slurp of her drink. "Well," she added, turning to April, "me and your sister."

April fiddled with a matchbook from the tacky dragon-shaped ashtray on the table.

To the wildest chick I know. Remember all the parties, and the ones still to come!!! That was how Nicki had signed April's last yearbook. And she'd ended with, Love you dearly, but not queerly.

Had friends of Katie's signed her yearbook that way, too? What had she thought about that?

✝

April wasn't at all surprised when Nicki pulled up in front of her house and Boyd was waiting half a block down the road. She stepped out of Nicki's car, waved her on, and started toward the Gran Torino.

Boyd met her halfway and steered her to the side of the house farthest from her dad's bedroom.

"You're out late," he said, pulling her close to him.

"Yeah. I told you I probably would be." She kissed his cheek.

"Who was with you?"

"Nicki drove us," she said.

"Yeah? Who else did you talk to?"

"No one in particular. It was just Nicki, and Mandy, and her boyfriend David."

"No other guys were there?"

"No, Boyd, no other guys." She took a step back from him. "Where did you go tonight?"

He cocked his head, like he was considering his answer and said, "I swung by Joey's to get some stuff."

134

"Some stuff?"

"Yeah." He wiped at his nose.

"Do you not want me going to Joey's with you anymore?"

"That's ridiculous." He took a step, closed the slight gap between them, and pressed against her. "Did you miss me?"

"Of course I did."

He leaned closer, and she felt the heat of the bricks against her back.

"You know why we're so good together?" He breathed in, smelling her neck. "Because we understand each other. My dad left me, and your mom left you. We understand." He kissed her hard on the mouth.

When he pulled away, he started talking fast. "I give you anything you want, right? And you take care of my needs. We're perfect together. Don't let anyone say otherwise."

"Who would?" she asked.

"I don't know. Your friends, maybe."

He nibbled on her neck, a little too hard, and she whimpered. He moved his mouth over the same area. She felt something hot and wet on her skin and reached up into the slickness of it. She leaned away from him. "Are you bleeding?"

"It's nothing."

She turned her head to see his face. "You are bleeding."

"It's just my nose. No big deal." He swiped at it several times, pressing a little harder each time.

"Easy," she said.

He leaned into her and slipped his hand between her legs. "Forget about my nose. Where were we? Oh, yeah, how perfect we are together. And how you take such good care of me."

She glanced toward the dark kitchen window. The Blue Dragon's Flaming Volcano burned in her throat, and she felt both excited and cautious. What if her dad saw them? She tensed.

"What, baby?" Boyd asked.

She took a deep breath, inhaling the smells of his stale cigarettes and her alcohol. His stubble scraped her cheek. His face wasn't usually so rough.

He grabbed her hand and pushed it between them. "Touch me," he whispered.

Her knees turned rubbery.

"Touch me," he repeated, louder. He started undoing her Calvins.

"Boyd, we can't."

"We have to." He pushed against her. "See. I have needs."

She worried about her father seeing them. That fear swirled around her, churning what was left inside her stomach into molten lava.

Don't be scared. Touch me, Bobby had said.

She froze with a sudden realization. The fear of her dad as he stood at the bottom of the basement stairs in Hillsboro far outweighed the fear of her cousin as he forced his big finger into her little body.

Touch me.

"No." She shoved Boyd backward. Her heart pounded as she looked around. There was no Bobby, no Dad, no Katie, no basement. Just Boyd and her and the heavy heat of the night.

"What's your damned problem?" Boyd growled.

They both jumped when the porch light came on.

"Shit," Boyd said.

"I better go in."

"Yeah, I guess you better." He wiped at his nose as he turned to leave.

†

April pulled the sheet over her head. She'd set the small trash can beside the bed, even though she was pretty sure she wouldn't get sick.

There had always been things about Boyd that reminded her of Bobby: the cigarettes, beer, even his fast car to some extent. But never before had the similarities struck her so strongly that she'd become confused. Never while she was awake, anyway.

For a brief moment, she'd actually expected to see her dad standing there with a shovel. And she thought she'd see Katie standing in the corner.

Why was Katie in the basement? The question had always been there, but she'd never let its implication form fully. What was Katie doing in the basement?

Lying very still, April concentrated, listening for any sounds from her dad. Nothing. She thought she heard him breathing, sleep sounds, but decided it was her imagination.

Katie saw everything.

She reached to the nightstand and pulled the phone into bed with her. Feeling for the position of the buttons, she dialed Katie's number. She was startled when Katie answered during the first ring.

"Hello."

"It's me," April whispered.

"Hello?" Katie repeated.

"It's me. April," she said, a little louder.

"I can barely hear you. What's wrong? It's late."

"You don't answer in the daytime."

137

The pause that followed reinforced the new tension between them.

"Have you been okay?" April asked.

"I'm fine."

April wasn't convinced. "Are you and your... friend... are you—"

Katie sighed.

"I'm sorry," April said. "Really."

"Everything is fine. Don't worry about me," Katie said.

April cringed at the amount of acid that dripped from the ordinary words. "Okay, then."

"Okay. Good night."

"Wait. Katie—" She saw everything that happened in the basement.

"What?"

"I... uh... I was wondering. Do you think the thing with me and Bobby made you afraid of guys?"

"I'm not afraid of guys."

"Okay, so maybe it made you hate them."

"I don't hate guys. I'm just not interested in them."

"But the thing with Bobby could have influenced you."

"Listen, you may want to blame Bobby for how you are, but that doesn't mean I—"

"How I am? What do you mean how I am?"

"You know, doing stupid and dangerous things, and sleeping with Boyd—"

"Sleeping with Boyd? Shit, at least that's normal."

"Normal?"

Katie saw that I didn't try to stop Bobby. April's face grew hot. "Yes. Normal."

She couldn't believe that Katie would try to turn this around on her after April had been so willing to try to understand this new information about her sister.

"You've spent the last seven years using Hillsboro as an excuse to shirk all responsibility," Katie spat.

Katie Hunter—the perfect student, daughter, sister. "And you've used it as a way to play the fucking martyr. Kate the damned saint."

"I covered your butt so many times. I always took care of you. Well, no more, April. I won't let guilt over that control my life for even one more minute."

April was stunned. She'd never heard Katie get so angry.

"Goodbye, April."

"Kate the saint," April hissed. The phone slammed in April's ear and her own anger rose. *Guilt?*

Of course, guilt. Katie hadn't tried to stop Bobby either.

April shakily placed the phone back on the table, then she leaned over the trash can and threw up.

†

Kate took several deep breaths as she resisted the temptation to hurl the phone across the room. She'd been expecting Lana to phone and apologize, but instead she got April calling to pick a fight. She jumped when she heard a knock. Her heart flipped and flopped. Kate stood to the side when she opened the door.

"Hey," Lana whispered. She slipped into the room and took Kate's hand into hers. "My God, you're shaking."

Kate yanked her hand away. "April had the nerve to suggest that I'm a lesbian because of what happened in Hillsboro. And then she accused me of playing the martyr over it!" She stopped when she realized she was screaming.

Lana took Kate's hand back. "Calm down," she murmured. "What happened in Hillsboro?"

Kate stepped away from her. "What?" she asked, confused and angry that she'd brought it up with Lana.

"Sweetie, I have no idea what you're talking about."

Kate gasped. "*Sweetie?* Don't call me that. You've been cheating on me this whole time. How could you?"

"God, I've been so anxious all night, wanting to get over here to explain things."

"I can't believe you stayed to work your shift. You had to know how upset I'd be." Kate plopped down on the bed and sat with her legs turned away from Lana.

"I couldn't come any sooner."

Kate folded her arms over her chest. "Yes, you could have."

"How would I have explained leaving to my boss, or to Richie?"

"Don't say his name. Don't you ever say his name in front of me."

"I'm sorry." Lana studied her feet. "I should have told you."

"Don't see him anymore."

Lana knelt in front of Kate. "Kate... I..."

"Aren't I enough for you? Don't I love you enough?"

"It's not about that. It's about the things my family would suspect if I wasn't dating a guy. My family isn't like yours."

"How is mine? Huh?" Kate thought about her family: runaway mother, distant father, drunk teenager, and lovesick dyke.

Lana swallowed hard. "When I was about thirteen, my mother caught me kissing a girl from school. Mom prayed for me day and night and told me God would punish me for doing those things. She said so many ugly, ugly things, that finally I'd had enough. I told her to tell God to bring it on, I didn't care. Two days later, my grandmother had a stroke and died."

"Oh no."

"All my mom said to me was, 'Well, He brought it on. Are you happy, because I guess I'll be next.' I swore to her I'd stop kissing girls. She didn't start talking to me again until a few months later when I brought home a boy named Robert. Those months when she was so upset with me were the worst in my life."

"I just want to be with you," Kate whispered.

"You are with me."

"Do you know there are places—bars—where we can go, and hold hands, and slow dance, and not hide what we mean to each other?"

"I can't do that. I can't risk my family ever finding out." Kate sobbed.

"This is all I can give." Lana opened her arms. She stood in front of Kate and held out her hands. "Come here. Dance with me."

"That's not what I had in mind."

"Let me hold you, Kate. Come here. Please."

Kate looked up at the tear-tracks streaking Lana's face, and her heart jolted. She stood.

Lana pulled her into her arms and started humming a song Kate didn't recognize.

Kate buried her face against Lana's neck. Their bodies fit together perfectly, unlike awkward embraces with clumsy, sweaty boys at the school dances before she finally just stopped going. That made her think of the time she had met Gregg Beech at the movies to see *Grease* before either was old enough to drive and before Kate decided not to even bother with boys in that way. Gregg had held her hand, and she was so distracted by it (what does that finger pressing there mean, and why is he moving his thumb like that?) that she barely remembered anything that happened in the movie. Except that her heart beat harder and faster during Olivia Newton-John's scenes than John Travolta's. She didn't understand it then, but she sure did now.

She savored the scent of honeysuckle. Yes, the way they fit, the way Lana felt against her, it was all simply perfect. But they were still hidden away in Kate's room. Kate would always be Lana's secret life.

"Do you love him?" Kate asked before she could stop herself.

"I care about him."

"But love?" Kate stepped back to see Lana's face.

Lana looked away.

"How about me? Do you love me?" A long silence followed. Finally, Kate placed her hand under Lana's chin and lifted. Looking into her eyes, she said, "Just tell me the truth. Do you love me?"

Tears trailed down Lana's face. "Yes," she whispered.

Kate stepped back into Lana's arms. "I've loved you since the moment I climbed onto the back of your scooter for the first time."

"I've loved you since I watched you carry boxes of clothes and books up to your room when you moved in."

Kate pulled away far enough to see Lana's face. "What?"

"Yeah. I was cutting across the campus, running late for work."

"And you saw me?" She couldn't believe there was ever a time she didn't instinctively feel Lana's presence.

"I not only saw you, but I stopped to watch. I ended up being really late for work. I wanted to offer to help you with the boxes, but—"

"But?"

"I was too shy."

Kate chuckled. "You? Really?"

"Yes, really. You know I only pretend to be confident and capable."

"You may pretend to be confident, but we both know you're quite capable."

"Can we lie down for a while?" Lana asked.

"All night, if you want."

"I'd love to—"

"But you can't." She led Lana to the bed.

As they curled themselves around one another, Kate thought about how they'd never before just laid down together, fully clothed, holding each other. She wanted to ask, 'What's next?' but was too terrified of the answer to pose the question.

Kate let her breathing fall into synch with Lana's.

"I need to go soon."

"I know," Kate said, just before drifting off.

Later, when Lana got up to leave, Kate kept her eyes tightly closed, choosing to pretend they'd wake up together in the morning.

†

Kate sat quiet and still in her car. She'd been watching the door to The Sea Scape for hours. Waiting. Her body jolted to attention when she saw him come out. Richie climbed into the passenger side of a beat-up Dodge van.

Kate gripped the steering wheel as she followed them through a maze of turns and swallowed hard when the van pulled into a dirt driveway.

She kept going. She watched in the rearview mirror as they got out of the van and sauntered up the driveway. The air-freshener swung in and out of her peripheral vision as she locked her gaze onto Richie.

Kate forced her eyes off him and gasped. She slammed on the brakes just short of running into the Dead End sign.

She knew they were staring at her as she backed up and tried to maneuver around in the narrow area. The back end of the car slid into the ditch. She pumped the accelerator to force the car forward, but her tires spun and she didn't move.

She jumped when Richie rapped on the back of her car. "Just a little gas… easy…"

She did as she was told and the rear end of her car lifted and inched forward. With all four tires on the asphalt, she stopped. Both guys approached on the driver's side.

"There you go," Richie said.

"Thank you. Really."

He leaned down and asked, "Do I know you?"

"No," Kate answered.

"Are you sure? You look familiar."

"Hey, Rich, you got a woman." The other guy gave Richie a playful shove. "Back off and let me have a chance to say hello to the pretty lady."

Richie rolled his eyes for Kate's benefit. He smiled as he wiped his hands on his pants. "You'll be okay from here?"

"Yeah. Thanks."

He straightened and stepped away from the car. "Anytime."

Kate drove away. *Hey, Rich, you got a woman.* The words taunted her and made her stomach churn.

Chapter Twelve

"Wow, you look rough," Nicki said.

"Gee, thanks." April sat up in her bed and glanced in the mirror over her dresser. Half moons of mascara loomed beneath each eye, and her face was paler than usual.

"What did you do last night?" Nicki plopped down hard on April's bed, causing April to groan.

"Partied in Norfolk," April said.

"Yeah? Where?"

"This guy named Richie's place." April thought about how uncomfortable she'd been there, trapped by the one-way-in, one-way-out arrangement of the converted garage apartment. On top of that, she'd been uptight, praying that Lana wouldn't show up, and that if she did, April wouldn't say anything she'd regret once she was sober and unstoned.

"Boyd knows the coolest people. You are so lucky you found him. Have I told you lately how lucky you are?"

"Yes, you've told me lately."

The night before, stoned, April had overanalyzed things, growing paranoid about changes in Boyd. Beyond the weight he'd lost, and how lately he didn't always smell his usual sexy-smoky-soapy way, something worried her, something she couldn't quite grasp.

She settled back against her pillow, her head pounding. Nicki was saying something about watching the hot Firebird guy again at McDonald's the night before, but April wasn't paying attention. April wanted to admit to Nicki that she was in over her head. That she wasn't as cool as she pretended to be, that she didn't really like getting stoned and was growing weary of hangovers.

An image, or memory, flashed through her mind. She'd felt in control as she straddled Boyd at the drive-in. The image of him entering her became more vivid, and she remembered repeating the words for him, just as he'd asked. *Fuck me.* Did she really remember that, despite how Quaaludes affected her memory, or had her mind fabricated the image in response to Boyd teasing her about it afterward?

"Hey, you haven't heard a word I've said," Nicki whined.

"I think I'm in trouble," April blurted.

"You think you're pregnant?" Nicki pulled her legs up under her and knelt on the bed. "How? We got on the pill together."

"No, not pregnant."

Nicki looked disappointed. "What other trouble is there?"

"I think I'm—" April took a deep breath. "I think I'm out of control."

"Out of control? You? You're the most together person I know. Your dad lets you do whatever you want; you're skinny; you have a hot boyfriend; and hell, your hair feathers better than anyone's I know."

April stared at Nicki. Why did she even bother? Of course Nicki wouldn't get it. But Katie would. Yes, Katie would get it, but she was also the last person April would admit any of it to.

†

April perched on the edge of the tub and worked the soap into a thick lather on her legs. She glanced around. Her Flicker wasn't there. She remembered she'd left it in her bag, in the other room. Her dad's razor—a bulky, metal beast—rested on the opposite side of the tub. She reached for it, but froze midway.

She remembered herself at nine years old as she stood naked in front of the mirror upstairs in her family's vacation home, disgusted by the smattering of hairs revealing themselves *down there*. Her breasts weren't yet more than bug bites, but she had to deal with hair? She'd snuck into her dad's room to borrow his razor. With the first drag of the blade through the shaving cream, pain seared through her and blood welled up through the suds. She wiped at it with her hand but that didn't help, so she got dressed and ran down to the basement shower.

And then Bobby and her dad and Katie were there... Katie.

Katie, who the day before had talked April into going into the basement with her to wait for the king snake no one but Katie believed would show up...

Katie, who wouldn't let April say anything while they sat among the spider webs and dusty jars of preserves that April imagined as hearts and tongues of deer and raccoons that Bobby had hunted, gutted, and cooked in the big pit behind Aunt Carolyn's house with the slanted porch and always-full clothes line...

Katie, who was usually too scared to go into the basement alone.

April shivered as she sat there, her outstretched hand still reaching for her dad's razor. The pressure of the cold porcelain tub numbed her tailbone. The soap on her legs stung the scab on her knee, the scab that made her think of Katie, even though she hadn't had anything to do with April's falling, that time.

She shivered harder and picked up the razor. The edge of the blade sank into the lather and she dragged it upward, toward her knee, forging a shaky, winding path.

Katie had started treating April differently after that summer. Their relationship could be bisected into pre- and post-Hillsboro. Before, April had to throw temper tantrums to get Katie to do anything with her. But in post-Hillsboro, Katie was always willing to play games with April, to let April tag along, to let her have her way.

Then Katie had started taking the blame for April. Little things at first, like leaving the milk out on the counter, and breaking things. When Katie let their dad assume she was the one who'd stolen his cigarettes, April knew she could get away with anything. She never questioned why.

Katie had let the key word slip the night before, and April was more confused than ever. *Guilt.* But could Katie's guilt over not trying to stop Bobby have lasted all those years?

She raked the razor over her skin and jumped when the blade bit into the flesh stretching over her bony shin. The soap turned a frothy pink.

While she rinsed, she thought about Boyd, hoping he would shave. Lately he'd gotten lazy about it, but she knew she shouldn't give him a hard time. He probably wasn't shaving as often because of the spot on his chin that didn't seem to want to heal.

Boyd's patience wasn't what it had once been, so April didn't want to keep him waiting. She hurried through the rest of her pre-date regimen and rushed out the front door just as he was pulling up in front of her house.

April slid into the Gran Torino. As Boyd pulled away
from the roadside in front of her house, she assessed him. He
hadn't shaved, but the growth was long enough that it
resembled a beard. It looked good. "Where're we going?"
"Richie's." He fiddled with the bottle of beer settled
between his legs.

"Richie's?" She knew her sister probably didn't want
anything to do with her, but she would rather go by there and
try to talk to her than go to Richie's. "Could you drop me at
Katie's on your way to his place?"

His eyes darted to the rearview mirror. "We're out
together. That means to-geth-er. And I need to go to
Richie's."

"Why?"

"He's getting some kick-ass crank."

"You just got some from Joey."

"It's gone."

"Gone?"

"What? Is there an echo in here? Jesus, April, I work
hard, you know. Can't a guy get a little chemical assistance
without a dose of crap with it?"

She recoiled and leaned against the passenger-side door.

Boyd sighed, the length of the bench seat heaving along
with his body. He pulled into the McDonald's parking lot.
"Sorry, baby."

She kept staring forward.

"Come here. Come closer."

She scooted over a few inches.

"Closer," he said. "I got something for you."

"You do?" A smile flirted with the corners of her mouth
as she turned toward him. "What is it?"

"You have to come closer."

She slid across the bench seat and settled next to him.

"Now close your eyes."

She did. The scent of beer, cigarettes, and mint toothpaste grew stronger, and April knew he was going to kiss her. His lips were rough as they grazed hers, then his finger was on her bottom lip. As he started to push a pill into her mouth, she tried to refuse its chalkiness by pulling away.

He held her firmly.

"What—" She knew by the familiar bulk of the pill that it was a Quaalude, not a Black Beauty or Pink Heart or Robin's Egg, like she would have preferred.

"Come on, baby. Just for you." He wedged his finger between her teeth, and her incisor gouged the lude. Then Boyd's beer bottle pinched a sliver of her lip. Afraid of chipping a tooth, she opened her mouth. The coolness of the beer washed over her tongue and threatened to choke her, so she swallowed, washing down the large pill on a river of beer.

The glass disappeared, and Boyd's lips gently found hers, but the lightness of his touch was overshadowed by the phantom pressure of his finger and the beer bottle. Her insides twisted, and she knew the awful feeling in her stomach had nothing to do with the lude or the beer.

†

Kate looked around her dorm room. She didn't know firsthand what Lana's bedroom looked like. She'd made Lana describe it on more than one occasion, but she had never, and would never, actually see it. Life with Lana would be restricted to Kate's dorm room or occasional late-night scooter rides to the marina or anywhere else they could remain hidden from the rest of the world.

She checked the clock on her desk. Lana would be there in a matter of minutes. She took several deep breaths. She glanced above her desk and immediately looked away from the table of elements. There was no way she was going to do symbol games in her head yet again. She didn't care about calcium or argon or even oxygen.

She whirled around and focused on the opposite wall. Her beloved map of the world. Her big map of the big world.

As a child, Kate would stare at her parents' globe-shaped bar and imagine traveling to faraway, exotic places. She thought about Japan, where the sake tucked away in the belly of the huge globe came from. Or Russia, where her parents' vodka originated.

After her mom left, Kate would use all her strength to spin the globe and poke at it over and over, slowing it down, until her finger finally stopped it. Then she'd imagine her mom at that exact spot, trekking the Sahara or navigating the Nile.

Kate vividly remembered the day she was adding water to the vodka bottle inside the globe-bar, covering for the fact that April had been helping herself to the booze. When Kate realized she hadn't played the "where's mom?" game with herself in years, she'd started sobbing, sloshing out the watered down contents of the bottle.

Her dorm room throbbed as the memories poured through her. She stood inches from the map on her wall. She splayed one hand across North America and the other over Europe and tried to feel the pulse of the world that she would never be allowed to share with Lana.

She backed away from it and sat on the edge of her bed. This room was the world, would always be, as long as Lana continued to come through her door. Realizing she was rocking, she dug her fists into the mattress on either side of her thighs to steady herself.

The cassette player beckoned her from its usual perch on the bedside table. She reached to it and pressed the Play button.

She knew even before she heard it that *Crimson and Clover* would assail her. She closed her eyes and her heart skipped a beat. Oh, God, she thought and jabbed at the Stop button.

Kate whipped her head up to stare at the painting hanging over her bed. The great blue heron always took her breath away, just like its artist.

She didn't need to go out with Lana, right? Being there with her was enough, right?

But sharing Lana with Richie? Her insides clenched. Kate didn't want to share Lana with him or anyone else. How could she make Lana see how much she loved her, would always love her?

She jumped at the knock on the door. "Come in."

Within seconds, Kate and Lana stood at opposite ends of the room, staring at each other.

"Hi," Lana finally managed to say.

"Hi," Kate whispered.

"Thanks for inviting me."

"Thanks for coming."

Lana's beauty threatened to reach across the small room and drown Kate in her own need.

"I brought some music." Lana held out her hand and offered the two cassette tapes to Kate. "One is Stevie Nicks, and the other is that tape I made for you with all the songs you like."

Kate smiled. *Gooey love music*, Lana had teasingly called it the week before. But Kate knew she wouldn't put either cassette into the player. She didn't want any competition from the music; she intended to memorize every sound Lana made.

✝

April reclined on the cushions strewn about Richie's floor. The lead singer of Heart roared about a barracuda. April tried to imagine Boyd picking out that kind of music and almost laughed. Or maybe she did laugh; she wasn't sure. Nothing else was clear, but April was pretty sure Richie was playing his girlfriend's tape. His girlfriend. Poor Katie.

April pried her eyes open when she heard Boyd yelling. He was up in Richie's face, calling him a liar. That didn't sound like a good thing.

"I told you, I didn't get any crank."

"Bullshit," Boyd yelled. "You're holding out."

Just when she thought maybe they'd start slugging it out, guitars and other things that made way too much noise filled her head, getting in the way of what Boyd was saying about Richie's crank.

April wanted to sing along with the song but didn't know the words and didn't know if she could get them out even if she did. When they'd first pulled up to Richie's, April had tried to work around the slur of the lude to tell Boyd how she was concerned about not having a favorite music group of her own. He just stared at her and picked at his chin until April could make out the glistening of blood under the new whiskers.

The next thing she'd known, they were inside and Boyd was having her swallow another pill. She did it without giving him any attitude because she didn't know where she'd put her attitude. Maybe she'd left it in Boyd's car. Then she

153

got irritated because she couldn't remember what she'd left in Boyd's car, or if she'd need it, or if she even knew where Boyd's car was.

Whoa, she thought. She felt swimmy-headed. Swimmy. What a weird word, but it was so... So what? She couldn't remember.

Richie rolled his eyes and mumbled something as he left his apartment. She wondered where he was going.

Then Boyd was standing above her, looking all sexy-wild with his almost-beard.

"Hey, baby, you look relaxed," he said in a thick voice.

Relaxed. Re-laxed. Yeah, she was.

Boyd's big hands were everywhere at once—her breasts, her neck and back. Ouch—inside her. *Damn, how'd he get there so fast?*

April stared up at Boyd as he lifted his weight off her with his strong, muscular arms. He had great arms. Covered in long, soft hair. She let the word "wheat" form in her mind. It was there, in her mouth, and she thought to whisper it, but it wouldn't cooperate. Wheat, wheat, wheat. The softness of the letters dissolved on her tongue before she could get to the "t." Just dissolved. Disappeared. Reappeared. Swaying.

Boyd's presence between her legs turned from a dull ache to a piercing stab. Was wheat supposed to hurt? She closed her eyes and thought back to the time when wheat was as soft as the "wh" in it. When wheat was romantic and gentle and fascinating.

✝

Kate's tongue danced across Lana's nipple. When Lana moaned, Kate's body reacted immediately—first making her wet, then making her stomach flip-flop as she wondered if

Richie's tongue knew how to drive Lana crazy. Did Richie know that if he concentrated on Lana's nipples, he could bring her to the edge without even touching anywhere else? And did he know that she loved to be brought over that edge with short, quick licks across...

She drew in Lana's other nipple with a growing fear that maybe Richie could reach parts of Lana that Kate never would. Kate brought her hand between Lana's legs. Lana gasped, and Kate increased the pressure and speed of her tongue on Lana's nipple and slipped a finger into her.

Lana raised her hips, and Kate let her teeth graze a hardened nipple. When Lana lowered her hips and brought them back up, Kate met her with three fingers poised to press into her.

"Oh, God," Lana gasped. "Oh, yes."

She started to move back to Lana's other nipple, but Lana pressed her hands to Kate's head, silently begging her to move her mouth lower.

Kate slid down the tanned length of Lana and drew her into her mouth, thinking that no one could convince her that Richie or any other man could do this better.

Lana's body rocked as Kate pulled her fingers out and plunged them back in, over and over, all the while driving Lana crazy with her tongue.

You'll never love her like I do, she thought to Richie. Never.

And she set about proving it, ignoring the cramping in her hands and the tightening in her jaw, in awe of her lover as Lana's body jerked and shuddered.

With one hand, Lana clutched at Kate's head, with the other she pulled Kate's hand away. "No more, please—"

Kate froze. How long had Lana been trying to stop her? She looked up at Lana. Sweat, or tears, or both, trailed down her face.

She slid back up Lana's body. Draped half across her, Kate held her, kissed her face and neck. "I didn't hurt you, did I?"

"No, you didn't hurt me," Lana whispered. She brushed at the hair plastered to the side of Kate's face. "Where did you go?"

"What?"

"For a minute it felt like you were somewhere else."

"But you liked it?"

"I loved it. I love it every time you touch me."

Her chest tightened and ached. "Better than with him?" The words had forced their way out, and she hated having asked but also felt relief knowing she was about to find out one way or another.

"Let's not—"

"We have to. Eventually, we have to."

"Not tonight. Not now," Lana pleaded. In one fluid motion, she rolled Kate over and glided on top of her. She pressed her thigh between Kate's legs.

"What would Richie do if he knew about us?" Kate asked.

"He can never find out."

"Would he break up with you?"

Lana shrugged.

"I bet he would." Kate heard the malice in her own voice, knew it should repulse her, but it didn't.

"Kate—"

"Go inside me."

She did.

Kate grabbed her hand and forced her fingers deeper. "You like it in there?"

"Yes." Lana's voice was muffled against Kate's neck.

"You like making love to me?"

"I love it."

Kate knew it wasn't fair—not the time or the place—but she couldn't stop herself. "Making love to me, or having sex with him?"

"Sshh."

"No. Decide which is more important to you."

Lana sank her fingers deeper into Kate and let her thumb slide the length of Kate's wetness.

Kate shivered under Lana's perfect touch. She would not be distracted for long, though. "You have to choose," she said.

Lana's lips found Kate's breast, and the electric current jolted through Kate.

She meant to tell Lana again to choose, but she couldn't find the words while her body pitched and her heels dug into the mattress. "Oh, Lana," she called out as her orgasm ripped through her.

Then she cried as she held Lana. She cried for what Lana's answer might be, she cried for needing an answer at all.

"I could tell Richie about us, and that would be that," Kate said.

Lana ran her finger across Kate's belly. "Don't even joke about it."

"Who's joking?" Kate grabbed Lana's hand and pressed it to her.

They held one another for a long time without moving, then Lana kissed Kate's eyelids, her nose, her chin.

"What does Richie do for you that I don't?" The bitterness of his name on her tongue made Kate want to retch.

"Kate, please, let's not do this."

"Tell me. I have to know." Her heart pounded, and she knew she wasn't going to like the way this ended, but she couldn't stop herself.

"Don't do this. Just accept things as they are. Accept me as I am." She stroked Kate's neck.

Kate pushed Lana's hand away. "Does he give you butterflies? Does he take your breath away?"

"Stop, Kate." She grabbed both Kate's arms and pulled her close. "Make love to me again."

She let Lana press into her, but she also kept up her questions, asking them into Lana's neck. "Does he make all your parts quiver? Does he make you quake?"

Lana slowly sank her teeth into Kate's shoulder.

"Can he get you drenched with just a kiss?" Kate asked. "Can he?"

"No," Lana whispered.

Kate let her mouth travel past Lana's belly to the closely cropped hair. "Does he kiss you down here like I do?"

Lana breathed in sharply. "No one could ever do that like you do."

She slipped a finger into Lana. "Does he make your toes curl?" she asked, her voice growing hoarse.

"No."

"Does he make you have to bite the pillow to keep from screaming?" She pulled out of Lana and went back in with two fingers.

"No," Lana gasped, arching her body up to meet Kate's.

Kate slipped in with three fingers. "Tell me—what can he do that I can't?" Tears coursing down her face, she went in deeper, harder.

Lana's breath turned ragged. "Oh, God." Her body jerked, and she held on tight to Kate. "Oh... oh... oh..." she repeated as she came.

Sliding up Lana, Kate covered her with her body, reveling in the exact fit, amazed that Lana could even try to deny how perfect they were together.

"Choose."

"No," Lana said.

"Why not? Why won't you leave him?"

Lana took a deep breath. "He can come to my home, sit and have dinner with my parents. He's proof to them, and to the world, that someone loves me."

"I love you."

"No one can know that."

"We can explain it to them. They'll understand if we could just—"

Lana shook her head. "For such a smart girl, you can be so naive. Sweet and wonderful, but very naive."

The intensity of the clash of sadness and anger in Kate's gut shocked her. How could she be so mad at someone she loved so much? And how could Lana say she loved her and then hurt her that way? As her thoughts collided, concussions of reality rocked through her.

Kate pressed her mouth to Lana's and kissed her long and deep as her tongue explored, her lips memorized.

"I love you," she whispered. Then she pecked Lana's cheek and said, "But I need all of you. Now please leave."

Lana's lower lip trembled. "We can keep things the way they were. You don't have to do this, Kate."

Kate took a deep, painful breath. "Yes, I do. Leave." She flung Lana's hand off her.

"Don't do this. Please."

"Leave." She rolled away and faced the wall. "Please," she whispered, using Lana's plea as her own.

✝

April opened her eyes and saw Richie behind Boyd.

"Jesus, take it easy," Richie said. "Seriously. Ease up, dude."

"Fuck off." Boyd rammed himself harder and harder into her. She wanted to say, "Stop," but the word got lodged deeper and deeper inside her with every thrust.

"I said, ease up." Richie was right behind Boyd. "Hey, she's a minor, and this is my place, and you need to knock it off."

"Fuck off," Boyd repeated.

Richie yanked at Boyd's AC/DC tour shirt. April winced. Nobody messed with Boyd's T-shirt.

Deep lines etched Boyd's forehead. He got to his knees, reeled half around, and swung at Richie.

April moaned as the shorter wheat-hair on the back of Boyd's hand struck her cheek, just below her slightly off-center bug-eye.

"Fuck! Look what you made me do," Boyd yelled.

"Me? You fucking psycho—"

April was unable to make herself get up, unable to form words, unable to do anything but watch as Boyd sprang to his feet and grabbed the baseball bat propped against Richie's wall. His face grew distorted as he raised the bat high. His teeth clenched together and a primal grunt-roar sprang out of him as he hammered the bat down on Richie's head.

Richie stood very still for a moment then dropped to his knees, and his eyes disappeared somewhere far away in his head.

With a whimper, he toppled over, and April imagined yelling, "Timber."

†

Kate waited until she heard the door shut behind Lana before she rolled away from the wall. She imagined Lana descending the stairs, opening the outside door that always needed the extra tug, crossing the parking lot. But Lana's pain lingered in the room, floated down through the air like the lightest of feathers, and landed on the carpet to wait for a draft to relaunch it or for decay to destroy it. Decay. Why was so much in nature heartbreaking?

Kate clutched at her chest. Staring at the ceiling, she began reciting. Aluminum—Al—Alabama. There were fourteen symbols that were also state abbreviations. Argon—Ar. Ne, Sc, Ga. What was Georgia's state bird? The stabbing in her chest worsened.

She glanced up at Lana's painting. The image of the heron was stunning. Just like Lana. Kate's face grew hot, and she jumped out of bed. She seized the painting off the wall and held it over her head. Aiming it at the bedside table, she froze mid-swing.

She gently placed the painting on her bed and ran her fingertips along the textured surface. She traced the long plumes that cascaded from the bird's head and shoulders. Just above where one of the legs disappeared into the murky water was a place where the steady brush-stroke faltered, and

Kate imagined the imperfection occurring when Lana thought about making love to Kate, her hand shaking with the lush memory.

Kate pictured Lana's tanned, slender fingers and brought her own to her face. She inhaled the scent of Lana's deepest, sweetest places, temporarily preserved on her flesh.

"Oh, God," she sobbed.

Kate yanked her clothes on as she stumbled across the room, grabbed her keys, and ran out the door. She bounced off the wall at the landing and barreled down the last of the stairs. Exploding out the door and into the parking lot, she searched for Lana. Remnants of exhaust mingled in the hot, thick air, taunting her.

Her car key gouged the Arrow's dusty paint as Kate missed the keyhole. She jabbed several more times before the jagged key slid in.

Her hands shook as she twisted the key in the ignition. Nothing happened. She cranked again. It whined. She closed her eyes and tried again. The Arrow trembled to life. She shoved the car into gear, and it lurched forward. The honeysuckle air freshener swung back and forth.

The car faltered when Kate gave it gas, so she gave it even more. The Arrow shot forward. She prayed she could remember how to get to Richie's. She felt sick, but didn't know whether it was because of Lana's indecision or because of what she was about to do.

She watched and listened, looking for the right roads, listening for the sputtering of a scooter. Her eyes were burning and her shoulders tense when she pulled up in front of the converted garage.

She got out of her car. She wanted to lash out at Richie, needed to make him break up with Lana. Lana had to be hers alone, whatever it took. And Kate was sure Lana would forgive her. If she could just get this guy out of her life, Lana would come around.

What would she say? That Lana loved her, and he needed to back off? She felt certain he would laugh at her. And then Kate would run away. Or worse, she'd stand frozen—just like the time she saw the bear at the garbage dump, just like when she had the chance to get Kristy McNichol's autograph but chickened out.

Or like with Bobby in the basement.

She took several steps forward. At least Lana wasn't there. At least Lana hadn't left Kate's bed to go to Richie. But Kate knew Lana better than that.

It wasn't too late. If she just left, Lana would never know how close Kate had come to betraying her.

Kate stared at the door. It was ajar. She gave a tentative knock, and it creaked open an inch more. "Hello?"

She peeked in. A picture on the wall sent a raging pain through her. Lana painted for Richie also. Kate's hands twisted into tight fists at her sides.

Unable to stop herself, Kate pushed the door open. She had to see what other things of Lana's were in Richie's apartment. She wanted to know if Lana had clothes in his closet, or if there were any signs that she spent entire nights in his bed.

She clenched and unclenched her fists. No. She didn't want to know. She didn't want to know about Lana's time with Richie, and she didn't want to betray Lana by telling him about them. How could she hurt the only person she would ever love?

Being there was all wrong. She had to get out. Turning to leave, she saw something by the end of the bed. Richie was on the floor. His head was twisted, and his mouth gaped open. She gasped when she saw the blood caked on the side of his face.

As she stared, her mind flashed to her dad hitting Bobby with the shovel. Bobby had fallen to his knees, and her father raised the shovel over his head again. When Kate cried out, he looked at his daughter and dropped the tool to his side. She didn't recognize the man who told her to take April upstairs. After that day, she no longer recognized any of her family.

Kate finally found her voice and whispered, "Richie?"

Her steps were slow and unsure as she moved toward him. "Are you okay?" Even as she asked, she knew he wasn't.

She knelt beside him and pressed two fingers to his neck. Did she feel a slight strumming, like little wings barely fluttering beneath his skin? She wasn't sure if it was his pulse, or if it was her mind willing the sensation to her fingertips. She studied his chest. It was still.

She grabbed the phone from the nightstand and stretched it over to Richie. She dialed with one hand while she felt again for a pulse with the other.

"I need an ambulance," she blurted. She looked again at the blood. "And the police."

She described Richie's appearance to the steady voice on the other end and did her best to give directions.

"Yes," she told the woman when she asked if Kate knew what CPR was. "But..." She could remember the atomic weights of everything from Hydrogen to Radon, but not the ratio of breaths to compressions. "How many times do I breathe?"

Kate followed the instructions, laid the phone down without hanging up, and straightened Richie's neck to get an airway. She squeezed her eyes closed as she pinched his nose and breathed into his mouth. He smelled sour and tasted metallic. *Copper... Cu.* Kate fought the urge to gag as she breathed into his mouth again.

When she pressed her hand against his chest, she was surprised by the amount of resistance. She counted out loud, her words becoming more and more labored with each set of breaths and compressions.

In a flurry of activity, people in a variety of uniforms burst into the apartment. A man with red hair knelt beside her and took over the compressions; another man pressed next to her, poised to take over breathing. Sweat dripped down Kate's face, and she allowed herself to collapse to the side. She had blood on her hands, and something had started to dry on her chin. More blood? Spit?

"No, no, no," a male voice boomed. "Christ, get her off the goddamned evidence."

All eyes turned to Kate. She looked down. She'd sat in a large smear of blood. A female cop had her by the arm and lifted her to her feet. "It's okay. Let's go over here." She led Kate to a small table by the front door.

"Make sure that gets on the contamination sheet," the male officer called after them.

Kate stood beside the table and stared out the window. The smudged glass over the crooked air-conditioning unit distorted the strobe lights flashing from atop the police cars and ambulance.

"I'm Officer Eliot. What's your name?" she asked Kate.

Kate looked back to where they were still working on Richie. "Kate Hunter." She bit her lower lip. "He's going to be all right, isn't he?"

"I don't know. Look at me, not at him."

Kate turned to face her. Officer Eliot's posture made her seem much taller than the two-inch height difference between them. Kate's gaze followed the strong jawline, but then she quickly looked away. The steel-blue eyes of the officer, Kate imagined, could eventually get anyone to confess to anything.

"Do you have ID on you?"

Kate pulled her driver's license from her back jeans pocket and handed it to her.

"You need to tell me exactly what happened," the officer said as she looked from Kate to the license and back to Kate again.

"The door was open, so I called to him, but he didn't answer."

"You can't go in there," another officer called out.

Kate looked over and saw Lana in the doorway. When Lana looked at her, confusion and disbelief were obvious on her face.

"What are you—"

Kate stepped back. She hoped Lana would understand that she wasn't going to betray her now. "I'm a friend of Richie's. I found him unconscious and—"

"Whoa," said the officer who'd followed Lana in. "You come out here with me," he said to Lana. His wide eyes made Kate wonder if he expected a catfight.

Lana turned in Richie's direction, and she visibly buckled. Kate's heart broke for her.

The paramedics pushed the gurney past Lana, and Lana glanced again at Kate just before rushing out after them.

Kate looked away. She couldn't watch the sadness, disappointment, and anger play across Lana's face. The silent acknowledgment of Kate's betrayal was too much for her. Just as one look made her smile, quiver, and grow wet all at once, this one branded, scorched, and eviscerated her.

Please don't hate me. She wrapped her arms around herself and sobbed. Oh, God, she doesn't think I did this, does she?

Kate looked out the window as Lana pushed her way into the ambulance with Richie.

"Ms. Hunter."

"Yes." She faced Officer Eliot but didn't look her in the eye. She swiped at her tears. "I'm sorry."

"So, the door was open, and you came in?"

Kate nodded.

"Was there anyone else here?"

"No. Just him. On the floor." The tears came faster, and her nose started to run. She wiped at her lips and thought about her mouth being on his.

"Did you touch anything?"

"Just him and the phone. And the blood I sat in," she said and sobbed.

Kate thought again about the CPR. Her mouth—her mouth that had just been all over Lana—was on his. On his mouth that had done God knows what with Lana. Bile rose in her throat. Her hand flew to her mouth.

"Shit. Not on my fucking crime scene," a gruff voice bellowed from the other side of the room. "Eliot, do something with her!"

A heave wracked Kate's body. Another officer, who originally looked as if he was going to stop her, stepped quickly out of the way and Kate flew out the door.

She leaned into the narrow space between the azaleas and the wall. It seemed to her that the vomit spewed in slow motion as her mind registered the glint of light. Even as she emptied her stomach onto the compost of leaves and petals and a silver ID bracelet, her mind alternated between being sure she'd seen that very bracelet before and doubt that she'd seen anything at all. She wasn't sure of anything. Not even whether or not it had been on purpose that she'd covered the jewelry that might have been there.

Chapter Thirteen

April's legs thrashed beneath the sheet. Through a dream-haze she watched Boyd then realized it wasn't him after all. Her cousin looked exactly as he had the last time April had seen him, seven years earlier. The dream swirled, and Bobby directed her to put her arm, palm up, on the table. He stroked the inside of her elbow, where the bend threatened to hide the perfect blue-green vein visible just below the pale skin. The slight rise of the vessel showed her need, her openness. She would not hide it, would not pull away from Bobby as his thumb and forefinger kneaded the flesh, pulled it taut, released it, then worked it some more.

He yanked off his belt, held it in both hands and snapped it to test its strength. His eyes stayed on April, testing her strength, her commitment to him. The belt was almost too big for her thin arm, but Bobby managed to pull it tight, all the while stroking the flesh around her vein. April looked away, but Bobby said, "No, watch." She saw him place the metal tip against her skin, knowing he was pausing to tease her, to make her beg. They both knew she would, silently with her eyes, with the slight opening of her lips, the tip of her tongue tapping her teeth just barely, just enough for Bobby to see how much she wanted it. The needle indented her flesh for a second before breaking through the skin, before slipping in, lingering, spilling its contents into her.

April sat up on the bed and immediately pawed at her arms. Even in the dim light of the desk lamp, she knew there were no track marks. It had been a dream. She looked at her wrists and grew confused over the pink welts she knew would soon be bruises.

Nicki stood next to the bed, her eyes wide.

April looked around Nicki's bedroom. She raised her hand to the throbbing below her eye. "What the hell?"

"Thank God you're awake," Nicki whispered. "We have to keep our voices down. Don't want to wake my parents."

April stared at her. "What am I doing here?" She started to get up, groaned, and sank back down. "Damn, what Mack truck hit me?"

"Is that what happened?"

"Huh?"

"Were you in an accident?"

April tried to clear her head. She hurt all over.

"My brother found you sitting on the front steps. Good thing it was Peter and not my parents. You were soooo out of it."

April's hand followed a jolt of pain to the inside of her left thigh. She was sore and sticky and more than a little disoriented.

"So, Peter helped me sneak you in. I've been watching you ever since."

"Watching me?"

"You know, just in case. I didn't know what you'd taken, and if you would choke or go into a coma or something. And girl, you are gonna have one nasty black eye."

"Where's Boyd?"

"I don't know," Nicki said.

†

Everywhere Kate looked in her dorm room, she saw Officer Eliot's steel-blue eyes trying to penetrate the armor of her loyalty to Lana. S. Eliot, as the name tag had read, must have sensed the chink of near betrayal left on the fragile exoskeleton Kate attempted to hide behind.

Kate had tried to use her customary periodic elements game to silently protect her from the same questions being lobbed at her over and over. "How long have you known Richard Davis? What is your relationship to him? Why did you come here tonight?"

But the game of distraction couldn't calm the roar of fear that invaded her head. All she thought about was wanting to console Lana, wanting to make Lana forgive her for almost betraying her. Nothing she recited to herself made the questions go away. And nothing could stop the fear and regret from congealing in her gut.

She clenched her teeth and marched over to the wall where the periodic table hung, mocking her. With a vicious rip, she tore it down. She flung it away, trying to hurl it against the wall, but it only collapsed into a crumpled heap on the floor.

"What time did you get here?" S. Eliot, with the piercing eyes, had asked.

She'd told the truth, that she had arrived only minutes before finding Richie and calling for help.

"Where were you the two to three hours prior to arriving here?"

"In my dorm room," Kate had answered. Then she'd squared her shoulders and added, "Alone."

Kate ran to her bed and buried her face into the pillow. Breathing deep, she thought she would suffocate in the heady scent of honeysuckle.

†

"You sure were thrashing around in your sleep," Nicki said.

"I was having a nightmare." April shut her eyes. "It started off with Boyd screwing me, and somehow turned into my cousin Bobby shooting me up."

"Your imagination is over the top. I wish I had dreams about hot men getting me high."

April rolled away and sank her face into the pillow.

"Do you have a cousin named Bobby?" Nicki asked.

April cringed. "Yeah."

"Did he ever shoot you up?"

She turned back toward Nicki. "Hell, no. I haven't seen him since I was nine."

"Hey, relax. Chill out."

"Sorry. I just feel like shit."

The sudden tapping on the window caused April and Nicki to jump. Nicki pulled the curtain to the side. "It's Boyd."

April got out of bed and grabbed Nicki's robe off the footboard. She pulled it tight around her.

"I'll go let him in." Nicki turned to her before leaving the room. "That is what you want, right?"

April nodded.

A few moments later, Boyd lingered in the doorway. When he stepped into the room, he stared at the floor.

"Mom and Dad left. They won't be home for hours," Nicki said as she looked from April to Boyd and back again. Then she left and shut the door.

Boyd leaned against the dresser. April sat on the bed, several feet away, hugging herself.

"What happened?" April finally asked.

Boyd took several moments to look around Nicki's room.

"Boyd? Boyd, look at me."

He glanced her way. "Shit," he whispered.

"What in the hell is this?" she asked, pointing to her face. "Tell me what happened." When he didn't answer, she added, "Now."

"Okay, okay," Boyd said, crossing his arms over his chest. "Richie hit you." He stared at the headboard to April's left, not making eye contact.

"What?"

He nodded. "Yeah."

She whipped open the robe. "He hit me here, too?"

Boyd's eyes grew wider, and he lowered his head. "I was hoping not to have to tell you that part."

"Tell me what part, Boyd?"

He picked up something from Nicki's dresser, realized it was her retainer, and tossed it down. He wiped his fingers across his jeans and looked up. "I went to the john. I guess that's when Richie came home. When I came out, he was on top of you."

"What?"

"He was…" Boyd scratched at the whiskers on his chin.

"He was what?" April screamed.

"You know."

"What?"

"Having sex with you."

"You mean raping me?"

Boyd grimaced. "I'm sorry, baby. I didn't know he'd do something like that. I pulled him off you and slugged him. And then we came here."

"You mean you dumped me here."

"I didn't know what else to do. I couldn't take you home. You were really messed up. All night you were wanting more ludes, and I wasn't sure how many you'd taken."

"What about Richie?"

"What about him?" Boyd scuffed his dusty boots into the shaggy carpet.

"Did you call the cops on him?"

"I couldn't. Then we'd get in trouble for all the drugs you'd taken. Damn, baby, I had no idea things would get so fucked up."

April sobbed. She tried to recall the night before, but the effort hurt her head and made her dizzy. "Richie raped me?" She couldn't wrap her brain around the idea of it.

"It's okay," Boyd said, stepping closer to April.

April's hands went up, warning Boyd to keep his distance. "Okay?" she screeched. "Look at me." She tightened the robe around her. "I am not okay."

Chapter Fourteen

Officer Eliot's voice had an edge to it. Distrust? Kate knew she deserved it, since she had lied, but wasn't certain that was what she had actually heard in the tone. "You know Detective Stewart's handling the case now," Eliot said.

Kate gripped the phone tighter. "I know."

"You want me to transfer your call?"

"No. Never mind."

"Kate?"

"Sorry I bothered you."

"It's just that I'm not involved in this case anymore. You should talk to Detective Stewart. If there's something you know, you need to tell him."

"I don't know anything." Kate's insides clenched. "Sorry."

She hung up the phone. There had been no reason for her to call Officer Eliot, other than that she was the only person that Kate had seen since finding Richie who hadn't treated her like a total leper. There was something patient, yet strong about Officer Eliot that Kate liked. She just wished she didn't have to weigh every word she said so carefully.

Kate thought about the first time Detective Stewart's deep voice reverberated through her. It was much like the time she accidentally turned the bass knob instead of the volume on her cassette player.

"Homicide investigation," Detective Stewart had said while questioning her the day before. Kate cringed at the memory.

She looked at the tape player on her nightstand. She wondered what *Crimson and Clover* would sound like with the bass turned all the way up. No. She could not tolerate their song, not distorted by bass or any other way.

She had to face the fact that Lana wasn't coming to her room. Then it dawned on her. Maybe it would be easier for Lana to meet her at the fountain. Maybe repeating how they'd first come together could be a cathartic act for them, a way to forge a new beginning.

She ran out of her room, barely shutting the door behind her.

†

The sun was painfully bright as it bounced off the slick marble surface of the fountain. The gurgling of the over-chlorinated water became a roar in Kate's head, churning, reminding her of the rapids running beneath the humpback bridge in Hillsboro.

She shook her head to dislodge the memory.

Droplets splattered from the rippled surface and pelted Kate's arms. She batted at her flesh and tried to swat away the offending water.

She thought of all the times she'd waited by the fountain for Lana, all the times Lana had come for her. She knew Lana wasn't coming this time. She sighed and thought about the first time she'd left this exact spot on the back of Lana's scooter.

That first ride was the beginning of her transformation, the first fluttering of wings growing and turning her into the woman she was meant to be.

Wings... wings that grew from the paper-thin mosquito wings to the heartbeat-fast wings of the hummingbird. Pointy, erratic swallow wings. Long, broad heron wings.

The fluttering in her gut increased until it was a painful thrashing. Her hand flew to her chest, and she took several gulps of air. "Oh, Lana," she whispered.

Would there be more of her and Lana together? And if not? Without Lana, what would become of the wings left to wither deep inside Kate? Would the fine, downy feathers dissolve and leave only the sharpened shafts to become brittle and splinter?

More water bullets ricocheted from the fountain, riddling her, taunting her.

Without the promise of Lana in her life, Kate would surely wilt. After knowing the beauty and grace that was Lana, how could she go back to her books and studies and be satisfied with just that?

Oh, if Kate had just left things alone. If she'd just stayed in Lana's arms that night—where she belonged—she could be helping Lana get through this ordeal now.

She stared into the water until her vision blurred and she was a child again, studying her reflection in the neighbor's pond. "Will Lana always need to be with someone else?"

Just as when she'd asked the water if her mom would ever come home, she already knew the answer.

"If not Richie, then some other guy? Someone who meets with the approval of Lana's family?"

She dipped her finger into the water but pulled it out immediately. "But wouldn't that be okay? Couldn't I be the one who was always there for Lana, the one living in the shadows, the one making all the sacrifices? And sooner or later, Lana would see the extent of my love and give herself totally."

Kate shuddered. "Oh shit," she whispered. April was right. "A fucking martyr" April had said about the way Kate had acted since the thing with Bobby in Hillsboro. "Kate the saint" April had called her.

Kate was jarred to attention by the sounds of a car engine and a male voice. She was certain the noises migrated the block and a half from the Quick Mart, from next door to the Sea Scape. She walked in that direction. Her gait increased to a jog and finally a sprint.

Breathless, she stood in the parking lot in front of the restaurant. She didn't know why she was surprised that the scooter wasn't chained to the No Parking sign. It wasn't there the last time Kate had checked either. And surely it wouldn't be there the next. Richie was dead. Of course Lana wasn't at work.

Dead. Dead. Dead. And Lana blamed Kate.

She ran back to campus.

✝

April sat in front of the mirror in her bedroom and patted the makeup around her eye, trying to use only what pressure was absolutely necessary to make it blend. The last thing she needed was her dad asking questions.

Not that he asked many.

And Katie. Miss Fix-Any-Mess Katie. What was she doing now? Was she letting Lana walk all over her? Was she so blinded by love that she would give Lana whatever she wanted? Her sister was like the antelope in the nature shows that always made Katie cry, the one tackled by the lioness and ripped to shreds. Yes, April thought, Lana would probably rip Katie's heart to shreds before it was all said and done.

April sneered. Then Katie could be one step closer to sainthood. She was oh-so-thrilled for her overachieving sister.

The blood pounded in her bruise and reminded her it was Katie she'd immediately thought of talking to about this mess with Richie assaulting her. Not just because she thought Katie should know that her girlfriend's boyfriend was a creep, but because she was— Well, Katie was her sister. And no matter how different they were, it did seem to always come down to that.

April looked in the mirror. The black-and-blue image that looked back wasn't smiling. She dabbed more makeup on her fingertips and smeared it across the blackberry-colored bruise. She winced at her own roughness but didn't stop.

†

"We should go to Joey's," April said.

"Nah," Boyd muttered as he turned down Leary's Lane.

"I don't understand why we don't go there anymore."

Boyd didn't answer. He drove halfway down the lane and pulled onto the shoulder, close to the briars.

She sighed when he turned off the car. Even in the half-light, she noticed his cheek was swollen. His broken tooth was probably infected, but she wasn't going to ask him about it. He never listened to her anyhow.

"Roll a pretty one, huh, baby? Then I'll show you the surprise I have for you."

"Surprise?" She opened the glove compartment. He reached across her and slammed it shut. "What?" she asked.

"Here. I have it here." He pulled the bag of pot from the sun visor and handed it to her.

April didn't bother trying to separate out any seeds or stems; she just pinched a bunch between her fingers and rolled it into an uneven, bumpy joint.

He reached under his seat and pulled out a bottle of Boone's Farm Tickle Pink. "Surprise. Your favorite."

She smiled. She was indeed in the mood for some wine. There was something almost innocent in the buzz from its sweetness, and she really needed to feel something like that. "Thanks, Boyd."

He poured some wine into an old Big Gulp cup and handed it to her.

She passed him the sloppy joint, knowing he wouldn't complain about it. He'd been so gentle with her ever since... well... She took a big drink of her wine.

Boyd fired up the joint. The paper caught and glowed orange. The slight illumination of his hair reminded April of the time she actually did go to Nags Head with Nicki's family. They'd gotten invited to a bonfire down on the beach by two older guys they'd met. As they sat around the fire, sipping beer, April watched with fascination as the eight or nine other people's faces were bathed in the soft yellow-orange light. Then she'd gotten busy fighting off the advances of one of the guys. In hindsight, she knew she was saving herself for Boyd. She hadn't met him yet but still believed in fairytale love.

After taking a second big hit, Boyd handed April the joint. She inhaled and shut her eyes as she held in the smoke. The image of Richie's ceiling drifted into her mind. It made her think of pain. Of pounding pain deep inside her. Her eyes flew open.

Boyd was looking at her, his brow furrowed. He took the joint from her, toked, and offered it to her again. She shook her head and sipped her wine.

Yes, he had been extra sweet toward her lately. Just like right after the first time she let him feel her up. And the first time they went all the way.

She drank more wine. That first time with Boyd had hurt like hell. And April had bled. And then Boyd bought her everything she wanted. Including the purple, feathery roach clip and the now misplaced diamond-chip earrings that she'd known he couldn't afford, but she had asked for anyway. Because that was how it worked. Enduring pain gained a person certain rights. Like how a moment of Bobby's big, dirty finger ripping into her had gotten her years of Katie's coveted attention and her dad's otherwise stingy permissiveness.

Her hand went to her bare wrist. Everything Boyd had ever given her had either been lost or, in the case of the feathered roach clip, caught on fire. She rubbed her wrist harder. She wasn't sure when it had registered that the bracelet Boyd had given her was gone, but she had a pretty good idea when it had disappeared.

She banished the thought by getting the joint from Boyd and taking a deep hit. A seed popped. She jumped when her shirt sparked. Boyd batted at the tiny, brown-ringed burn mark, and April recoiled.

She realized she was reacting as much to her own thoughts as she was to his touch.

"Look," he said as he turned to face her, "I know you're still sore, but there are things we can do that won't hurt you."

"Please, Boyd, not now."

"Damn, why are you acting so cold? Why can't we just go back to the way we were?"

He grabbed his cigarettes and lit one. He took a long drag and exhaled into the car.

Wonderful. Now he's gonna be an ass.

"We won't ever go near Richie again. I promise I won't let him ever hurt you again," Boyd said.

April felt the tears on her face before she realized she was crying. "What part of the reality of me being raped are you not getting?"

"Come on, it's not like he forced you. You were so out of it, you didn't even know what was happening."

"Because I didn't scream and say 'no,' it's not such a bad thing. Is that what you're saying?"

"Well, yeah."

"I can't believe you."

"What?" he asked.

"He fucked me," she said. "Don't you get it?"

He gave an exasperated sigh. "That's what you're so upset about? That another guy—" He took her hand in his and kissed the back of it. "It's okay, baby. It's not like you cheated on me or anything."

"Good God, Boyd."

"What?"

"Please just take me home."

"Just as well." He started the car. "You're really killing my buzz."

Chapter Fifteen

Kate knew exactly where the tape was positioned in the cassette player. She held down the Rewind button. "One-one-thousand, two-one-thousand, three-one-thousand—"
Her finger flew off the button as a high-pitched squeal assaulted her ears. She stared at the player for several moments before pressing Play.

Garbled nonsense crackled out of the tiny, built-in speakers. She turned it off.

Ruined. Her Crimson and Clover was ruined. How appropriate. How damned appropriate. Her anger startled her.

She pressed the Eject button and pulled out the cassette, leaving behind a trail of glossy tape. She grasped the thin ribbon, wrapped it around both hands, and yanked. She meant to snap it in half, but it stretched instead and cut into her hands. Her head still reeled with the squeal of the cassette, and she felt as stretched and distorted as the brown tape was.

She shook it off her, let it fall to the floor, and followed it. Crumpling onto the carpet, she hugged her knees to her chest and cried.

Something dug into her thigh. She shifted her weight and pulled the plastic cassette case from beneath her. The light played off it, at first blinding her and then illuminating the pink background.

She stared at the picture on the front. Those intense eyes stared back at her. She knew it was cheesy, but she wanted to be as strong as she imagined Joan Jett would be. Okay, she'd never be Joan Jett-tough, but she wasn't going to lie on her dorm room floor and decay either. She looked again at the image of the heavily made-up eyes and smooth skin.

She got off the floor. She would be strong. She would go out—to one of *those* bars. Turning to glare at the painting of the great blue heron that she'd left leaning precariously against the wall, she took a deep breath.

"I'll show you," she said.

✝

April sighed as Boyd drove down Leary's Lane. Here we go again, she thought, slugging down half the cup of wine. *Could you be any more predictable?* she wanted to ask. Instead she swirled the cup and decided to count her blessings. At least Boyd had gone back to his old habit of hooking her up with Boone's Farm. She finished the cup and reached for the bottle. Ah yes, such a sweet buzz.

Boyd parked the Gran Torino and opened the little baggy of powder. "Just what the doctor ordered." He pulled a cutoff straw from the visor.

April wondered when he'd started carrying that around with him.

"This will make you feel better."

"I got what I need right here," she said, indicating the bottle.

"This crank will make it even better."

"I don't want any."

"Sure you do." He stuck the straw into the bag and turned toward April. "Ladies first."

"You heard me," she said through clenched teeth.

"Suit yourself." He brought the straw up to his nose.

April turned to look out the window. She heard Boyd snort and felt his hand on her leg. The muscle in her thigh twitched.

"How long is this gonna last?"

"What?" she asked, not turning back to him.

"This frigid act. I swear, if you toot just a little of this, you will forget all about the... the incident."

"The incident?" Wasn't that what her father and Katie had called what had happened with Bobby in the basement the one or two times it was even mentioned? First there was The Hillsboro Incident. Now she had The Richie Incident. Terrific.

Boyd leaned into her. She twisted around and tried to keep him off. He wrapped his arms around her, pinning hers to her sides. "Baby, I hate seeing you like this."

"I can't help it." She trembled.

"What can I do to make it better?" He kissed her neck, and she shuddered.

"I'm sorry." She felt bad about withdrawing from him but couldn't stop. She tried again to twist away, but he held her tighter.

"Baby, baby, baby," he whispered. "It's okay."

"It's not okay. I can't stop thinking about him doing that. I can't stop—" She choked back a sob as her body heaved several times. "Him inside me," she moaned.

"It's okay. Baby, it's okay. Richie was never inside you," he whispered against her neck.

"I know he was. I was so bruised, inside and out. I know he was."

"No, baby. It was just me. It was only me."

Her shoulders tightened; her entire body stiffened. "Don't lie to me just because you want to get laid."

"I'm not lying. I swear to you, no one but me had sex with you."

"But the bruises…"

"Just me," he said, still holding her. "It was just me."

She sobbed. "You did it?"

"Yeah, it was only me. You weren't raped. We just got a little carried away, that's all."

"Why did you tell me it was Richie?"

"All that matters is that you weren't raped. See? We can get back to normal now." He caressed her back. "I love you so much." Tears streamed down April's face, and Boyd wiped them away with a gentle sweep of his finger. "It was just an accident. Now you know, and we can get back to how things used to be."

She tensed. "An accident?"

"I know you're still sore. We can wait as long as you need to for *that*, okay?"

She wasn't sore anymore. No, just numb. He'd lied to her. Lied. How else had he deceived her?

Boyd had the tiny bag of crank between them and was forcing some of the powder up his nose. "Come on, do a little for me."

"No."

"I want you to party with me. I want you to feel as good as I do right now."

She turned away from him.

He reached down and undid his zipper. "I know what we can do that won't hurt you."

Through her numbness, she felt him putting pressure on the back of her head and had an overwhelming need to scream or throw up or both. She tried to pull her head away, but he held her firm. She smacked his arm away.

"Jesus Christ!" he yelled. "What's your fucking problem?"

"Take me home."

"What's wrong with you, April?"

"Take me home right now, or I'll walk." When he rolled his eyes, April opened the door and got out. She started to walk back toward the main road.

"Come on, get in."

She kept going.

He stepped out of the car. "I'm not mad at you. Come back. I'll take you home."

She walked faster.

"Get back in the fucking car," he yelled. He started after her.

April cut to the right and dodged between two patches of briars. She ran and could tell by the string of cuss words that Boyd hadn't done such a good job of avoiding the thorny bushes.

As she bolted through the woods, she tried to remember where on Route 17 she would come out, but she couldn't focus. She heard Boyd thrashing through the woods behind her. Her lungs wheezed and ached. Her heart pounded in her chest, below her eye, between her legs. Was this how a wild animal felt when it was hunted? Was it how a deer felt, running from her cousin Bobby's rifle, his serrated knife?

As April emerged from the woods, she realized she hadn't heard Boyd behind her for several minutes. Just as her tennis shoe hit the asphalt, she saw the headlights. She slid to a stop, in front of a skidding Firebird.

The driver's door opened, and a guy jumped out. "Jesus, you almost ran right into me." He looked her up and down. "Shit, are you okay?"

April nodded.

"Can I do something?"

She looked behind her, then down the road.

"Let me give you a lift."

"No. Thanks." She looked up when she heard another car. What if it was Boyd? Seeing Boyd was the last thing she wanted. Not until the numbness wore off. "Ah, okay. Sure."

When she got in the car, he turned the radio off. "I've seen you around before." He cocked his head. "Cruising McDonald's."

She looked at him. Dark eyebrows and thick lashes contrasted with his sun-bleached hair. His neck was thick like a jock's. It was Nicki's hot Firebird guy.

"Can you take me somewhere?" She took a deep breath and gave him Joey's address.

†

Kate's nerves calmed, and the bar noise settled into a steady chatter. After the unfamiliar traffic and the trickiness of finding a parking space behind the club, she was glad to be settled on a stool, leaning on the bar with both elbows.

She didn't recognize the song. It wasn't the same music she heard on the top 40 station, nor was it like the compilation of gooey love songs Lana had put together for her. This had a beat that started inside Kate's chest and kept pounding, unrelenting, trying to thrust its way out from deep inside.

The volume decreased slightly as one song bled into the next, and Kate looked up when the collision of pool balls crashed over the pause in the music. A blonde carrying a drink tray was congratulating a tall, slender woman on her break. Someone else was challenging her to run the table. She answered something along the line of preferring to run the waitress but settling for finishing the game of pool.

Kate looked away from the pool table, unable to watch the easy intimacy between the women for too long.

"What can I get you?" The bartender smiled.

"Screwdriver?" Kate asked, not quite sure what wouldn't make her too drunk.

"Sorry. We only serve beer and wine."

"Oh." Her gaze settled on the silver ID bracelet the bartender wore. She swallowed hard and tried not to think of the other bracelet she'd seen recently.

The bartender grinned again. "Wine?"

Kate forced a smile. "Gives me a headache." This woman didn't have to know she'd only tried wine once and had never quite gotten past the smell of beer. She glanced around to see what the other customers were drinking.

"You don't like beer?" the bartender asked.

"Sorry, I'm taking way too long."

"I know what to get for you. Hang tight." She moved around the other bartender, placed a hand against the small of the woman's back to signal her presence, and squatted in front of the cooler. When she returned, she placed a small bottle of rosy liquid on the bar.

Kate eyed it.

"Malt Duck. Try it and tell me what you think."

Kate took a sip. "It's good." *Maybe too good.*

"I know it's your first time here, but is it also your first time in a women's bar?"

"First time in any bar," Kate said.

The bartender nodded. "Ah. Welcome."

Kate pulled money from her pocket, but the bartender waved her away. "First drink in your first bar is on me."

Kate's heart did a little flip, and her gaze went back to the bracelet.

"You like that?" the bartender asked.

Kate nodded.

The bartender rested her wrist on the bar next to Kate's drink. Kate reached out and touched the engraved part. The coolness of it against her fingertips made it less ominous, and she could almost forget why it kept demanding her attention.

"Dee," the bartender said. "That's what it says. It's my name."

As if on cue, someone called out to Dee that she needed another drink.

She sauntered away, and Kate couldn't help but notice how attractive she was. And the way she moved with the other employees behind the bar, like dancing—a gentle touch to this woman's back, a playful pat of that woman's butt—all while reaching and pouring and serving.

Oh, and her quick, easy smile. In that sense she reminded Kate of Lana. Just not as pretty. No, she warned herself. She was not going to compare everyone in the place to Lana.

Kate sipped her drink and looked around at all the people. A woman standing on the opposite side of the bar was kind of cute, except for her posture. She didn't carry herself as confidently as Lana. That was the first thing Kate had noticed about Lana—the way she sat so sure and straight on the scooter.

Kate adjusted her bra strap. It wasn't just any bra, but the one she'd been saving to wear on a real date with Lana. She was also wearing the blue shirt Lana loved, the one Lana said brought out the color of her eyes.

Another woman caught Kate's attention. Her eyes were sexy, except that they didn't crinkle up at the corners when she smiled, like Lana's.

Kate took a big drink of her Malt Duck. A woman in a black cowboy hat had nice arms. They looked strong. She thought about Officer Eliot's arms, muscled and tanned. Wow. What if Officer Eliot was... What if she came to this bar? The idea of seeing the cop there both frightened and excited Kate. Just then, she felt eyes on her and turned, expecting to meet the penetrating gaze of her favorite police officer.

The woman who stared back wasn't Officer Eliot. She didn't have Eliot's intense eyes or strong arms. And she didn't have Lana's incredible smile and perfect body. When she smiled, Kate quickly looked away.

The lace around the semi-padded cups of Kate's new bra itched. She tried to be discreet as she moved her arms across her breasts to relieve the tormented skin.

Dee placed another Malt Duck in front of her. "From the woman in the hat," she said. Then she winked, and Kate turned away, trying to hide her blush. She turned toward the end of the bar, and Ms. Strong Arms raised her drink in a toast.

Not knowing the proper etiquette, Kate smiled and raised her drink, just a little, in a shy gesture. She worried about the woman coming over and wanting to talk. What did you talk about in bars? Should she put it out there right away that she had a girlfriend? The thought made her chest ache. She didn't have Lana anymore. And she didn't think she'd ever get used to that idea.

She gulped her drink. The pink stuff did go down easily. She drank some more. As she placed the empty bottle on the bar, Dee replaced it with a new one, strolling away with a sneaky smile and sexy sway.

Strong Arms wasn't still at the end of the bar. Kate saw her wedged between the jukebox and a table, making out with someone. She figured the drink didn't come from her. She took another swig, not caring where it came from, just that it was there. She was feeling better already. She lifted her bottle and toasted herself, a silent self-congratulation for moving on with her life.

"Last call," one of the bartenders sang out. There was a flurry of activity as a wave of women moved in to order.

Kate pushed herself away from the bar. Another drink was the last thing she needed. She did, however, need to relieve herself.

She joined the line for the restroom and realized the women were using both the women's and the men's. She hadn't known how tense she'd become until her body relaxed when it was her turn and it was the women's room that was available.

When Kate left the restroom, the bar's lights had been turned up.

"Breakfast?" Strong Arms was asking the slim pool player.

"Yeah," she answered and turned to the group of women that had formed by the door. "You guys going to Steak 'n Egg?"

"Yep," several women said in unison.

Kate envied their ease with one another. Their familiarity made her wish she had friends she'd known for years. Or, better yet, that she and Lana could leave the bar together and go to Steak 'n Egg for waffles and juice and the joy of each other's company.

"Okay, ladies, time to go," the blonde waitress in the skimpy shorts called out.

Kate discreetly shifted her bra and moved the lace to alleviate the itch. She walked out behind a small group of women and imagined for a fleeting moment that she was part of their camaraderie.

She almost tripped on a pothole in the parking lot. Her face grew warm, but then a sense of detachment washed over her. She stared at her car for what felt like an eternity. She knew better than to drive.

"Car trouble?"

Kate looked at the woman in the tiny MG. "No," she said. "Driver trouble, actually."

The woman laughed. Kate wished someone could make her laugh like Lana could.

"Hello?"

Kate looked at the woman. "Oh, sorry."

"I do believe you need some food. Want to get some breakfast?"

Kate envisioned being accepted into the late-night-breakfast-with-lesbians club as she pulled up to Steak 'n Egg with this good-looking woman in her hot little car. "Yeah, sure."

The woman motioned to her with a nod. Kate shoved her keys into her front pocket. She looked back one last time, remembering her passenger door no longer locked, but decided she didn't care. There was nothing in her car worth stealing.

Kate grew dizzy as she climbed into the MG, and she was sure it had as much to do with the sense of excitement building in her as it did with the Malt Ducks.

†

Joey handed April another beer. "I wish you'd tell me about that bruise." He sat in the recliner, across from where April perched on the edge of the sofa.

"It's nothing. Really." April sipped.

"Did Boyd do it?"

She didn't answer. Her stomach growled. She could tell Joey was trying to pretend he didn't hear it. He was sweet like that. It growled again. Loudly. "Sorry," she said.

"If you're hungry, we could scrounge around in the fridge for something."

"No, that's okay. I'm fine. I just haven't been eating lately." Feeling self-conscious, she held up her beer. "Liquid diet."

He held his up for a toast. "Here's to beer, my favorite of the four food groups."

April giggled. "What are the other three?"

"Cannabis, pizza, and more beer."

"Ha. I'll drink to that." And she did.

April looked at the ashtray on the coffee table and realized Joey hadn't been smoking. He'd stubbed out his half-smoked cigarette when she'd first gotten there and hadn't lit another. She was touched that he'd remembered, and cared, that cigarette smoke bothered her.

"Hey, seriously now, tell me about the bruise."

She waved him off. "I have a question for you first."

"Fire away."

"It's about when that Doug guy overdosed."

"Oh." Joey's forehead crinkled. "You know, Boyd asked me not to say anything to you about that. He said it really freaked you out."

"I need to know when he died."

"When?"

"You know, exactly when."

"On the way to the hospital."

A lump grew in her throat. "So he wasn't already dead when the cops and ambulance got here?"

"No. But damned close. Why? Is that important?"

The implications slammed into her gut. Had Boyd misled her about Doug already being dead, or had she heard what she'd wanted to? She shivered at the thought that he could have been saved when she found him on Joey's floor, needle dangling from his arm.

She swallowed hard. What else had Boyd misled her about?

Joey gave her a quizzical look as she chugged the rest of her beer. "You *are* on a liquid diet."

She nodded and pushed the thoughts of Doug out of her head. She couldn't deal with that on top of everything else. Instead, she thought about Joey. How easy he was to talk to. How conscientious he was—about not smoking, about letting her hang out with him even though Boyd could show up at any time and get really pissed at her being there.

She closed her eyes for a moment and tried to imagine being with someone as nice as Joey. She liked the picture it created. Hell, he was probably the type of guy who'd actually take her out to dinner. Or to a movie *she* wanted to see.

She imagined Boyd's rage if she and Joey ever got together. No, she told herself, I will not think of Boyd now.

She drank more beer and allowed the liquid courage to wash over her. "Right now, I'd really like for you to kiss me."

He laughed.

"That wasn't a joke."

He took a sip of beer. "I like you. Hell, I've always liked you. But the bottom line is that you are Boyd's girl. And you just don't mess with Boyd's girl." Joey fidgeted with the tab on his beer can. "Especially the way he's been acting lately."

She found it endearing that Joey all but admitted he was afraid of Boyd. She took a gulp of beer. "I can handle Boyd. I can handle anyone and anything."

Joey laughed.

"What's so funny?" She wished she hadn't slurred her words. It was hard to be taken seriously when she couldn't quite spit it out.

"You are so cute, sitting there trying to act like such a bad-ass. So cute, it'd almost be worth the risk."

"Almost doesn't count," April said.

"Except in horseshoes—"

"And hand grenades."

They both laughed.

Joey went to the kitchen to get two more beers. When he returned, he opened one and handed it to April.

"This has been really nice." April took a sip. "It's nice being with someone I can actually talk to."

He smiled, and a new kind of warmth rushed from April's neck to her face. He really was cute.

"Thanks," she whispered.

"For?"

"Being here."

He stared at her. "Okay, I confess. Being with you would definitely be worth the risk of Boyd finding out. No 'almost' about it."

He put his beer on the table and walked to the sofa. He took April's hand and pulled her up. "Now, what were you saying about me kissing you?"

Her head spun—with passion, or beer, or both, she didn't know—just that she liked it. She liked him. She answered by letting her lips brush against his.

He traced his fingers along the outline of her jaw and rested them under her chin. He kissed her, and she kissed him back and shuddered as he ran his hands along her sides. She couldn't believe how tender his touch was. The taste of beer in her mouth mixed with his. Her pulse raced. *So sweet, so good.* This was how it should be. Someone who could be sexy and gentle at the same time.

"Damn, I want you," he whispered.

"Make love to me."

He pulled her toward him. "Yes?"

"Yes." She kissed him harder. "Yes."

He pulled away. Into her neck, he mumbled, "Shit."

"What?" Please don't turn me away now.

"I… I don't have any protection."

April froze.

He put a hand on each side of her face and kissed her. "I'm sorry."

She glanced at the spare bedroom. Did she dare? "There's—" She took a deep breath. "I know where one is."

He turned toward the spare room, the room he'd let Boyd sleep in with April so many times. "Are you sure?"

"Yeah, I saw one—"

"No, I mean are you sure you want to use one of his?" He kissed the top of her head. "Are you sure you want to with me?"

She smiled. Joey cared what she thought, what she wanted. "Yes," she said. "I'm sure."

She touched the side of his face before walking away.

It took both hands to open the warped drawer of the nightstand. April reached in for the condom. She looked down just as her fingers brushed the side of the slick foil wrapper.

She yanked her hand way. "Oh, God," she said. Then, louder, "Oh my God!"

Joey ran into the room. "What's wrong?"

The blood drained from her face as she stared at the pipe. The one Lana had painted. The one Boyd had eyed so intently. And there, smeared across the yellow sun rays, was a dark brown smudge.

As Joey came up beside her, she trembled.

"It's just a bowl," he said.

She shook her head, over and over. "It's not just a bowl. It's Richie's bowl."

✝

"Where are we?" Kate asked.

"My place. Well, it's part my place. I have two roommates, but they're out of town for the weekend."

Kate had expected a restaurant, not this woman's house. She tried to remember what the woman had said her name was. Terry? Tracy? Tina? Oh no, what was her name?

"Come on in. I won't bite." She laughed. "Unless you beg me to." She ran her hand along Kate's thigh before opening her car door.

As Kate got out of the car, it crossed her mind that it would serve Lana right if she met someone new, someone who didn't mind being seen out in bars with her, someone who didn't need to hide behind a boyfriend.

Kate jumped when she felt the hand on her back.

"Relax," Ms. T. said.

She looked at the woman and decided yes, she was quite attractive, and no, Kate would not compare any part of her to any part of Lana.

The next thing Kate knew, she was inside her door—this woman whose name she didn't remember, but who let her see where she lived and who obviously wanted her.

She pulled Kate close, and their mouths came together with a hunger that made Kate's nipples harden against the woman's breasts. The itch of her lacy bra rubbed her sensitive flesh in a way that turned her breath ragged.

Just as Kate was getting lost in the new sensation, Ms. T. tugged at her bra, a clumsy attempt to free Kate's breasts. Kate tried to back away, horrified that she would be so rough with Lana's bra.

Kate knew Lana would have taken the time to notice. Lana would have whispered, "beautiful," and her eyes would have gone to Kate's, and Kate would have been jolted...

"No," Kate whispered.

Ms. T. kissed her again, and Kate's head reeled. Kate parted her lips and let out a little gasp when her tongue danced with the other woman's, their lips pressing frantically together. But then careless hands were pulling again at the delicate lace.

"Stop," Kate said. "Please."

The woman scrutinized her. "The words are coming out as 'no,' but your body is definitely saying something different."

Kate looked away.

"So, which is it—yes, or no?"

Thoughts of Lana flooded over Kate. "No," she whispered. "I'm sorry." Kate pulled away. "I should get back to my car."

"It's late. The cops will be out this time of night, just looking to harass people like us."

Kate thought about Officer Eliot. She wouldn't harass them. Of that, Kate was certain.

Ms. T. ran her hands along Kate's sides. The touch felt good, but not right. Not Lana.

"I need to go."

"I swear I won't try to get into your pants if you stay the night. We'll sleep. I'll just hold you." Even as she said the words, her hands gripped Kate's rear.

Kate pulled away again. All she could think about was Lana, and how with her, there was never even a sliver of doubt. Hell, from the first moment with Lana, Kate couldn't get enough of her.

"I really need to leave."

Ms. T. gave a gusty, annoyed sigh. "I'm way too tired to drive. Come on, I won't touch you, I promise." She started toward the bedroom door. "When you change your mind, I'll be in here." She unbuttoned her shirt as she made her way across the room.

Kate waited until she heard what she imagined was the bedding being turned down, and then she fled.

†

April pulled the seatbelt across her chest. Joey's car smelled like Boyd's: cigarettes and testosterone. Not unpleasant, but very different from Nicki's or Katie's. She cast a sidelong look at Joey. "I'm sorry about... ruining the mood."

"Hey." He brushed the back of his fingers along her cheek and gave her hand a quick squeeze. "Don't worry about that. I'm just sorry you got upset." He pulled his Charger out of the apartment complex. "Do you want to talk about it?"

She shook her head, and the movement dislodged tears she hadn't realized had formed. She didn't know whether she was reacting to the frustration and confusion over all that had happened or to the sincerity of Joey's concern.

Joey glanced at the blood-smeared bowl they'd placed in a sandwich bag and tucked into the drink holder. "Boyd could have bartered some drugs for that," he said. His tone told her he was trying hard to make her feel better.

"No. You don't understand," April said and sobbed. "Richie would never willingly part with it."

"Then Boyd stole it. No big surprise." When April took a deep breath, Joey said, "Okay, so tell me more about the bowl."

"I can't."

"The bruise. Questions about Doug's overdose. The bowl." He looked back and forth between her and the road. "Girl, what is going on?"

"I'm not sure." The tears came faster. He reached to take her hand. She let him.

When they stopped for a light, April knew by the way they gripped each other's hands they'd seen him at the same time.

"Shit," Joey whispered. He looked across the road to the 7-Eleven parking lot. Boyd leaned against the hood of his car and chatted with two rough-looking guys as he sipped a beer and took a drag of his cigarette.

April's entire body tensed. Did he still have that inexplicable, dangerous effect on her?   Joey extricated his hand from April's. She glanced at him and saw him staring at the passenger door, as if he expected her to vaporize through its hinges, back to Boyd.

She looked again at Boyd then turned to Joey and thought about the gentleness in his touch. She took his hand. "Let's get out of here."

He looked both ways then into his rearview mirror. When the light turned green, he crossed over two lanes to turn right.

The unexpected turn made April brace herself with her hand against the dash. She stared straight ahead. She had it in her mind that if she didn't look at Boyd, he wouldn't turn and see her.

Moments later, Joey was on the back roads, which he navigated with ease. He rested his hand on April's knee. It wasn't lost on her that his was a gesture of compassion, unlike Boyd's, which would have been one of possession or control.

April reached for the door handle when Joey pulled in front of her house. "You better go, in case Boyd drives by. He's got a bad habit of that."

"I'm worried about you. Are you gonna be all right?"

She knew her nod wasn't convincing. Leaning across the car, she brushed her lips against his. "Thanks for being here for me."

"Of course. Anytime," he whispered as she got out of the car.

She walked across her lawn and glanced back at Joey. He was leaning down to watch her through the passenger window. She waved him on.

The harshness of the porch light made her squint. Joey pulled away as she stepped inside. She leaned against the safety of the locked door and stared at the plastic baggy dangling from her two pinched fingers.

She needed to talk to someone about that night at Richie's and about finding the bowl. Katie, she thought. She should go to Katie. Her sister would know what to do, would help her. For the first time, April was glad Katie was so sensible, so together.

†

As she walked, Kate tried to remember the direction from which they'd come. She wished she'd paid closer attention to the streets instead of watching Ms. T.'s hands maneuver the steering wheel. If only she hadn't been so focused on the short, clean fingernails, or the way the little car seemed to purr under Ms. T.'s touch.

She adjusted her bra and looked down the front of her shirt to see if the lace had been permanently distorted from the rough handling. Her lower lip trembled as she thought about the way Lana would have stroked her through the fabric.

"Where are you?" Kate whispered. "How are you?" A chill ran through her as she recalled all the manic thoughts she'd been having. What if Lana needed her? What if something horrible had happened to her, and instead of trying to find her, Kate had been out whoring around? Not knowing tore at her.

The grinding of gravel under car tires made her jump. A battered Cadillac pulled up beside her. All the windows were up, but Kate could make out two guys up front and one in the back.

The front window cranked down. "Hey, gorgeous," the passenger said.

Kate glanced at them and quickly looked away.

"What's a nice girl like you doing in a—"

"Oh, dude," the guy in back said, "you'll have to excuse my friend's lame line. You deserve so much better."

The car came to a complete stop, and the passenger door opened. Kate thought about running. She realized that if the guys wanted her in the car, they could force her inside. She tried to swallow past the lump forming in her throat. Wouldn't it just serve her right if something horrible happened to her when she should have stayed in her room, waiting for Lana?

The guy in the passenger side climbed in back to let Kate in up front. She got in willingly. Maybe that way they'd at least be nice about whatever they had planned. She willed a message to Lana: *If I die tonight, please know I'm sorry I hurt you—and that I love you.*

"Dude, she reminds me of my sister."

"Is that a problem?" the driver asked.

The dark-headed guy with a uni-brow just shrugged.

Kate glanced around at the three guys. None of them would come across as particularly malevolent if alone, but together they made her jaw tense painfully.

"I'm Tom. And back there is Dick and Harry." He pounded on the steering wheel as he laughed. "God, I crack me up."

From the backseat, Dick, or Harry, asked, "So, where you headed?"

"Back to my car." Kate was afraid to tell them where her car was.

"And where would that be?" the driver asked. "We aren't mind readers, you know."

"I am," the stocky guy in the backseat chimed in. "And right now, you're thinking that I'm the best looking of the three of us."

Kate figured the big guy was Dick, since the bushy-eyebrowed one *had* to be Harry. Her musing stopped when she felt hot breath on the back of her neck. "Bullshit," the guy behind her mumbled.

Kate leaned closer to the door, trying to put distance between her and the unwanted closeness. But the breath and voice moved along with her. "I'm the one you'd rather make it with, aren't I?"

The driver laughed. "Dude, you're gonna scare her." He put his hand on Kate's leg. "Trust me, we're harmless."

Kate swallowed hard as she stared at the large, rough hand on her leg. Then Tom gave her a playful slap on the thigh and put his hand back on the steering wheel. He turned left at a Stop sign without bothering to actually stop. Moments later, he looked into the rearview mirror. "Shit." He glared at Kate as if the flashing lights behind them were her fault. "Nobody say a word. I'll handle this." He opened the car door and started to get out.

"Stay in the car," a deep voice boomed from behind them.

Tom raised his hands but didn't get back in. "Is there a problem, Officer?"

Kate jumped at the thud. The cop had the guy's face pressed against the side window.

"Next time, stay in the car like you're told."

Time froze as Kate studied the distorted facial features mashed against the glass. He didn't seem real. Nothing, she thought, would ever be real again. Not without Lana.

Kate pivoted to watch through the back window as a second set of flashing lights pulled up. She looked at Harry just as he reached under the front seat.

"Don't move another inch."

Kate stopped in mid-turn as she saw the glare of the officer's gun in the smudged glass. She held her breath.

In a blur of motion, Kate was yanked out, barely avoiding hitting her head. Held against the car, she felt her feet being nudged apart. She thought she'd get sick when the pressure on her back increased and hands ran down her legs and across her belly. Then her driver's license was pulled from her back pocket.

She turned her head slightly and saw that all occupants were out of the car, being frisked.

The officer let go of her. "You go sit over there, and don't move." He pointed to the side of the road.

She twisted her ankle as she fell onto the curb. Her legs were rubbery, and she thought she might pass out. She put her head in her hands and tried to control her erratic breath. She wondered if April felt this bad after drinking. And if so, why did she do it?

Kate looked up as another cop car pulled up to join the others. The cop who'd taken her license leaned into the window. A minute later, the new arrival parked in front of Kate.

Officer Eliot waved her over. "Get in," she mouthed.

Kate obeyed. As she shut the car door, Eliot threw her license into her lap.

"Are you drunk?"

"Not anymore," Kate muttered.

"What are you doing out here?"

"I got stranded."

"Do you know those guys?"

"No," Kate managed to say.

"What in the hell possessed you to get in the car with three men you don't know?"

Kate watched as the driver was handcuffed.

"Don't look at them, look at me." Eliot glared at her. "There were drugs and a gun in that car. Do you know what could have happened?"

Kate shrugged.

"Lucky for you, the officers believed those guys when they swore you didn't know what they had in the car. That's the only reason you aren't in big trouble." She sighed. "Officer Parker recognized your name from the Richard Davis case and radioed me."

Kate stared straight ahead.

"But forget the legal aspect. Do you know how dangerous that was?"

Kate didn't respond.

"What were you thinking?" Her steely eyes bore into Kate. "Really, what in the hell were you—"

"I'll tell you what I was thinking—that I don't care. I don't care anymore what happens." Kate knew she sounded like a spoiled eleven-year-old, but still the words spilled out. Tears followed, and she shook all over.

"Nothing matters," she said. "All I've wanted is to see her. To know she's all right. God, I just wanted to know." Tears streamed down Kate's face.

Eliot turned almost sideways in her seat.

"I'll say anything you want me to, anything. Just tell me Lana's okay." Kate realized she would be willing to confess anything, do anything, just to see Lana. "Please just tell me nothing bad has happened to Lana." Her shoulders heaved with her sobs.

"Oh boy," Eliot muttered. She looked up as one of the other cops approached her car. Her brow furrowed, and her hand gripped Kate's shoulder. "Don't say another word."

Eliot's tone and touch kept Kate frozen.

The officer leaned into Eliot's window. He looked closely at Kate, turned back to Eliot, and said, "Everything okay?"

"Fine, Parker."

"Can you do something with her?" Officer Parker asked.

Kate read the expression on the officer's face as, Please, don't make me put this crying bimbo in my car.

"Yeah, no problem," Eliot answered.

Kate took a deep breath in an attempt to get herself together. She watched as the officer walked back to his car.

Eliot turned to her. "Okay, what's going on?"

Oh, God, Kate thought, I said Lana's name. The adrenaline of the moment wore off, and Kate started to shiver.

Eliot adjusted the AC.

Kate hugged her arms to her body. She shook her head, over and over. "No," she whispered. "No, no, no."

After several long moments, Eliot asked, "Where's your car?"

Kate's face warmed. "Umm... between some church and a laundry place."

"Can you tell me which ones?"

Kate looked down.

"Seatbelt," Eliot said as she put her car in gear.

Kate did as she was told.

Eliot drove, without further instruction, to the bar between a church and laundry place. She pulled up beside Kate's Arrow.

Kate found some relief in the knowledge that her favorite police officer did know this bar.

Eliot handed her a tissue. Kate wiped under her eyes, blew her nose, and wrapped her arms around herself.

"Still cold?" Eliot asked.

"No." In her peripheral vision she saw Eliot lean back against the headrest. She imagined she could feel the rhythm of Eliot's deep, controlled breaths. She closed her eyes and concentrated on the soothing quality of hearing nothing but their breathing.

Then Eliot broke the spell by clearing her throat. "How do you feel?"

"Fine," Kate murmured.

"You must have had quite a bit to drink." Eliot contemplated her several moments. "Anything you need out of your car?"

"What do you mean?"

"I'm driving you home."

"You don't have to do that."

"Yes, I do. So, if you need anything—"

Kate shook her head. "How will I get my car?"

"I'll bring you back in the morning."

"Why?"

"Why what?"

"Why are you being so nice to me?"

Eliot scrutinized her a moment, turned away, and smiled. "Beats the hell out of me."

Chapter Sixteen

April opened one eye. The sun winked at her from between the slats of the blinds. Thoughts of Joey warmed her, and a smile spread across her face. She still felt the light touch of his hands moving up and down her sides... his tongue exploring her mouth...

Both eyes flew open. Her stomach lurched as she remembered finding Richie's bowl. She tried to convince herself she was overreacting, but she knew in her gut something was terribly wrong.

Her head pounded a complaint, and her stomach answered with a gurgle. God, she hated feeling this way in the morning. She crawled out of bed and crept out the door and down the hall.

Please don't be home, she willed her father. She wasn't in the mood to make nice with him, or with anyone, for that matter.

Once sure she was alone, she pulled open the fridge and stared. Nothing looked good. Ginger ale always made her stomach feel better, but caffeine would help her head. She wrestled a handful of ice into a glass and winced as it clanked and clattered.

She filled the glass halfway with ginger ale. Adding cola, she slopped some onto the counter. She smeared it with the palm of her hand and wiped it against her T-shirt. She

210

used her finger to stir up all the fizz and wiped that on her shirt, too.

She took a gulp of her drink. Closing her eyes for a moment, she tried to imagine molecules of carbonated bliss traveling to her aching head. She still felt like crap.

She slinked back to her room and set the drink on the table beside her bed. She crawled in and pulled the covers up to her chin.

It was time to admit to Katie that she'd long been in over her head. She groped for the phone, picked it up, and dialed.

It rang. "Please," she whispered. And rang. "I'm begging you." After nine rings, she hung up. *I need you, Katie.* She curled into a fetal position, hugging her legs to her chest. *Where are you?*

✝

Kate stood in the corridor at the police station and watched as Officer Eliot shoved a folder into a file cabinet. Two hours earlier, when Eliot dropped Kate at her car, she'd given her instructions to meet her back at the station. Kate didn't know why she wanted her there but wasn't about to push her luck by asking.

Eliot looked up. She gave Kate a slight smile and nodded to her left.

Kate's gaze followed Eliot's gesture. She reeled backward two steps when she saw Lana.

Excruciatingly slowly, Lana turned to face her. Kate's breath caught as she watched Lana nibble on her lower lip. So sweet, she thought. Until she looked into Lana's eyes and saw the anger and confusion. Kate glanced at Eliot, who was feigning interest in a file, and turned back.

Lana took tentative steps toward her. When she was within a few feet, she said, "Excuse me," and moved to the side, as if to go around Kate.

"Lana," Kate whispered, "please talk to me."

"You want to talk? Okay. What in the hell are you doing here?"

Kate was caught off guard by the coldness. "I..." She crammed her hands into her shorts pockets and took a moment to steady her voice. "I guess I'm here for more questioning." It wasn't really a lie, since she didn't know exactly why Eliot had arranged their "accidental" meeting.

"Questioning?" Lana looked around. "What questions?"

"I don't have an alibi for when Richie was..." She couldn't say the words, not to Lana. "Alone in my room isn't an alibi."

"They can't seriously think you... Oh, come on."

Kate sobbed.

"Don't cry. That's just stupid. You wouldn't hurt anyone." She touched Kate's arm.

"I miss you so much," Kate blurted.

Lana jerked her hand away. An officer walked by, and Lana blinked several times as she took a few steps back.

Kate cocked her head. Was that fear on Lana's face? Or worse, disgust?

Anger flooded over Kate. She thought about the sense of desperation that had driven her to the bar the night before and the confusion that propelled her into one dangerous situation after another.

"Don't worry, I won't tell your dirty little secret."

Lana looked down at her feet.

"No, I won't tell them who I was with, what I was doing," Kate said, tears flowing freely down her cheeks. "Or what was being done to me." Her voice had turned into a hoarse hiss.

When Lana didn't speak or look at her, Kate turned and ran from the building. If Eliot had wanted her there for any other reason, she'd have to come get her.

✝

Kate didn't remember driving to the marina. The edge of the bulkhead was hard on her backside as she sat listening to the lapping of the water. It took several moments for her to become aware that she was staring at a great blue heron. A mere fifteen feet from the bird, she'd never before been so close to the shy species.

Another layer of sound joined the water's rhythm, and Kate knew it was the low honk of the heron. The rapid beating of her heart joined the percussion. She couldn't believe the intimacy of being that close to something usually so elusive. Her favorite bird. Whose image would be the only painting Lana would ever do for her.

Lana. The thought of Lana's contempt was like a punch to her gut. Kate's involuntary gasp registered with the heron, and it took off in a great blue-gray riot of color and sound.

Secretive and shy, Lana had also taken flight from Kate's life.

✝

"Katie, it's me." April read obvious disappointment in her sister's sigh. "I need to talk to you. Something bad has happened." April sobbed. "Can you come home?"

"Is it Dad? Has something happened to Dad?"

"No," April said.

"So, what is it then?"

She stared at Richie's bowl. "We should talk in person. Please come home."

"I'm sorry, but I can't. Whatever it is, it's probably not nearly as bad as you think."

"I really need you," April whispered.

"I'm sure it can wait. I've got my own things going on right now."

"This is serious," April said.

"So, talk. It's this or nothing. Tell me what it's about, or I'll have to hang up."

April clenched her jaw and slowly ground her molars, then she slammed down the receiver.

✝

April couldn't return Joey's smile when he opened his door.

"I would say this is a pleasant surprise, but judging by the look on your face, I guess not."

April looked over her shoulder to where Nicki had parked when she dropped her off. She waved Nicki on, praying she'd keep her promise and not tell anyone— especially Boyd—where she was. She slipped into the apartment and followed Joey to the kitchen. He opened the fridge and pulled out two beers.

"No thanks," she said.

He put them both back.

"Do you still want to hear about it?" April asked.

"Yes." He led April to the sofa, but she refused to sit. He leaned against the arm.

She took a deep breath. "Here goes. Boyd assaulted me at Richie's place and tried to tell me the bruises were from

Richie. He said he hit Richie to get him off of me. I was wasted on ludes, so I didn't know what happened. When he finally told me the truth, it was only to make me feel better so I'd have sex with him."

"The black eye?"

"Boyd."

Joey's fists clenched at his sides.

"And now with Boyd having Richie's bowl—"

They both jumped when the thudding started at the door.

"Dude, it's me. Open up!"

Ice ran through April at the sound of Boyd's voice.

"Man, I know you're in there. I ain't leaving until you let me in."

Joey silently ushered April into his bedroom. He gave her a quick peck on the lips before leaving the room and closing the door behind him.

April squeezed her eyes shut as she leaned against the wall. She didn't move when she heard the front door opening.

"Hey, got any weed?"

"Yeah, man. Let me get it." She heard Joey go to the "fun drawer" in the kitchen.

"How about some crank?"

"Nope, just the pot," Joey said.

"Come on, I know you got some crank."

"It's been dry as hell around here lately."

Boyd mumbled something that April thought sounded like "something's better than nothing." She cringed. Wasn't that what he'd said the last time he tried to get her to give him a blow job?

"Where you going?" Joey asked.

April's breath caught. Did Boyd suspect she was hiding in Joey's bedroom? And what would he do if he found her?

She heard the spare room door open. Her stomach slammed into her throat.

"Hey, dude," Joey said.

April knew the next sound—the scrape of the nightstand drawer. Rustling... then, "Where's my fucking bowl?"

"What bowl?"

Not very convincing, April thought.

"My new bowl that was stashed in here."

"I haven't seen—"

The rustling grew, and stuff was obviously being dumped on the floor.

"Hey, Boyd, that is so uncool."

"This is bullshit," Boyd yelled.

April shuddered.

"Hey, chill out. Maybe you took it with you last night."

"I wasn't here last night."

"The hell you weren't. You drank about every drop of beer I had."

April slowly exhaled. For just a second, she worried Boyd wouldn't believe the lie.

"Which reminds me," Joey said, "you were gonna bring some brew by here. What happened to that?"

"I... ah..."

April pictured Boyd shuffling his feet. She wasn't at all surprised that Boyd had been so messed up he didn't even remember where he had been just the night before.

"Don't worry about it," Joey said.

"So, do you have any beer?"

"No, sure don't. Listen, I gotta jump in the shower. I have to go to my parents' and act like I'm not a major fucking disappointment to them."

"Too bad. I guess I'll check you later then."

"Yeah, later."

The door squawked as it opened and whined when it shut behind Boyd. Even the apartment was glad to see him go.

April stayed where she was. She wouldn't feel safe until Joey came to get her.

†

"What now?" Joey asked.

"I still feel like I should talk to Katie before I do anything."

Joey handed April the phone, then he walked over to the window and looked out, giving her a little privacy.

She glanced at him as she dialed. He nodded his head. When Katie answered, April blurted, "Okay, it's about Richie."

Katie exhaled long and hard. "There's nothing I can tell you that I haven't already told the police. I'm sorry, but I'm tired and—"

"The police? Why the police?"

"Gee, April, that's who usually gets involved when someone is killed."

"Richie?" The name came out high and squeaky. Nausea swirled through her stomach and forced its way into her throat.

"You didn't know?"

"What happened?" she whispered, needing to hear it.

Joey walked back over to her.

"All I know is that he wasn't breathing when I found him," Kate said.

"You found him? What were you—"

"*That* I don't care to discuss." Kate took a deep breath. "He died on the way to the hospital."

Just like with Doug when he overdosed. Shit, shit, shit. A flash of memory: the baseball bat. April could see Boyd picking it up. Getting into a batter's position, ready to swing. That was the first night they'd met Richie. But she also had an image of seeing Boyd a different time, holding the bat over his head...

"How did he die?" she asked.

Kate sniffled. "Crushed skull."

April used both hands in an unsuccessful attempt to steady the phone. "Do they know who did it?"

Kate's laugh boomed through the phone, dry and brittle. "I guess I'm their only suspect."

The bile in April's throat solidified, and she had to force her voice past the boulder. "You?"

"I don't guess they really think I did it, but they're convinced that I know more about it than I'm telling."

"Do you?"

"April!"

"I mean, do you think you know who did it?"

"I don't know. Do you?"

The boulder in April's throat crumbled, and she sobbed. "I really need to see you, Katie."

"You do know something."

"Will you please come?"

"I'll leave right now."

"Wait." April looked at Joey. "Let me give you the address."

"To where?" Kate asked.

"Joey's. I'll explain it all later." She gave Katie the address. "Just come, please."

Chapter Seventeen

Kate pulled into a parking space at the police station, turned off the engine, and glanced at April. She remembered the last time she'd been to the station, when Lana was so angry, so disgusted. She turned to April. "What happened to the bracelet you were wearing when you and Boyd surprised me?"

April rubbed her wrist. "I lost it."

Kate had known all along she had seen it there in the bushes outside Richie's apartment. No matter how she had tried to convince herself it might have been her imagination, she'd always known in her heart that her vomit had covered an important piece of evidence.

She held up the plastic bag and stared at the ceramic pipe. She'd never seen one before, so she brought it closer for a better look. The style and colors of the painting were unmistakably Lana's. She cringed at how the darkened smear of blood debased it. Kate moved her face closer to the pot pipe and could make out the ridges of a fingerprint. She looked at April.

"Don't worry, there's no way that's my print." April hesitated. "Unless…"

"Tell me," Kate said.

"Unless when I was passed out…"

"Crap," Kate whispered. "Damn it, April. This is very bad. This I won't be able to get you out of. "

April sobbed. "I know that. And I deserve whatever happens."

Kate gingerly set down the bagged bowl and took April's hand. "We'll get through this, you know. It may not be pretty, but we'll get through it."

"I can't believe you're saying 'we,' not with how I've treated you all these years."

"We'll talk about that later, but for right now, you have to make sure you want to go in there. Once we do, there'll be no going back."

"I know that. Could we please get this over with?"

"You're sure?" Kate asked.

April answered by opening her door. "You really do need to get this lock fixed."

Kate bit her lip. April's attempt at nonchalance stirred up a new kind of protectiveness. She forced a smile, and they walked toward the police station.

†

"Kate." Officer Eliot stood as they approached her.

Kate studied her face. Eliot's eyes seemed warmer, less intense than usual. Was it just her imagination?

"Thanks for… you know, the other day," Kate said.

"You're welcome." Eliot glanced at April.

"Officer Eliot." Kate squared her shoulders. "This is my sister, April."

Eliot extended her hand; April hesitated before shaking it. "It's nice to meet you," Eliot said.

April mumbled something in return, but Kate couldn't make it out.

Kate turned back to Eliot. "We have something to tell the detective, and I would like it very much if you could be there with us."

Eliot gave a slow nod. She turned to April. "How old are you?"

"Sixteen," she managed to squeak out.

Kate put her hand on April's shoulder.

"Should we call your parents?" Eliot asked.

"Our dad's in Dallas," Kate answered. "Mom's... just gone."

"How about a lawyer?"

Kate turned to her sister. When April shook her head, Kate answered. "Not right now."

Eliot nodded. "April, could you excuse us for a minute?"

Kate followed Eliot to the other side of a filing cabinet.

"If this is about Lana, about where you were that night, you don't have to do it."

Kate cocked her head.

"Lana came to see me. She told me where you'd been."

"Lana?" The blood rushed to Kate's head. Her legs were unsteady, shaking slightly. "She told you?"

"Yes." Eliot put her hand on Kate's arm. "You okay?"

Kate couldn't answer. All she could think of was how much she wanted to see Lana again. If she could just touch her face one last time... whisper to her that she'd always love her...

"You have your alibi. Do you still want to see the detective?" Eliot asked.

Kate nodded. "April has something to give him."

They both turned in April's direction. Eliot's slight tensing told Kate she'd finally seen the baggy dangling from April's fingers. "Evidence?" Eliot asked.

"Yes."

Eliot took a deep breath. "Okay then. You ready for this?"

The warmth in Eliot's voice almost brought tears to Kate's eyes. "Yeah, let's do it."

†

Kate watched April stare at her hands; she was pretty sure April was focused on the ink smudged across her fingertips.

She let her gaze drift from Eliot, to Detective Stewart, to April. Every now and then, Eliot's eyes met hers.

Kate remembered how scared she'd been of Officer Eliot that night at Richie's. She'd feared that Eliot's ice-blue eyes could see into her very soul. Sitting across from her now, she hoped they could.

Detective Stewart let out an exaggerated sigh. "You sit there and expect me to believe that shit?" His deep voice bounced around the room and echoed in Kate's head.

April looked at her sister.

"Excuse me?" Kate's voice squeaked out from her tightening throat.

Stewart held up a hand, silencing her. "Ms. Hunter," he said to April, "can you seriously expect me to believe that your boyfriend killed Richard Davis in front of you, and you didn't remember it until now?"

"Yes, s-sir. I—"

"And what did Boyd Smith use to kill Richard Davis?"

"A bat, I think."

He slammed down the pen he'd been fiddling with. "You think?"

April didn't look up.

Kate's stare was riveted on the detective's underarms, where huge sweat marks stained the material of his button-down shirt.

Detective Stewart leaned forward. "And where is this bat?" he asked April.

She shrugged.

"Good God. Give me a break. And don't try to sit there looking all—"

"Detective Stewart," Eliot said.

Stewart glared at her. "I don't have to allow you, or her"—he gestured toward Kate—"in here at all. So, if you don't mind, let me do my damn job."

April's lips trembled. Kate's insides started freezing up, much as they had in Hillsboro. *No. Not here, not now.* She took several deep breaths.

"Detective Stewart." Kate paused, surprised by how steady her voice was. "Maybe you'd like to replace me and Officer Eliot with my father and his lawyer."

He grunted a dismissal, but it only emboldened her further.

"April, you don't have to say anything else," Kate said.

"Young lady," Stewart yelled at Kate.

"Detective," Eliot said in a low voice, "may I have a word with you?"

They all turned at the knock on the door. An officer stuck his head in. "Sir, I have something for you."

Eliot followed Stewart into the hall.

"Hey," Kate whispered, "how you holding up?"

April shrugged without looking at her.

They both jumped at Eliot's raised voice. "That's bullshit."

Kate stared out the door.

"*Officer* Eliot, don't you have traffic citations to write?"

The color on Eliot's face rose.

"There is a reason the word 'Detective' comes before *my* name."

Eliot glanced in at Kate then looked to the man who'd joined them. "What's up?" the new man asked.

The two men stood facing one another. They were the same height and had similar slicked back hairstyles and matching pot bellies that hung over their belts.

Kate strained to hear.

Stewart crossed his arms. "Wes, could you put your officer to work? She seems to have forgotten who does what around here."

Kate knew Eliot saw the smirk that passed between the two men.

"Officer Eliot," her boss said.

"But, sir—"

"Not another word. In my office, now."

Even when Detective Stewart came back into the room, Kate's eyes stayed on Eliot. Kate tried to read the expression on her face but couldn't. Eliot gave her one last look before following her boss down the hall.

"Ms. Hunter, based upon preliminary analysis of the fingerprint found on the evidence you finally deemed important enough to bring in, it appears you will be spending some time with us here."

April turned to her sister. "Katie."

"Big sis can wait for you or not, I don't care." He smirked. "Officer Williams here will escort you to your nice, quiet cell. After you've had some time alone to relax a bit, maybe you'll remember more of the details."

April stared over her shoulder at Kate as the officer led her away.

When April was out of sight, Kate let the tears flow. She started to shake then made herself focus.

She paced the hallway, frantic. She wanted to call her dad, but wasn't sure where he was, let alone how to reach him. That wasn't unusual. Bitterness rose in her throat, and she considered how her dad hadn't been there for her for a very long time. And he'd done April a huge disservice by not reining her in.

The stench of stale smoke and the glare of the fluorescent lighting made her head pound. She massaged her temples while she tried to think.

She stared in the direction Eliot had disappeared. As much as Kate wanted Eliot there with her, she knew she had to handle it herself. There were no other options. She swallowed all the anger toward her dad, the detective, and Boyd. And herself. She sat on the stiff bench along the pale yellow wall, determined to wait there until April came out, no matter how long it took.

She stared at the pay phone several feet away and felt tremendous loneliness at not having anyone to call.

A thought almost paralyzed her. What if there was more to what April didn't remember than they'd imagined? What if... No, Kate would never believe that of April. Even if it did turn out to be April's fingerprint on the pot bowl, there was a perfectly logical explanation.

Something nagged at Kate. What was Eliot talking about when she told the detective something was bullshit? What did the other two men not want Eliot telling her?

Kate looked back at the payphone, then toward Eliot's boss's office. He was making his way across the room. She dug a quarter out of her front pocket and moved to the phone, where she stood with the coin poised. When the pudgy cop was halfway down the hall, she deposited the quarter. When he was almost within earshot, she pretended to dial. He was right behind her when she started talking.

"Is this WAVY TV 10? I have a story you might be interested in. It's about the police harassing a minor. Yes, I can be there in fifteen minutes. Thank you."

She dawdled toward the door, giving him plenty of time to catch up to her.

"Ms. Hunter—"

She turned to him and gave him her best look of innocence. "Yes, sir?"

"Your sister's almost ready to leave. If you'd like to wait—oh, let's say about fifteen minutes—she can go home with you."

"Yes. I'd love to wait. Thank you."

✝

April stared out the passenger window as I-64 streamed by. She balled her hands into fists and concentrated on the low rattle of Katie's car.

When they got to the tunnel, April unfurled her fingers and studied the ink smudged across the tips. The pulsing light inside the tunnel made the mess look surreal. She'd nearly panicked when they printed her. But when they put her in the dirty, smelly cell, all she could do was sit there and cry. She'd finally found something with Joey, and now she'd probably end up rotting in a cell just like the one she was in. She'd even wondered if Officer Eliot would maybe visit her, offer her an extra ration of bread and water.

April had liked Officer Eliot immediately, liked the way she didn't seem to judge. If the officer only knew the truth about how big of a fuck-up April really was. She'd watched as the cop turned to Katie. There was a gentleness about

Officer Eliot that April wouldn't have expected, even more so when she spoke to Katie.

"You do understand what Detective Stewart told you, right?" Kate asked.

April nodded.

"Under no circumstances do you go out of town."

"I know." April kept staring at the littered shoulder of the interstate.

"And you do not go anywhere near Boyd."

"I know!" April squeezed her hands into fists. "I know," she repeated.

She didn't understand why Katie was acting so snotty now. When April had come from her cell at the police station, her sister had been happy to see her. She supposed Katie's temporary, yet fiery, portrayal of the protective sister had already fizzled out.

April stared at the lone evergreen in the median. There were no decorations. The American flags and red, white, and blue ribbons most likely had been knocked off the last time it rained. The tree was naked. And vulnerable. April watched the tree go by as Kate drove. She'd never before passed it going only the speed limit.

She turned back to the front of the car, and her eyes met Kate's for a second. Then they both looked forward.

"That tree," Kate said in a low voice, "it's hard to look at around Mother's Day."

April stared at her sister. Her hands relaxed at her sides, and her chest fluttered slightly as she thought, Katie hurts, too.

Kate nodded toward the shoulder of the interstate and gave April's leg a light, playful nudge. Looking at a yellow tractor, she said, "Hey, remember when we were kids and Eric Rogers started one of those things?"

April laughed. "And then he couldn't stop it."

"And the cops came. They couldn't believe someone had left the keys in it."

"It wasn't like a nine-year-old could have hot-wired it."

"That's all everyone talked about for weeks."

April wondered if their mom leaving was what had finally shifted the attention off Eric Rogers and the tractor. She didn't remember and wouldn't ask Katie.

"We're gonna have to tell Dad about all this," Kate said.

"I guess," April said.

"When's he coming home?"

"I don't know."

"Where is he?" Kate asked.

"I don't know." They looked at each other and both laughed.

"Okay," Kate said. "Maybe we don't have to tell dad." She glanced at April. "I can't believe that bastard let you think it was your fingerprint."

April almost choked.

"What?" Kate asked.

"That 'bastard'? My, my, college sure has broadened your vocabulary."

"Yep. Nothing but the very best education for me."

"What are you going to do now?" April asked.

"Take you home."

"No, I mean after that. You know—"

"I'll get on with my life." Kate laughed, high and unnatural. "What else is there to do?"

April didn't answer.

"I'm gonna drop you at home and go back to my room to grab a few things."

"We could have gone by there after leaving the station."

"No," Kate said. "I need to go there alone and put some things in my head to rest."

April nodded.

"And I think I'm going to transfer to Old Dominion. A change of scenery, and major, will do me good."

"What about Lana? What if she comes around, what if she—"

"She's not coming around. It's over."

†

April cut across a neighbor's lawn. She glanced at the pond and thought of Katie spending a lot of time hanging around there when they were young. She never understood Katie's fascination with the dingy water.

She veered around a stack of firewood that hadn't shrunk or grown for as long as she could recall. She remembered how she and Nicki would hide behind the crooked woodpile and get stoned. Now she couldn't understand her fascination with that.

When April emerged onto her road, two blocks from her house, Joey was there waiting for her. She slipped onto the seat beside him and gave him a weak smile.

"You okay?" Joey asked. When she nodded, he added, "Are you sure?"

"Yeah."

"What's the latest?"

"They're looking for Boyd. To question him."

"Any regrets about going to the police?"

"No."

"Not even a little?"

April smiled at Joey's insecurity. "Not even an atom's worth." She paused. "I wonder if that's something Katie would say."

"Would that be so bad?"

Katie had really impressed her at the police station— first sticking up for her, then waiting around after April was locked up. "Maybe not so much."

"I always wished I had a brother or a sister," Joey said.

"You get along good with your parents though, right?"

"Yeah."

"So, what you said to Boyd about being a disappointment to them?"

"I was just being cool."

"It may have worked with Boyd, but I know better," April teased.

"That's only because you've seen me being very uncool, cruising McDonald's on a Friday night."

"You may not have been cool, but you were cute. Nicki even said so." She glanced into the side mirror when a car approached them from the rear.

Joey's gaze followed hers. "What do you want to do today?"

"Anything. As long as I don't leave town. And no more jail cells. I've had enough of that to last a lifetime."

He took her hand. "It's gonna be all right, you'll see. No more cops, and most important, soon, no more Boyd."

She looked again into the side mirror. "One part of me believes that, another part just can't shake the feeling that Boyd's everywhere. I keep expecting to see him in my room, at Nicki's, behind that tree—"

Joey lifted her hand to his lips and kissed her knuckles. "I won't let anything bad happen to you, ever."

"I know." He would protect her to the best of his ability, but April wasn't sure if that would be enough.

"We probably shouldn't be just sitting here." He started the car and pulled away from the side of the road.

"Where can we go? He'll go to your place for sure," April said.

"I know, let's go sightseeing."

"Sightseeing? Where?"

"Right here. When's the last time you were to Yorktown as a tourist?" He laughed when she shrugged. "Yorktown it is."

Chapter Eighteen

Kate slammed the gearshift into park in front of her dorm and ran to intercept Lana. She stepped in front of the sputtering scooter. Lana stopped a foot away from her, and they stared at each other. Lana gunned the engine, and the machine lurched forward until the front wheel was between Kate's knees.

Kate didn't flinch, didn't blink. She held Lana's gaze until Lana turned off the engine.

"Come up to my room," Kate said.

"That's not a good idea."

"It's a terrific idea." Kate brushed the backs of her fingers along the side of Lana's face. Her heart pounded when Lana didn't push her hand away. "Let's end this right."

After several moments, Lana leaned the scooter against the brick wall lining the walkway to Kate's dorm. They entered the building and ascended the stairs without speaking.

Kate froze when she saw the back of a painting leaning against the wall beside her door. She slowly turned it around to face her.

Lana shuffled her feet. "I hadn't planned on being here when you found that."

Kate stared at the portrait, studying how the cautious, whimsical strokes of the hair—her hair—transformed her lackluster straw into brilliant gold threads. Her pale skin, a trait she never liked on herself, was luminescent and beautiful. She wondered if Lana really saw her like that. And if she did, how could she walk away? She took another deep breath and thought that maybe the representation of her was how Lana wished she looked.

She turned to Lana and saw she was holding her breath. The gesture was so pure, so sweet, all doubt fled. She unlocked her door, and Lana carried the portrait into the room. Kate shut the door behind them.

"I'm sorry things turned out this way," Lana said.

"Shh." Kate went to her.

Lana placed a hand on each side of Kate's face. She leaned closer, keeping eye contact, and asked, "Are you sure you want to do this?"

"Yes," Kate whispered.

Lana stared at her for a long time before pulling her into a fierce hug. When she sobbed, Kate asked, "What?"

"I don't want to let you go."

Kate pulled away enough to look at her. She put her hands on the sides of Lana's face. They kissed through the tangle of hands, and Kate backed Lana up to the bed. "Then don't let me go. Ever."

Kate's clothes dropped off like protective feathers molting, floating down, leaving her vulnerable. And glad. Such a simple word, "glad," but a perfect one, too.

Lana's clothes landed on the floor with Kate's, the fabrics rumpling together. Kate slowly lowered herself onto Lana. She pressed against Lana and rocked harder and harder, wetness to wetness. Within moments she was grinding frantically and crashing over the edge. As soon as she caught her breath, she shifted her hips just enough to slip a hand between them. She found Lana's wetness and gasped.

Lana dug her fingers into Kate's back as Kate slid two fingers into her. The rising of Lana's hips was enough to spur Kate on, and she added another finger. She left a trail of kisses, tasting every inch on the path down Lana's throat, breasts, belly. When her mouth joined her fingers, she pulled out far enough to add her pinky to the thrusting.

Lana bucked. "Yes. Just like that. Just like that."

Twisting her hand slightly, Kate pushed deeper and deeper into Lana. She needed Lana's scent to cover as much of her as possible. She wanted to always smell this precious moment, to feel the memory of Lana's yielding to her own flesh.

Kate squeezed her eyes shut and tasted her tears as they mixed with Lana's wetness.

Lana took a deep breath and held it a few moments before letting it rush out, accompanied by a loud moan.

Kate used her free hand to hold Lana's hips down as she twisted her four fingers deep inside. Lana's body clenched around her, holding Kate's fingers in her as she shuddered and trembled and writhed.

When Kate finally, slowly, pulled her fingers from the last spasm of Lana's orgasm, she marveled at the slickness that covered her hand. She would forever remember how Lana's juices were like a second skin, a sacred second skin.

Kate ran her fingertip along Lana's collarbone, as she had so many times after making love to her, then she brought the wet finger to her mouth. The smell of Lana on her fingers, the saltiness of her sweat on her lips, all made Kate's breath catch in her throat.

Lana sobbed.

"Don't cry, baby, please don't cry."

"I don't want to lose you," Lana whispered.

"You don't have to. I love you so much. I want to be with you so much."

"I don't know if I know how."

"How to what?" Kate asked.

"Be with you the way you need me to be—open and out there. I'm not ready to come out to my parents. Or the world."

"It's okay. You come out at your own pace. No pressure from me."

"You promise to be patient with me if I promise to try?" Lana asked.

"Do you love me?"

"Yes."

"And only me?" Kate asked.

"Yes."

"That's all I'm asking." She pulled Lana closer.

†

"You sure you don't want me to come with you?"

"I'm sure. You stay here and rest," Lana said.

"Hurry back."

"I'm just going to grab a few things. Your fridge is barren."

"I didn't think I'd be staying here, so I haven't shopped for groceries."

"But you are staying. With the college and with me," Lana said.

"Yes, I am. Now hurry up. I miss you all ready."

"I'm happy, Kate. Very happy."

"Me, too."

Lana stopped at the door, looked back at Kate, and smiled. She turned the knob and was thrown backward as

Boyd barreled through. He kicked the door shut and lunged at Kate. He grabbed her by the shirt collar and pushed her against the wall.

Boyd pressed a knife under her chin. Lana gasped. Boyd swung around and pulled Kate with him, until she was between him and Lana. He kept the knife against her flesh.

"Move, bitch, and she's dead."

Lana looked at Boyd then at Kate.

Boyd reeled around and shoved Kate back against the wall. "Why couldn't you just stay away from us?"

"I—"

"Shut up! Shut the fuck up!" Boyd swallowed hard and licked his lips over and over. "You poisoned her. You turned April against me. God damn you."

He started to sob but clenched his teeth and pressed all of his weight against her. "You fucking bitch." His spit splattered her face.

The steel of the knife tip pierced Kate under her chin. She whimpered and heard Lana gasp.

Boyd shoved Kate away, and she landed against the edge of the portrait. He raised the knife.

"No!" Lana screamed.

Boyd jerked at the sound of Lana's voice and brought the knife down, slashing through the canvas. He lifted the knife again as Kate tried to crawl away.

Lana grabbed the lamp from the desk. She yanked its cord from the wall. Holding it by the cord, she whipped it around. The ceramic base slammed squarely against the side of Boyd's head. He fell against Kate. She pushed at him as she rolled away. He crumpled to the floor.

"Oh, God, Kate. Your arm, your chin…" Lana took several steps toward Kate. When Boyd moaned and tried to sit up, Lana froze.

"It's not deep. I'm fine." Kate shook as the adrenaline wore off. Sweat coated her forehead and back. Her arm was warm with the sticky, slow trickle of blood.

"But you're bleeding."

"Just a little." Kate looked down at Boyd. "I'll call the police."

Lana put her hand up as Kate moved toward the phone. "He'll talk his way out of this. You know he will. And we'll never be totally free of him. April for sure won't be."

"But what else is there?" Kate's eyes widened as she stared at the cracked lamp still gripped in Lana's hand. "You can't mean—"

"We have no choice. He'll never leave April alone."

"That's wrong." Kate's voice broke. "We can't." She shook her head over and over. "I better call the police now."

"Kate," Lana pleaded.

"We have to call them." Her hand trembled as she grasped the phone and dialed.

"We can't let him get away with killing Richie. Or hurting April. He'll do it again."

Kate blurted her name and address into the phone. "I need the police. And an ambulance."

Kate fixed her eyes on Boyd as she hung up. The blood on the side of his face brought the memories rushing in. She could almost taste the blood from Richie's mouth as she had tried to resuscitate him.

Boyd got to his knees. "Stay down," Lana yelled. "You son of a bitch."

"The cops should be here any minute," Kate said.

"How's your arm?" Lana asked.

"I'm fine. Really." Kate's quivering voice wasn't supporting her claim.

Boyd reached for the side of the bed to steady himself.

Lana jumped. "Down," she screamed.

"I gotta take a leak," he muttered. He twisted the bedspread into his fist.

"You can pee on yourself for all I care," Kate said in a nasty tone.

Lana looked at her and cocked her head.

Kate knew right away where the hostility had come from. What she saw was Bobby on the ground in the basement. And her dad standing over him with the shovel. And the fear that flashed through her mind for years after they left Hillsboro that last time—that Bobby would hurt other young girls. She wondered if her dad regretted not finishing the job.

I didn't protect you then, April. But this time will be different.

Boyd yanked at the bedspread and pulled it halfway off the bed as he boosted himself onto his wobbly legs.

Kate kicked at his left leg, and he went back down. "Oh, God." She'd frightened herself with her own reflexive move.

"Why'd you kick me?" he whined. "Damn. I really gotta go."

"He's going to get away with everything," Lana whispered. "Everything."

Kate glared at Boyd. "No, he won't," she said, her words slow, measured. She held Lana's gaze for several moments then stared at the lamp.

Lana held it out, offering it to Kate.

"Me?" Kate whispered. "I don't think I—" She shuddered.

Lana didn't answer, but Kate read it all in her eyes.

Sirens screamed in the background; lights strobed through the curtain. Boyd got to his knees again, and they both jumped.

Lana lifted the lamp.

"You won't do it," Boyd growled.

She lifted it higher.

Boyd's eyes grew wide, and he raised one arm to cover his head. "No. Please."

"Did April plead with you not to hurt her?" Lana's voice was barely above a whisper. "Did Richie beg for his life?"

"Fuck this." Boyd scrambled to his feet. Kate screamed as he lunged at Lana. He threw a punch at Lana, and she sidestepped. He recovered his balance and threw himself at her again. She managed to get the lamp in position just as he came within inches of her. The sound of shattering ceramic echoed through the room.

Kate grabbed Lana to her. "Are you okay?"

Lana buried her face against Kate's neck. "I had to do it," Lana said, sobbing.

"I know. I know."

Lana pulled away enough to look into Kate's eyes. "I love you." She gave Kate a soft kiss.

"I love you, too."

They jumped at the splintering sound of the door flying open.

"Police!"

But the noise that ensued was obliterated, no match for the perfect echo of their words. *I love you.*

Chapter Nineteen

"Kate? How's your arm?" April had made a pact with herself to finally call her older sister *Kate,* as she had requested long ago. April figured it would be a sign of how much she had matured in the last few weeks. She held out a glass of water and a pain pill.

Kate looked up from where she sat cross-legged on her dorm bed, leaning against the headboard. She curled one side of her upper lip. "Not another pill. God, I hate the way those things make me feel. I will never understand what you people get out of altering your—"

April started to back away.

Kate grabbed her arm. "I'm sorry. Please stay." She took the water and pill from April and put them on the table next to her juice.

April studied Kate and thought about their last night in Hillsboro. Kate had brought a game to April's bed, and they played for a while, longer than they ever had. Then they lay in the bed together, staring at the moon's reflection on the peeling, yellowed walls, and listening to the wail of the train.

A lot had happened in the seven years since The Hillsboro Incident. A lot had happened in the last three weeks.

She climbed into bed with Kate, stretching perpendicular to where her sister sat. She spread the driver's booklet out in front of her. After several moments of feeling her sister's eyes on her, she looked up. "What?"

"What do you mean, 'what'?"

"You're staring at me."

"I just think it's cute."

"Cute?" April shut the booklet.

"That you're nervous about taking your driver's test."

"I'm not nervous."

"Are, too."

"Am not." April laughed. "Okay, maybe just a little."

"You'll do fine. Better than fine." Kate grabbed the orange juice off the nightstand and took a sip.

"I'm glad you're taking me."

"Me, too," Kate said.

"So, did you tell Dad you want to switch your major from pre-vet to psychology?"

"Yeah."

"He took it well?" April asked.

"After the shock wore off. He's glad I'm staying at Lillian Wilde College, though." Kate smiled. "Tell me more about Joey."

April wanted to say, "Thank God he's not Boyd," but couldn't bring herself to. As bad as Boyd had ended up being, she couldn't ignore the fact that she'd once loved him, or at least thought she had.

Of course she was sad that he died, but she had to keep it in perspective. Boyd had killed and could very well have done it again. It was bad enough that he'd murdered Richie, but April wouldn't have been able to deal with it if he'd killed Kate.

April banished Boyd from her thoughts. "Joey's a welder at the shipyard."

"Yeah?"

April smiled when she thought about talking to Joey about his job. "One time he got flash-burn at work. He didn't know it until 2 o'clock the next morning, when he woke up and it was like someone had thrown sand in his eyes. No matter how much he rinsed them, they didn't get any better."

"Ouch," Kate said.

She picked up Kate's ugly red throw pillow and started kneading it. "When I asked him what he did next, he said, 'Called my mom.'"

Kate laughed.

"He was so embarrassed and so cute when he told me that." April sighed. "God, he's sweet. And you know, it's the little things. Like not smoking around me. He knows smoke bothers me, so he doesn't do it."

"He does sound wonderful."

"He is. Okay, your turn," April said. "Tell me about Lana. You're seeing a lot of each other now, huh?"

"Yeah."

April was amazed by the speed of Kate's blush. Had she ever seen Kate's color rise because of something good?

"When is Lana come back?"

"After work. She's spending the night."

"Oh yeah, she's got it bad for you. And she saved your life."

April stopped teasing when Kate's color drained as fast as it had risen. She stared at her sister, but Kate had suddenly become quite engaged with the condensation on her glass of orange juice.

"Hey," April whispered.

Kate looked up.

"Whatever it is you're thinking about, I'm sure you did the right thing."

Kate looked away again.

April didn't want to directly address what had happened in Kate's room between her and Lana and Boyd. If her sister ever decided to tell her about it, she'd listen.

April casually picked up the driving booklet. "It's nice to be able to relax. I like not feeling I have to constantly look over my shoulder."

Kate nodded but still wouldn't make eye contact.

The booklet made a swishing sound as April ruffled through the pages. She closed her eyes for a second then stopped the movement with a flourish. "Okay, brainchild. What distance do you keep behind a stopped school bus?"

Kate sat up straighter as she looked at April. "I have no idea."

"Well, that's a first."

Kate ripped the pillow out of April's hand and tossed it at her. "Brat."

"Thank you, Kate," April said.

"Don't thank me. I owe you an apology. For Hillsboro. For not being strong for you then."

"You were a kid."

"I froze when you needed me in that basement."

"You were a kid," April repeated. "And you sure had my back through this last mess."

Kate didn't say anything.

"Do you remember the train in Hillsboro?" April asked.

"Yeah."

"Where was it coming from? Where was it going?"

"I don't know," Kate said.

April looked at her sister then averted her gaze. "I used to be so scared you and Dad would get on that train and leave me."

"We didn't leave," Kate whispered.

"I'm glad."

"Me, too."

"I like this," April said, gesturing between herself and Kate. "I like where we are now. And where we're going. Us as sisters, and me with Joey, you with Lana."

"I like this, too," Kate said. "A lot."

"I know it won't be easy, but with your help, the first thing I'm going to do is clean up my act. And Joey and I are going to get some new friends."

"Probably not a bad idea," Kate said.

"What about you and Lana?"

"She's agreed to go out to that women's bar with me next weekend."

"Wow. That's great."

"It's a start. I just hope I'm strong enough to be as patient as she needs me to be."

"You're strong enough to do whatever it takes," April said. "We both are."

About the Author

Renee MacKenzie

As a Navy brat, Renee lived on three continents before her family settled in Virginia. She currently resides in Southwest Florida with her partner, Pam, and their poodle, Sabrina. Renee works and plays in the swamp, where she enjoys wildlife photography, kayaking, and hiking. Even though Renee has been paid to do all sorts of jobs, ranging from dental assistant to bartender, data entry clerk to maintenance worker, and field sampler to pet-sitter, she insists she's only had one job—writer—and all the rest has just been research.

Other Books from Affinity eBook Press

The One—JM Dragon.. Rosa Moran is a woman with a mission. Born in China but educated in Britain, she has come back home to China to work as a missionary helping the many orphans who need help there. Philomena Casters is the pilot sent to bring Rosa a letter that encourages her to return to England when a family member falls ill. When Rosa refuses, Phil is intrigued and some months later, she flies back to the mission, to save a set of twins from a corrupt Chinese official. Phil and Rosa find their lives intertwined in an effort to transport a handful of children to safety leading them to the surreal private paradise of Langshow. Even though caught up in the maelstrom of war, the two forge an unbreakable bond built on a platform of duty and a belief in a common good. The One is a delightful, gender-bending romance with everything—love, intrigue, misunderstandings, and two women whose faith and trust allow them to overcome all obstacles thrown at them.

The Chronicles of Ratha: Book 2 A Lion Among The Lambs—Erica Lawson   It has been three years since Jordana Laren's path first crossed the Noorthi's—three years since she's had a drink, had sex, and a life of her own. Her only excitement has been spent keeping up with her two year-old daughter, Rice, who is definitely a chip off the old block. All has been peaceful until one of the colonists becomes sick. Bad news shifts to worse news when the disease spreads through their community. Unable to get proper medicine, Jordana is forced to rely on the Noorthi healers to come up with a cure. Soon the herbs run out, leaving her with no choice but to search for more on the Noorthi home planet. What is supposed to be a simple pick-up flight turns into a nightmare. Can Jordana believe in herself like her Noorthi sisters do? Only then can she fulfill her destiny as The Chosen One. Follow the colorful cast of characters in this action-packed adventure sequel as they traverse the galaxy. Of course, nothing ever goes smoothly when Jordana is involved.

Cowgirl Up—Ali Spooner When the new ranch hand, Coal Bryan, arrives at the MC2, the last thing she's looking for is love. Her co-workers are surprised when Coal turns out to be female. Coal, used to the reaction, quickly earns the respect of the crew with her work ethic and skill with horses. Coal uses the strenuous work and friendship of the ranch hands to try and forget her broken past. Melissa Conway, owner of MC2, offers Coal a place to live in her home. The both are shocked to find they are linked in a way neither of them imagined. Mary Leah, Melissa's sister, arrives at the ranch to recover from a recent tragedy. The attraction between Mary Leah and Coal is instant and mutual. Can the three women survive their personal dilemmas? The love and friendship they develop certainly helps but will it be enough to bring them together. Ride along with the crew of the MC2, for boot scootin', butt kickin', dirt eatin', rodeo adventures, with a love story thrown into the mix.

The Chronicles of Ratha: Book 1 Children of the Noorthi—Erica Lawson Jordana Laren is a hard-drinking, hard-fighting womanizer, who works as a freighter pilot in her spare time. Her latest customer drugs her, steals her ship, and abandons her on a desert hellhole called Rigeus, infamous penal planet for the worst women criminals. Her chances of survival aren't looking good. She has no food, water, or weapons, and the nearest bar is a million miles away. Just when she's ready to write her last will and testament, Jordana is rescued by a group of barely-clad women. Has she found nirvana? Her own personal harem seems like a possibility, until the intercession of their enemy, the Velkren. Their leader, Vel, remembers Jordana well, and not fondly. But why is Vel on this planet, surrounded by murderers, thieves, and bad-tempered bitches? Jordana knows Vel isn't a prisoner, so why is her nemesis on Rigeus mining mud, of all things? Jordana knows only one thing. She has to get off the planet before Vel kills her. Unfortunately, the women who saved her reveal themselves to be holy. They are the Noorthi, and Jordana's dream of endless debauchery becomes a nightmare of eternal servitude. The Noorthi make her one of them, marking her with a wrist tattoo, and leaving her no choice but to protect them with her life. The last thing Jordana wants is to become involved in galactic politics or heroic actions. But the tattoo ochre in her body is suddenly giving her morals and scruples, not to mention a better vocabulary! And she really can't pass up a chance to outwit Vel, whose megalomaniac plans are endangering not only the Noorthi, but the civilized galaxy itself. But Jordana is torn. Does she stop Vel at all costs, or does she get out from under the thumb of the Noorthi while she can? Some things were never meant to be easy...

Renee MacKenzie

If I Were a Boy—Erin O'Reilly Katie McGuire appears to have it all. A devoted husband, a job she loves, and a comfortable lifestyle. Helen Swenson is a successful financial director of a prominent investment firm, with an unfaithful husband, and few friends. Their husbands' annual trip to Padre Island National Seashore to reunite with their air force pilot squad becomes a pivotal point for the two women. Their lives take on a completely new meaning when an undeniable magnetism between them draws them together. Passion and secrecy becomes the norm, as they have no choice but to surrender to their attraction. Can the vacation love affair continue? When they leave for their respective homes, will they regret what happened? Life is not that easy to change and the people around them are the hardest to convince. There is no more powerful motivation than love. Except hate and there are plenty of people who want to see their relationship destroyed. Will Katie and Helen be able to make a life together work or succumb to doubts and the pressures of family? This story will fill you with the thrill of passion and the tenderness of love.

Nesting—Renee MacKenzie Macy Stokes, a divorced mother who is struggling with her sexual identity, jumps at a once-in-a-lifetime opportunity to help her friends. She doesn't foresee it will put her in jeopardy of losing her son, Jeremiah. Fresh out of high school, Cam Webber travels to Augusta, Georgia, to reconcile with her aunt. When she learns that's impossible, she determines to gain acceptance from her aunt's partner, Sharon. Meanwhile, Cam sets her sights on Macy, but Macy has other ideas. Kenny Brewer is a good old boy who loves his wife, Dorianne, even when he thinks she's gone totally off her rocker. Dorianne gets it in her head that a local woman is her long-lost half-sister. But soon, her obsession with that is eclipsed by medical problems that involve them all. Set in Augusta, Georgia, *Nesting* explores the age-old issues of guilt, regret, and redemption, and the part they play in driving people to create and protect family-at any cost.

Reece's Faith—TJ Vertigo   In the return of the main characters from the bestselling novel *Private Dancer*, we see the blossoming relationship of bar owner, Reece Corbett and actress, Faith Ashford. The two women explore new, uncertain territory together, using sexual intimacy as a glue of comfort, helping them become strong and whole. A trusting Reece shares with Faith the sordid tale of how she became *The Animal* and Faith finds herself newly empowered by Reece's ongoing trust and support. Jealousy arises when Faith has to kiss a man on her TV show and two amorous women stalk Reece. When Faith is outed on her television show, things get crazy. With the arrival of her parents on the scene, the craziness escalates. As Faith tries to justify her lifestyle and defend her love for Reece, she discovers that nothing about her parents is as she once believed. This, not to be missed passionate and erotic romance, will have you begging for more.

Starting Over—Jen Silver   Ellie Winters, a successful potter, is living on a remote hilltop farm inherited from her parents. Her well-ordered life is shaken apart when her past meets her present. Robin Fanshawe, Ellie's philandering long-term lover, has a fragile truce with Ellie. The arrival of women from Robin's present threatens to break that tentative pact. Charming Dr. Kathryn Moss, an archaeologist and an old lover of Ellie's, arrives on the farm searching for a new site to dig. When she discovers a previously unknown Roman settlement and ancient burial site on Ellie's farm, Ellie allows her to start an archaeological dig of the area. Will Ellie also allow the rekindling of an old romance or will she stay with Robin? Can that long term relationship, albeit tentative, recover from this collision or will an old romance trump everything she knows? Will Robin, seeing the interaction between Ellie and Kathryn, leave her womanising ways behind? Will she take a chance on giving herself wholly to the woman she loves? These questions and the mystery of whose royal resting place is disturbed at Starling Hill are answered in this classic romance of simmering passions, anguished loss, and the wonder of love.

Twisted Lives—Ali Spooner A twist of fate leaves Bet and her daughter Kylie stranded at the entrance of the home of Alex Graves, as she flees the control of an abusive husband. When custom–homebuilder Alex arrives to find steam boiling from Bet's car and a beautiful child asleep in the passenger seat, her heart goes out to them. Alex offers shelter to the pair setting off a chain of events that bring both mother and daughter close to her heart and danger to her door. A heartwarming story of true love that will keep you smiling long after you've finished the book.

Malodorous—Del Robertson Sequel to My Fair Maiden Something in Fairhaven stinks. Other than the mutton stew, that is. Gwen thought life after being a virgin sacrifice would be a bed of roses. Bodhi was just looking for a wench to bed. Neither less-than-dashing hero nor not-quite-so-pure maiden imagined they would meet again, much less be trapped together in a city the likes of the ill-named Fairhaven. There's a killer on the loose. Fairhaven's on lockdown, its citizens fearful for their lives. The local guards are corrupt. And, Bodhi's been accused of murder...

Desert Blooms—Dannie Marsden Luce's story continues in DESERT BLOOMS... When we last met Luce Velazquez in Desert Heat, she went through hell and back to salvage her soul and reputation. Hoping to get her life back on track with lover Beth Ryan, a woman who understands her pain and can relate on every level. Instead, Luce is in the hospital, and Beth in protective custody. Jessica Sullivan, Luce's friend and ex, has big doubts about the sincerity of Beth's love, and is in no hurry to release her from custody. Can Luce's new found happiness last, or is Jessica correct in her doubts? A heart stopping romance that will fill you with the wonder of friendship, anger of betrayal, and the everlasting vision of love.

Finding Her Way—Riley Jefferson Is it love or just great sex? After ending an abusive marriage, Jerrica Kerrison is finally alive and she's apologizing for nothing! She has a job with a financial firm in Boston, a townhouse in Newburyport, and a sports car she drives way too fast. Jerrica has everything except that indefinable emotion called love. Madison Jeffrey is a lost soul. A PR job in the south has always protected Madison from the pressures of her family. But one day, fate brings her back to New England, forcing Madison to face her long buried demons, and a sister who despises her. When a chance meeting brings Jerrica and Madison's separate worlds crashing together, the attraction is instantaneous. After one passionate night together, Jerrica retreats into the safety of her world, leaving Madison to figure out what happened. Will Jerrica open up her heart to the idea of love? Can Madison finally believe that she is worthy of unconditional love? Or will a devil hiding in the shadows tear them apart?

HER—Lisa Ron Fox has been looking for that one person who will make her feel complete-her perfect match. Together with her friends, Megan and Tree, Fox continues her quest while dodging exes and clingers, laughing a lot along the way. When she meets Madeline, she instantly knows that she has found HER. Madeline has her own problems-notably a domineering husband. Can Fox win her heart? Can they make a life together? This story will make you laugh, cry, and hold your breath as the story unfolds. With the right person love can conquer all.

Bayou Justice—Ali Spooner Hell hath no fury like a woman scorned. When Kara, Sasha's new lover is taken hostage as a diversionary tactic to allow the drug dealing Bellfontaine brothers to escape justice, Sasha springs into action. Kara is released physically unharmed, however her emotions and budding career in the District Attorney's office are left in shambles when she is held to blame for their release, Appalled by the failure of the criminal justice system, Sasha exacts her own brand of justice for the acts committed against her lover. From the Bayous of Louisiana to the jungles of South America, Sasha plots her revenge.

Out of Retirement—Erica Lawson Melanie Stokes was a doctor—a very good one, or so she hoped. She was calm and cool under pressure, and very little fazed her. Until…Caitlin Joseph ran a small retirement home for older women in need. The fact that everyone in the house was gay was a coincidence, although it did cut down the number of women agreeing to live there. Mel took up an offer to do some relief work for a local community center when their regular doctor was away on holidays. As soon as she arrived at the home she knew something was different about the place. Was it the little old lady chasing the paper boy down the street or the sign saying "Dykes Retirement Home"? But there was something about the place that also appealed to her. Sure, Caitlin was cute as a button, but it was more the fact that she took very good care of her charges despite their rather bizarre behavior. The older women seized the opportunity to introduce a woman into Caitlin's lonely life, using any means possible to keep Mel coming back. Their plans were boosted by the introduction of another woman into the house, who set hearts a fluttering and blood pressure rising. Now if she was a lesbian it would have been perfect…

Letting Go—JM Dragon A failed relationship puts Stella Hawke's life on the brink of chaos. When her grandmother falls gravely ill in Ashville, Stella ends her army career to take care of the woman during her last weeks. Little does she know that an old army comrade, socialite Reggie Stockton, whose family owns the local newspaper, also lives in Ashville. Will she allow herself to accept Reggie's help to turn her life around and let go of the past? This is a journey where both women re-evaluate what they want out of life. Will that path lead to happiness or to a parting of the ways?

E-Books, Print, Free e-books

Visit our website for more publications available online.

www.affinityebooks.com

Published by Affinity E-Book Press NZ LTD
Canterbury, New Zealand

Registered Company 2517228